W9-AHA-272

POISON SPRING

OTHER FIVE STAR WESTERNS BY JOHNNY D. BOGGS:

The Lonesome Chisholm Trail (2000); *Once They Wore the Gray* (2001); *Lonely Trumpet* (2002); *The Despoilers* (2002); *The Big Fifty* (2003); *Purgatoire* (2003); *Dark Voyage of the* Mittie Stephens (2004); *East of the Border* (2004); *Camp Ford* (2005); *Ghost Legion* (2005); *Walk Proud, Stand Tall* (2006); *The Hart Brand* (2006); *Northfield* (2007); *Doubtful Cañon* (2007); *Killstraight* (2008); *Soldier's Farewell* (2008); *Río Chama* (2009); *Hard Winter* (2009); *Whiskey Kills* (2010); *South by Southwest* (2011); *Legacy of a Lawman* (2011); *Kill the Indian* (2012); *And There I'll Be a Soldier* (2012); *Summer of the Star* (2013); *Wreaths of Glory* (2013); *Greasy Grass* (2013)

POISON SPRING

A FRONTIER STORY

JOHNNY D. BOGGS

FIVE STAR

A part of Gale, Cengage Learning

GALE
CENGAGE Learning·

Farmington Hills, Mich • San Francisco • New York • Waterville, Maine
Meriden, Conn • Mason, Ohio • Chicago

GALE
CENGAGE Learning·

Copyright © 2014 by Johnny D. Boggs.
Five Star™ Publishing, a part of Gale, Cengage Learning.

LIBRARY OF CONGRESS CATALOGING-IN-PUBLICATION DATA

Boggs, Johnny D.
   Poison spring : a Frontier Story / by Johnny D. Boggs. — First Edition.
     pages cm
     ISBN-13: 978-1-4328-2765-6 (hardcover)
     ISBN-10: 1-4328-2765-0 (hardcover)
     1. Frontier and pioneer life—Fiction. I. Title.
   PS3552.O4375P65 2014
   813'.54—dc23   2013041348

First Edition. First Printing: April 2014
Published in conjunction with Golden West Literary Agency
Published by Five Star™ Publishing, a part of Gale, Cengage Learning
Find us on Facebook– https://www.facebook.com/FiveStarCengage
Visit our website– http://www.gale.cengage.com/fivestar/
Contact Five Star™ Publishing at FiveStar@cengage.com

Printed in the United States of America
1 2 3 4 5 6 7 18 17 16 15 14

For Megan Varela
and the 2012-13 Fifth Grade Class
at Eldorado Community School

CHAPTER ONE

That was the year we had no food.

The cornfield Papa had cleared lay fallow, as it had for going on two years now. Oh, Mama had a little garden out behind our cabin, but this was the 1st of April, so we didn't know if anything we had planted would make it. Winter had been hard, and a late freeze had killed the blossoms on our apple trees.

Not that we were starving. Not yet, anyway. From last harvest, Mama had put away jars of preserves, and there were still some potatoes and carrots left in the root cellar that hadn't rotted.

Besides, we had Miss Mary Frederick for a neighbor, and Miss Mary had to be the richest woman in Ouachita County. She was always bringing us leftovers, plus cakes or cookies or pies. She'd bring us everything but coffee. Mama dearly loved coffee, but that was one product nobody was getting in Arkansas. Even if you could find it, you couldn't afford it. Well, maybe Miss Mary could have, but she said she never cared much for the stuff.

That spring of '64 had been so wet, so miserable that when our baby brother Hugh had walked out into the old cornfield, he had sunk in mud up to his waist. When Edith and I had pulled him out, the thick goo had sucked off his shoes and socks. Baby Hugh hadn't minded one bit. That boy loved running around barefoot.

It seemed to be raining all the time, that spring. In fact, it was raining the evening when Uncle Willard paid us one of his visits.

Like Miss Mary, Papa's brother always brought us things, too. Not food, but money, which Mama always refused, although Uncle Willard would leave it when he rode back to Camden. At first, when we found some state script or gold coin left under the wash basin or stuck inside a coat pocket after he had gone, Mama would throw what Papa always called a "hissy fit"— yelling and breathing hard and moving around, banging dishes, pulling her hair, doing everything except cussing. After two years, however, she had grown resigned to the fact Uncle Willard would leave money behind, and it would wind up in the church collection plate. Taking leftovers from Miss Mary was one thing, but Mama never would accept anything from Uncle Willard.

All of us Fords could be mighty stubborn, but none ever came close to matching Anna Louella Graham Ford's mule head.

Uncle Willard was three years older than Papa, and might have been just a hair less richer than Miss Mary. Miss Mary, why, she had always been rich. She'd let you know that the Frederick family had been wealthy when they had been in Germany, back when they had spelled that name with an *ie* and an *ich,* and they had been rich when the Fredericks had settled in Pennsylvania in 1732, and they had made even more money when her side of the family had moved to Virginia in 1785, and her Grandfather Frederick had made a fortune in Cincinnati packing hogs in the early 1800s, and, twenty years ago, when Miss Mary's father had gotten sick of hogs and had moved the family to Arkansas, they had gotten even richer on cotton.

Uncle Willard, though, made his fortune another way. He called himself a trader, but what he traded were men, women, girls and boys my age, even younger. He once bragged to me, back when Edith and I were nine years old, that if our skin were darker, if we were colored, he could sell us each for $900. He had laughed when he had said that, kept right on laughing even after Edith and I started crying, until Papa had told him to shut up.

Edith and I had been born in this cabin thirteen years earlier. My twin sister was older than me by a few minutes, which she bragged about while bossing me around. While we were born in Arkansas, where slavery was a fact of life, we Fords didn't own slaves. Papa always told his brother that, if he couldn't do it himself or pay a worker for an honest day's work, he didn't want it done, but I think the real reason we didn't have any was on account of Mama. Mama hailed from Illinois. Once, she had even seen Abraham Lincoln walking down the streets of Springfield long before he was elected President and sent us into war.

No food. No sawmill. Just a war. And rain. Nothing made sense to me any more.

How come it was Papa who was fighting with Slemons's cavalry while Uncle Willard stayed in Camden to trade slaves and get richer? Papa wasn't a soldier, or hadn't been before the war. Jokingly he would sometimes tell us he wasn't a farmer, either. He was a furniture maker, a carpenter, but mostly a sawyer, yet, for two years now, we hadn't heard the whining at Papa's mill. Still, Papa had joined of his own accord, although I guess he didn't have much choice. Not after the spring of '62, when the Confederacy had enacted a Conscription Act, meaning any man between eighteen and thirty-five years old, and later from seventeen to fifty, had to serve in the army for three years.

At first, you could hire a substitute, someone to fight for you, but that was later outlawed in December of '63. Uncle Willard, however, was exempt from service on account that he owned more than twenty slaves. The closest Uncle Willard got to fighting came on his weekly patrols, when he and some other grown men who hadn't joined the Confederate Army rode around the county looking for runaways or slaves, as Uncle Willard said, "up to some cussedness."

Which is what had brought him by our cabin that rainy day on the 1st day of April.

Nobody in our family cared for Uncle Willard, not even Baby Hugh, who wasn't a baby any more, but going on seven years old.

When the war broke out, back when I was just a kid ten years old, Papa hadn't run off to enlist. He had told Uncle Willard that he ran a sawmill and was not a soldier. Besides, the South would have the Yankees whipped in six months, if not sooner.

That, of course, had not happened, and with Yankees pressing their cause up in Missouri and over in Tennessee in the early spring of '62, and with the Conscription Act about to take men and boys from their homes and jobs, a new rallying cry went across Arkansas for more troops, more soldiers, more fighting men. So Papa had mounted Nutmeg, his brown mare, ridden off to Hampton over in Calhoun County, and joined up with a cavalry company a fellow named Alexander Mason was organizing. Later, they had gone to Memphis, Tennessee, and became part of General William Slemons's command. We hadn't seen Papa since.

He had written, of course, from camps in Tennessee and Mississippi. Not that his letters revealed much, though Mama would read them over and over till the pages got so smudged that you couldn't tell what Papa had written. Even then, she would still sit in her rocking chair and pull them from their tattered envelopes and read them, from memory now, again. By April of '64, however, letters had become more scarce than coffee. The last we'd heard from Papa had been during the previous summer, when he was riding with the 2nd Arkansas Cavalry with Major General Nathan Bedford Forrest.

Arkansas had not escaped three years of fighting unscathed. In 1862, the Yankees had defeated the Confederates at Elkhorn Tavern, Prairie Grove, Hill's Plantation, Arkansas Post, Fayetteville, and other places now forgotten. Bluecoats controlled the port city of Helena on the Mississippi River. They had captured Fort Smith on the western edge of our state, and in September of '63 they had taken Little Rock, forcing the state government to retreat and set up a new capital down south in Washington.

To a thirteen-year-old boy, all this became hard to comprehend. Connor Ford, sergeant, Company A, 2nd Arkansas Cavalry, was fighting for the South, or at least, Arkansas. Yankees were the bad guys. Yankees were the invaders. How could my father, could we, be losing this war?

War was not supposed to come to Ouachita County, but Uncle Willard came to tell us that it was coming here. Real soon.

"It's darkest before the dawn," he said, then rubbed his rough hands in my hair, tangling my long locks and pulling that dark mane of mine till I squirmed. "But we'll whip 'em curs, give 'em tyrants a taste of buck and ball, drive 'em back to Springfield, and leave that city in ashes and ruins. Ain't that right, Annie Lou?"

Mama pretended she had not heard. Springfield had been her home before marrying Papa. Her name was Anna Louella. She hated anyone to call her Annie, let alone Annie Lou.

He let go of my hair, and spit tobacco juice into a tin cup.

Thunder rolled, and Uncle Willard left me to my *McGuffey's Reader,* went to the window, pushed back the curtain, and stared outside at the gray skies. Rain kept falling, as it had for most of the day, but I guess my uncle wanted to make sure that sound had indeed just been thunder and not distant cannon.

Satisfied, he turned back toward us. "Old Pap has his boys in Camden," he said, "just waitin' for 'em Yanks to dare show their faces on this side of the Ouachita River." Old Pap was General Sterling Price of Missouri, hero of Wilson's Creek and Lexington. "Old Pap has whipped the Yanks ever' time they dared clash with his boys."

Uncle Willard moved over to torture Baby Hugh. My uncle must have forgotten the battles of Elkhorn Tavern, Corinth, and Iuka. Like every other Southern general, Price lately had been losing battles and men. The mention of Price's name, however, stopped Mama from peeling potatoes.

"Price?" Lowering the knife, she looked at Uncle Willard. "Price is in Camden?"

"Yep. The city again is awash in butternut and gray."

"Is Connor with him?"

He spit again, wiped his mouth with his shirt sleeve, and shook his head. "I doubt it, Annie Lou. Ain't seen him, nohow. Reckon my brother's still busy ridin' rings 'round the Yanks with Bedford Forrest." With a smile, he turned back to me. "I ever tell you that I know Bedford Forrest?"

Only a million times, I thought, not looking up from the *The Eclectic Fourth Reader.*

"Did some tradin' with him at his business on Adams Street in Memphis. Quite the speculator, and quite the businessman. But I got the better of 'im in all my deals.

"But, Annie Lou, the Yanks will be marchin' this way. Pret' soon. If I was you, I'd move these young 'uns to Camden. I got plenty of room. I can load y'all up right now, fetch you to Camden. It'll be safer there, and you won't have to work so hard to scratch out a livin' if you. . . ." He stopped himself, but I knew what he meant. *If you could call this living.*

"Thank you, Willard, but the children and I will make out fine here." She went back to her potatoes.

"How?" Uncle Willard spit again. This time, juice dripped and darkened the brown stains of his prematurely white beard. "You got no mules to work that bog you call a cornfield."

Last summer, scavengers or deserters or runaway slaves had stolen our two jennies.

"You got one old milch cow . . . is she still givin' any milk, Travis? . . . and I bet your chickens ain't even layin' no more," Uncle Willard went on. "You won't let me take over Connor's sawmill. Why, with my slaves, I could turn y'all a tidy profit. Lumber's one thing that ain't scarce in these parts."

He paused, waiting for Mama to say something. Uncle Willard had made his pitch to operate Papa's sawmill with his slaves many times before. Like his money, Mama wouldn't take that offer, either. She went right on preparing supper.

After dribbling more juice into his spit cup, Uncle Willard said: "You're alone here, Annie Lou, a good-lookin' woman with three kids. Nearest neighbor's five mile down the road, and that's a crazy ol' biddy who ain't got a lick of sense. They be deserters, Yanks and Southern trash, scavengers. And they's plenty of contraband. Runaway slaves, headin' north to Little Rock to escape their masters." He swore underneath his breath, but not loud enough for Mama to hear.

"As you always say, Willard," Mama said, "it's darkest before the dawn. Thank you, kindly, but I am not moving my family. This is our home."

"Yanks get here, you might not have a home no more. Best remember that."

Instead of answering, Mama asked: "Will you be staying for supper, Willard?"

"Need to be gettin' back to Camden. Just stopped by after our patrol to see how you and the kids is farin'. You sure I can't take y'all home to Camden?"

"We're fine. Thank you."

He sighed, shook his head. "At least let me send you some slaves to work that mill, Anna." We knew he was serious. He hadn't called her Annie Lou to irritate her.

His answer was the patter of rain on the roof.

With nobody giving him any attention, he rose without another word, fetched his wide-brimmed hat and India rubber poncho off the antler horn on the wall, dressed, and left, hollering out the door for one of his slaves to help him to his carriage. His last words to the house were: "You're as mule-headed as that hard-rock brother of mine, Annie Lou!"

"Mama!" Baby Hugh had gotten up to peer through the window. "He left two of his boys out in the rain. Why did he do that, Mama? His boys might catch cold."

"They are not boys, Baby Hugh," Edith pointed out. "They are slaves older than Uncle Willard."

"He calls them his boys," our brother pointed out.

"He calls them a lot worse, the sorry old. . . ." I hadn't intended for Mama to hear, but she did. Once, Papa told Mama: "Anna, you could hear Miss Mary drop a pin while she's darning socks in her parlor during a thunderstorm." I should have kept my thoughts to myself. I didn't have to like my uncle, but Mama certainly would not tolerate a thirteen-year-old showing disrespect to his elders.

"Travis Connor Ford," she barked, and I knew I was in trouble on account that she'd called me by my full name and not just Travis. Closing my *Reader,* I stood up, and her angry eyes stared me down. For a moment, all I could hear was pounding rain. Baby Hugh and my twin sister stared, holding their breath, waiting to see if I got a switching or scolding.

Instead, I got neither. "Travis," she said, her tone softer now. "Go to the barn. Milk the cow. Bring in some more firewood."

Just my normal chores. I felt lucky.

As I put on my coat and Papa's boots he had left behind,

Edith shouted: "Mama!"

Uncle Willard had left $100 in Arkansas bills on the seat of his chair.

"Leave it on the table, Edith," Mama said, without looking up. "We'll give it to the Reverend White the day after tomorrow."

CHAPTER TWO

Our home lay in the woods just off the Camden-Washington Pike. It was only a dogtrot cabin, two rooms separated by a covered breezeway, which, coupled with the shade from the pines and oaks, kept the house cool during the summer. The east side was the kitchen, where we had been talking with Uncle Willard while Mama prepared supper. Although Papa had bought a cook stove from Mr. Kroger's mercantile just before he left with the Confederate cavalry, Mama still did most of her cooking in the fireplace. You walked through the breezeway to get to the bedroom. Mama slept downstairs. Edith, Baby Hugh, and I bunked in the loft. There was a fireplace in that room, too. Two rooms. Two fireplaces. A covered porch with a slanted roof of wooden shingles. Windows with wooden shutters on the east and west walls next to the fireplaces. Front doors to each room, as well as the doorways through the breezeway, which we usually kept open when it turned hot.

That was it. Nothing fancy. Nothing to brag about, the way Miss Mary often talked about her vast brick house with the white columns and two stories and the porch swing and the verandah and gazebo and whitewashed picket—not split rail, she'd remind you—fences. But, to us, the cabin, those woods, always felt like home.

While we certainly weren't rich, the roof usually did not leak, the fireplaces kept us warm during the winter, and the cabin was solid. The furniture, what little we had, Papa had made himself. He was proudest of the rocking chair, which I heard squeaking on the front porch the morning after Uncle Willard had left. I heard something else.

Birds chirping. No rain.

Baby Hugh and Edith still slept, and it must have been an hour past dawn. Usually we were doing chores by that time of day. Hurriedly I dressed, came downstairs, through the breezeway, and found Mama rocking away, staring down the path that led from the road to our house. Staring at nothing.

Papa had dug the well in a little clearing in the front. The water was cool, refreshing, with not a taste of iron. Behind the house stood the barn and chicken coop, and a lean-to filled with firewood and hay, though the hay pile kept getting lower. Off to the west stood the cornfield, which now stank of mud, the run-down corncrib, and Mama's garden, where the first sprouts had just started to pop up through the soil. Or had been before the big rains came. For all I knew, last night's storm could have washed everything down to Poison Spring.

A few miles from our house, Poison Spring trickled through the hilly woods. Nobody knew where the spring got its name. The water didn't smell bad, and I'd seen deer and squirrels drinking out of it without keeling over dead. Still, I never drank from it, even when Edith double dared me to. She called me a baby when I had refused, but when I told her to taste it, she had said: "It would not be proper for a lady to drink out of a spring like some animal." When I'd cupped my hand and splashed water at her, she had dashed away, crying all the way back home.

"Good morning, Travis." Mama kept rocking. You couldn't sneak up on her, never in a hundred years.

"You want me to milk Lucy?" Lucy was our cow.

She rocked, lost in her thoughts. I was about to ask her again, when the chair stopped, and she pushed herself up. Mama

17

didn't look at me, but moved to the rough-hewn column, looking down the path, then stepping down off the porch. I didn't see anyone coming to pay us a visit.

"Would you like to walk to the sawmill with me?" This time she turned around, looking at me with a certain light in her eyes, an idea formulating in her head.

She would get these notions, and, once one took root, she'd tear into it like a dog feasting on a meaty bone.

"Sure," I said, but gestured through the breezeway. "But should I milk Lucy first?"

"She can wait. Are Edith and Hugh still sleeping?"

"Yes, ma'am. Should I wake . . . ?"

She had turned, her long legs moving down the path. I ran back inside, grabbed my hat and a canvas sack for kindling. By the time I caught up with her at the main road, my lungs heaved for breath.

Mama wore a cotton work dress of red and gold plaid and flat-heeled button shoes. She had forgotten her bonnet or straw hat, but the sky shone blue, and the pines blocked most of the sun.

Always, this land had been thick with forests. I figured it would take a hundred thousand years and ten times the number of slaves Uncle Willard had to clear the land for farming. Walking down the road often seemed like walking in a cave. Those pine trees stretched all the way to heaven, and oaks and dogwoods had just begun to blossom. I would stop to collect pine cones and twigs for kindling—though they were soggy from all the rain and would take a good long while to dry out—sticking them in a burlap sack I'd grabbed, then hurry to catch up.

Twenty minutes later, we turned down the woods road that led to Papa's sawmill. Well, once it had been a road. Now the grass grew so thick you couldn't see any ruts from the wagons that used to haul lumber to Camden, there to ship timber up or down the Ouachita, or winding down the Princeton Road to Harmony Grove, or sometimes to the Tate family's place on the river at Tate's Bluff. Now the road, like Papa's mill, had been all but abandoned.

A half mile later, we reached the mill.

I think Papa would have preferred to have become a furniture maker, or just a carpenter, but, as long as I could remember, he had been a sawyer. He had joked—or I'd assumed he'd been funning us—that when he first bought our land, he had discovered the pond. First, he tried fishing, but the catfish and crappie were too smart, so he decided to make the pond a millpond.

Usually a sawmill was located next to a river, but we were too far from the Ouachita. Papa had dammed a creek from the pond, and put up the mill. To turn the water wheel in the mill he had built, all Papa had to do was open the dam. The water flowed, the water wheel turned, and the shafts inside the mill pushed the muley saw up and down. Muleys were old-fashioned, slow. The saw cut only on the downstroke, and ours was a small operation.

Rarely did Mama, Edith, or Baby Hugh come to the mill. Papa had never wanted them around here, especially when running the muley. Even away back at home, the buzzing of that saw could be heard, and it often had made Baby Hugh cry. But Papa would let me sweep up sawdust, or coat the machines with oil to keep them from rusting. Once, I'd even helped one of Papa's workers clamp a log on the carriage. Another time, with Papa and a freedman named Jared Greene smiling over me, I'd burned Papa's timber mark, *FFM*—Ford Family Mill—onto a two-by-four. That had to have been five years ago. Usually I just marveled at the workers Papa had hired to help him out. Every one of them was missing a finger, some more than one; one fellow even wore an eye patch and had a hook—like a pirate—for his left hand. Jared Greene had lost two fingers on his right hand. It felt funny whenever he would shake my hand.

Ford Family Mill. I reckon I was doomed to fail Papa if he wanted me to take over the mill. Writing, reading, telling stories fueled my passion, though I had no idea how one did that for a living. I had no interest in becoming a sawyer, yet I had to admit that I always enjoyed the smell of sawdust and grease and freshly cut trees.

That pleasant smell no longer entered my nostrils. I smelled only the wetness of the forest. A pine tree had fallen, crashing through the roof of a privy. The tool shed remained unscathed, but the main building had also been wrecked by another falling tree, an oak. One of the old wagons appeared rotted. A squirrel stood guard, angrily chirping at us from the open door. Or should I say, the missing door. I guess the squirrel had decided a shanty made a better nest than one up in a tree. Which would have struck me as funny, but Mama choked out a sob. She hadn't been up to the mill in a 'coon's age, either.

There were few scraps of lumber to be picked up for kindling, no grease. Nobody working. It looked like a ghost town. Only mountains of sawdust, some of which bulged out of overfilled baskets or barrels, the rest on the floor. I drew in a deep breath. I'd always loved the smell of wet sawdust. Wet sawdust didn't sting one's eyes and nose. Wet sawdust didn't remind me that, when Papa would let me work with his crew, my job had been to sweep it up. Those overflowing baskets and barrels were filled with my labor. Labor I hadn't done for years.

Squirrels leaped across the tall pines. Birds chattered. A gust of wind caused the trees to rustle. Finally Mama sighed.

"I don't think we can do it, Travis," she said after the longest while.

"Do what, Mama?"

20

"Run the mill."

I blinked incredulously. "Who? Uncle Willard . . . ?"

"No," she snapped. "Not Willard." As Papa would often tease—or maybe he wasn't teasing—Mama was "getting her Abolitionist up." Her head shook again, and she said softly: "I was thinking we could do it. Ourselves. You, Edith, and me. Let Miss Mary look after Hugh."

My mouth dropped open.

Moving over to me, Mama smiled and tousled my hair. "Not a big operation, Travis. Nothing like Connor was running. Just cut a few boards. Just enough to earn some script, or enough to barter with Mister Kroger at the town mercantile. But I don't think that's feasible, after all. Do you, Travis?"

Of course, it wasn't feasible. It was inconceivable. Even compared with other family-run sawmills in the county, the Ford Family Mill had been downright tiny, four or five hired men and Papa. The Fountains owned one, The Fountain Timber Company, on the other side of Camden along a stream that flowed into the Ouachita. But the Fountains had three brothers, and those brothers had eleven working-age boys—three already married with kids of their own—and still Ezekial X. Fountain III hired five or six others to help haul, cut, stack, and sell lumber. I was just thirteen, but I had enough sense to know that if Mama, Edith, and I tried operating the mill by ourselves, we'd likely wind up looking worse than Jared Greene or that fellow with the hook and the eye patch who had so intrigued me back in 1860.

But I said: "I don't know, Mama. We could, I reckon, try."

"No." She squeezed my shoulder. "That was a forlorn hope. We'll find another way. Let's go home. Get you some breakfast."

She steered me out of the mill, away from the wet sawdust, and back down the path.

"How'd we get to be poor, Mama?" I asked.

"We're not poor," she said. Not defiantly. No embarrassment or hint of a lie in her voice. "We have each other. We have our health. Most of all, we have the Lord's blessings. I'd say that makes us far from poor, Travis, but rich. Yes, we are very rich, indeed."

Which brought to mind something else Papa was always telling my mother. *Anna, you missed your calling, girl. You should have become a preacher.*

I could picture Papa at the supper table, saying those words, Mama shaking her head, maybe mentioning that she'd heard that from Papa more than a million times but laughing anyway, as she topped off his cup with coffee. It brought back a lot of good memories, but then my smile vanished, for it seemed that all I had now was memories of those good years.

Yet a thirteen-year-old boy in Ouachita County, Arkansas, didn't have long to feel down. Not in 1864. Back home, chores awaited me, so while Mama went into the kitchen, opening a window so it wouldn't become an oven in that part of the dogtrot, I went about my work. Milking the cow. *Yes, Uncle Willard, Lucy still gives milk,* I thought while filling the bucket. Chopping wood. Gathering kindling. Fetching eggs, which I turned into a game.

Since I was seven, I'd been adding ten years to my age, during my imaginary games—so in my mind I was now twenty-three-year-old Travis Ford—Confederate spy, out to steal the battle plans from the Yankee invaders and deliver them to Bedford Forrest and turn the tide of the war. I had overheard Uncle Willard talking to the preacher about how misplaced battle plans had helped the Yanks win a battle near Sharpsburg, Maryland, so it was my turn to save the day for the Confederacy. As I looked for eggs, I pretended I was sneaking into Sibley tents, hotel rooms, county plantations captured by Yankees and turned into headquarters where I would find the battle plans, general orders, or sacks of coffee for Mama. And I would get out, alive, before the hens noticed what I was doing and could come after me with blood in their eyes.

Lieutenant Travis Ford, C.S.A., special courier for Bedford Forrest, under the command of recently promoted Colonel Connor Ford, walks through the Yankee camp, bold as brass. Only twenty-three years old, yet already the Southern newspapers compared him to the likes of Revolutionary War heroes Nathanael Greene, John Laurens, and Francis Marion, the famed Swamp Fox. Ford makes a beeline for the general's tent, sharply saluting a major chomping on a cigar. The major straightens, returns the salute, and goes back to doing what he did best. He picks his nose.

Stopping at the fire in front of the general's tent, Ford pretends to warm his hands, all the while glancing at the major, the other Yankees. Ford himself wears the blue, which comes from the officer he killed in the woods with his bare hands. If discovered, if caught, well, an enemy captured wearing the wrong uniform behind the lines . . . that meant only one thing. Hanging did not appeal to Lieutenant Ford.

No one is looking. This is his chance. He darts inside the tent, finds the papers, grabs two of them, then barges out of the tent, ready to fight.

No one has noticed him. The Yankees go right along pecking the ground, scratching the earth, clucking like the cowards they were. Ford stops fingering the ivory grips of his LeMat revolver. He would not have to fight his way out. Yet.

He has the plans. He can leave now, but then he sees the patrol bringing in the gray-clad prisoner.

"We've captured Colonel Ford!" a red-bearded sergeant brags. "The war is ours!"

Travis Ford stares as the Yankees ease Colonel Ford, his father and commanding officer, off a mule. He watches the miserable curs shove the Confederate hero into a prison pen, and the young lieutenant knows one more mission awaits him. Slowly he crosses the Yankee camp, picking up another egg, then his LeMat is in his hand.

He shoots the nearest guard, turns, fires three more times in rapid succession. Just as rapidly, three more Yankees fall.

"Come!" he yells, shooting the sergeant off his horse, leaping into the saddle, reaching down with his free hand. His father grips it. They smile at each other.

"What is going on?" the Yankee major says.

Lieutenant Ford aims the LeMat, pulls the trigger, and the cowardly Bluecoat is dead.

"Long live the South!" both father and son shout, and gallop out of the Yankee camp, firing, shouting, laughing.

Once I had retrieved the Yankee plans to capture Camden, which also revealed all the weaknesses to hold onto Little Rock, I hurried back inside with a dozen eggs, delivered those to Mama, and then heard the jingle of a wagon trace outside.

"Who is it, Travis?" Mama asked.

Edith, who had finally awakened and was bringing Baby Hugh into the kitchen, answered first.

"It's Miss Mary, Mama."

CHAPTER THREE

She had arrived in a fancy touring carriage, custom built by Chase's Carriage Factory in Camden, the side curtains rolled up, pulled by a matching pair of gray mares. I never understood why Miss Mary needed a wagon that big. It would seat six or eight people, and she was alone except for the Negro driver, who was helping her down from her throne in the back.

When Miss Mary Frederick turned to reach back into the wagon, Baby Hugh freed himself from Edith's grip and bolted, never touching the steps, practically flying across the yard toward the carriage, the slave, Miss Mary, and the covered dish she had retrieved.

"Miss Mary! Miss Mary! Miss Mary!" Baby Hugh screamed loud enough that I feared he might startle the team. The slave, old Mowbray who had been with Miss Mary as long as I had known her, must have thought the same, because, although he grinned widely, he quickly moved to the two horses, whispering something and rubbing the heads of the animals.

"What'd you bring us? What'd you bring us? Is it cake? It sure looks like cake. Chocolate? I love chocolate." At least Baby Hugh had the decency to wrap his arms around Miss Mary's waist and say: "It's great to see you, Miss Mary. How you been?"

"Is it great to see me, Baby Hugh?" Everybody called our brother that. Somehow, Miss Mary maintained her balance and did not drop the dish into the wet pine needles. "Or is it great to see half a carrot cake?"

Our brother backed away, his smile evaporating. "Carrot . . . cake?" He gulped.

I imagine his face paled, his stomach turning over, and him falling to his knees and wailing. He despised carrot cake, even though he'd never tasted it. I reckon he thought it was good for you, or maybe he—like most of us by that year—had grown sick of carrots.

Edith had managed to leave the porch. She grabbed Baby Hugh's upper right arm and chicken-winged him back toward the house. "You go wash, Baby Hugh. Face and hands and behind your ears. Breakfast is ready." Then she bowed, like she was curtseying to a queen. "It is wonderful to see you, Mary," she said. "Mama's fixing breakfast. Won't you join us?" She relieved Miss Mary of the dish.

"Breakfast?" Miss Mary clucked her tongue. "Child, it is almost time for dinner. Are y'all sick?"

"No, ma'am."

"You've wasted half the morning. You're just getting up?"

"Well. . . ."

I couldn't help myself. "I've been up, Miss Mary," I announced proudly. "Went with Mama to the sawmill."

That was the wrong thing to say.

"Goodness gracious," she said, stepping around my twin sister and making her way to the steps. "Sawmill. Why on earth would you go to that wretched, noisy place?"

"It isn't noisy, Mary." Mama had stepped out of the kitchen, drying her hands on her apron. "Unless you mean the squirrels. They've practically taken over the mill." She sighed. "But I think wretched describes it accurately."

I was making a note to myself to look up "wretched" in our Webster's Dictionary: Unabridged: Pictorial Edition. But after hearing Mama's last statement, I decided I knew the meaning.

"Won't you join us, Mary?"

"Eating this late in the morning, Anna Louella, would spoil my dinner." Mowbray, the slave, was helping her up the steps. "But . . . I suppose. . . ." They embraced under the dogtrot, and disappeared inside, though Mama quickly reappeared.

"You wash, too," she instructed Edith and me. "Both of you."

"But, Mama," I protested. "I've been up and washed already."

Which might or might not have been the case. Honestly I couldn't remember.

"Yes. And you've been in the barn and gathering eggs. *Wash.*"

You have to give Miss Mary credit. She might discreetly, or maybe bluntly, chastise Mama's sometimes relaxed discipline or her Yankee sensibilities and politics, but never did she turn up her nose at our table. I'd never been inside her house, but I imagined her breakfast consisted of poached eggs, and fried ham, and buttermilk biscuits with jellies and preserves and tons of butter, mountains of hot cakes, and sausages, and bacon and grits, and tea and milk and apple cider. Served by an army of slaves marching in and out of the kitchen, summoned by silver bells.

Scrambled eggs, fried potatoes, and a cornmeal gruel must have been unappetizing to her, but she sipped hot tea, and made no comment about our breakfast. The towering bald slave profusely thanked me when Mama sent me out with a plate filled with more food than Edith, Baby Hugh, or I ever got. Usually our leftover breakfast became our dinner, but Mama had scraped the skillets clean to give Mowbray some food. From the looks of him, I figured Miss Mary fed him pretty well. He wasn't starving. But he sure acted like it.

"I must practice my French, Anna Louella," Miss Mary said, and, as was their custom, they spent the next five minutes talking in that poetic but foreign language. None of which we children really understood. Miss Mary said it was the language of genteel society, even if her family had been Germans, and Mama said she had learned it in Illinois, which didn't sound French to me, at all. But hearing them talk always reminded me of Alexandre Dumas, *The Three Musketeers,* and *The Count of Monte Cristo.* Adventure stories that I dearly loved.

"Have you heard from Connor, Anna Louella?" Miss Mary set the tin cup—I bet she always drank from china—on the rough table. The French session had ended.

Mama stood over the sink, scrubbing the cast-iron cookware clean. Since Papa rode off to war, rarely did Mama eat with us, always cleaning while we ate. I guess she ate when we were finished. She wouldn't eat now. All the extra food had gone to Mowbray.

"No, Mary. Not in a few weeks." She set the last dish out to dry, then began drying her hands with a towel.

Edith and I exchanged a quick glance before quickly returning to the eggs, which were good, and the potatoes, which weren't, and the corn mush, which made the potatoes seem savory. *A few weeks?* It had been months. No letter had come at Christmas. No word since last fall.

"Well, Mowbray is taking me to Camden today. I could check at Darius's store, see if there's a letter for you."

Darius was Darius Kroger. He ran the largest mercantile in town, which also served as the post office.

"Thank you, Mary, but Willard was here yesterday evening. He would have brought a letter had one been waiting for us." She thought about that, however, still rubbing her hands on the towel though her hands had to have been dry by then. "But if it's . . . if it's no bother."

Miss Mary smiled. "It's no bother at all, Anna Louella. Perhaps. . . ." Now it was our rich neighbor's turn to pause. Sipping her tea again, her pinky finger held up just like a real lady, she turned to me, then faced Mama again. "Perhaps Travis could accompany me."

I stopped eating. Sat erect. Put my hands underneath the table and crossed as many fingers as possible. I tried not to look at Mama, but couldn't help myself, though I hoped my face remained passive, not pleading.

She had tossed the towel aside, and picked up her own cup of tea. "I don't know . . . ," Mama began.

Often, Miss Mary let me ride into town with her. There was one shop in town that I dearly loved, and Miss Mary did, too.

"Oh, let him ride with me, Anna Louella," Miss Mary said. "It's a dull ride to Camden with only Mowbray to talk to. And Travis could help me pick out some new fabric for the curtains in our formal parlor. That blue is just so dreadful. Just dreadful. Every time I see it, I think the Yankees are invading. Now, Travis has an eye. He could help me."

My fingers uncrossed to grip my thighs. I didn't think I wanted to be known as the boy with the eye for picking out drapes for a formal parlor. I would much rather have been Lieutenant Travis Ford, spy for the Confederacy, a hero in the mold of Nathanael Greene.

"Well. . . ." Mama had weakened. "I suppose it would be all right . . . if you finish your chores first, young man."

"Yes, ma'am." I was up in an instant. "I'll start right now."

"You'll do no such thing. Finish your breakfast. It's rude to leave the table when company is still here."

I sat back down.

"I want to go, too, Mama!" Baby Hugh started pouting. "I want to go to town, Miss Mary. Why does Travis always get to go?"

"Hugh Ford!" Mama snapped.

Yet Miss Mary remained calm. "Would you rather ride all the way to Camden or stay here and eat cake?"

"I don't like carrot cake," he said.

"It's not carrot cake," Miss Mary said.

"You said it was."

"I said . . . 'Is it great to see me, or is it great to see half a carrot cake?' I did not say I had brought half a carrot cake."

He contemplated this. Mother was smiling again.

"Is it chocolate?" Baby Hugh asked.

"Mon Dieu," Mary said, shaking her head, to which Mama said: "Mary Frederick!"

"No," Miss Mary told Baby Hugh, ignoring Mama's reprimand. "It's pound cake. And you know how well my Sallie makes pound cake."

"I'll stay," Baby Hugh said.

"Well, you're not having cake till you've dressed," Mama said. "And you've gotten your chores done, too, young man. And started your lessons."

At last, Edith, Baby Hugh, and I were excused, so we left Miss Mary and Mama to their gossip and went about our chores, fetching a bucket of water from the well, gathering more firewood and kindling and moving on to the garden.

The corn hadn't been washed away by the rain. Turnips, beans, radishes, and carrots were popping up in Mama's garden. In fact, even the cornfield looked good, except the spot where Baby Hugh had bogged down a while back. When the last of the chores was finished, we went back inside, nodding a greeting at Mowbray, who sat on the front steps, smiling, waiting for Miss Mary.

Baby Hugh took his *Reader,* and Edith and I took ours off the bookshelves, and retired to the front porch.

"Why does Miss Mary always let you go to town?" Edith asked. Jealous. She was always jealous. "I'm older than you are. I should go. I could pick out a fine fabric for curtains."

"I'm good company." I turned to the poem.

"You are not."

Ignoring her, I began reading where I had left off.

Baby Hugh was reading aloud, making it hard for me to concentrate, and then he stood up and walked to the steps.

"Hey, Mister Mowbray," he said, and thrust the *Eclectic Spelling Book* in front of the slave. "What's this here word?"

Edith and I practically leaped up.

"I wouldn't know, sir," the slave said.

"D-o-s-t," Baby Hugh spelled it out.

"Dost," Edith said. "It's dost. It's old English. It means does."

"Well, that don't make a lick of sense," Baby Hugh said.

"I reckon not," Mowbray said, "but I'd take your sister's word for it. She's right smart."

"You ever heard that word?"

"Dost?" Mowbray chuckled. "I reckon not."

Baby Hugh shoved the book under the slave's nose. "That's it!"

"Hugh Ford!" Edith snapped in horror. I just stood there, mouth open.

"Is that so? Now I reckon I have to take your word for it, Master Hugh."

"What you mean?"

"Hugh! You come up here right now." But Edith wasn't moving. I guess she was curious. Same as Baby Hugh. Same as me.

"Well, it's this way, Master Hugh. I can't read."

"You can't?"

"Not at all."

"But you're older than. . . ."

"Than Methuselah? Reckon I am."

"And you still can't read."

He shook his head.

"Well, it's easy." Hugh turned the pages. "See. This here is an A. That's the capital A, and that's the baby a. And that there's a picture of . . . what?"

"Looks like an axe," Mowbray said.

"That's right. Axe starts with an a. And you see this one? That's a C."

"Looks like a cat, Master Hugh." Mowbray's voice trembled, and I decided it was time to move.

I left Edith standing, holding her *Reader*, and moved to the step. "Hugh," I said softly, dropping the Baby. "You need to leave Mowbray alone."

"I'm just learning him his letters," he said.

"Yes, but, well. . . ." I didn't know how to explain to him.

"It is against the law to teach a slave to read." Miss Mary stood underneath the dogtrot, Mama beside her.

I tugged Baby Hugh up, away from Mowbray, who rose and handed his empty dishes to Edith. Glancing back at him, I thought I detected fear in his eyes as he faced Miss Mary.

"You ready to go now, Miss Mary?" he asked.

"Yes," she said stiffly. "Master Travis will accompany us to town and back."

The thought of going to Camden had excited me. Now I dreaded the journey.

CHAPTER FOUR

"Red would be a nice color for drapes," I said.

"Garnet or cherry?" Miss Mary said.

"Garnet." I had no idea what the difference between garnet and cherry was.

"Well, let's see if Darius Kroger has something in garnet."

We fell silent. The carriage rolled along the road, splashing through puddles, Miss Mary looking straight ahead, Mowbray holding the leather lines, keeping the two grays at a steady pace. I watched the passing pine trees.

As things turned out, the ride wasn't bad at all. Miss Mary never brought up the fact that she could have sent Baby Hugh to prison. Well, maybe not, but she did not rebuke Mowbray, and seemed to have forgotten everything by the time we reached Camden.

Sight of the town revived everyone.

It always did.

Camden was a pretty city—the biggest I had ever seen—standing atop the red bluffs overlooking the bends of the Ouachita River. The streets wound about, over bridges across ravines, lined by giant oaks and pines. We rode down Washington Street, one of the few streets named after U.S. Presidents that the city officials had not changed. At the corner of Washington and Adams, where the Ouachita Hotel stood guard, someone had Xed out *Adams* on that street sign, and painted above it *Davis*. Polk Street was now Lee Street. Jefferson had become

Stonewall. Madison was Cleburne, named after one of Arkansas's favorite sons of the Confederacy. Taylor Street had been turned into McCulloch, after the Texas general killed at Elkhorn Tavern. Jackson Street remained Jackson Street, either because Andrew Jackson had been a Southerner by birth or perhaps because the city fathers had decided Jackson could refer to the late Stonewall Jackson, even though he already had Stonewall Street renamed in his honor.

We didn't reach Monroe Street, or whatever it had now been christened, for which I was grateful. Uncle Willard's Trader House was down Monroe at the edge of town.

The streets might have new names, but Camden looked the same. At first.

For a boy on a farm and sawmill in the country, Camden excited me.

This was "The Cincinnati of Arkansas"—bustling with men and women, black and white, with merchants, vendors, and ordinary people. White houses lined the residential streets. Walls of cotton bales lined the front of the warehouses and the wharfs, waiting to be shipped to. . . .

To where?

Yankees controlled the Mississippi River. They had a blockade along the Texas coast. Maybe that cotton would never be sold. Maybe it would never leave Camden. I wondered if those bales were the same ones I had seen the last time Miss Mary had brought me to Camden. That had been . . . when? . . . back in December, a week before Christmas?

Then I saw something I hadn't seen on my last visit. Filthy, bearded soldiers in butternut rags, straining to get cannon and caisson out of the mud on Jackson Street. An officer on a blue roan barked orders, brandishing a saber, cursing the men and two mules that seemed disinterested in pulling their load out of the quagmire. Other soldiers walked along boardwalks. A patrol of six men, in blue shell jackets and ostrich-plumed Hardee hats galloped past us, and I began inventing adventures for those men, replacing the captain with the scar across his cheek with my twenty-three-year-old imaginary hero.

Leaning out the window, I looked behind me, and, sure enough, I saw more soldiers. Some in gray. Others in butternut. Many in blue denim, tan duck, or dirty muslin. The flag flapped in the wind, and standing atop the roof of the Ouachita Hotel were three sentries, one of them peering off toward Little Rock through a spyglass.

"Don't get muddy, Travis!" Miss Mary called. "Your mother would have us both ruing the day."

I slipped back inside the carriage.

"I didn't think town would be so busy," she said.

"No, ma'am," I agreed. "Me, either."

Camden had grown, sure enough. The way Papa told it, Camden had started down along the river around 1830 when a trader built a cabin to trade with the hunters in the area. Ouachita County had been formed in 1842, and merchants, farmers, settlers, and sawyers like my father had arrived. When Papa arrived with Willard in 1848, Camden boasted a population of eight hundred. Camden had grown into the second-largest city in Arkansas, just behind Little Rock. More than two thousand white people lived here. There had to be that many soldiers in town on that April afternoon.

We rode past more cotton bales, more wagons, more soldiers, more people. Past the Planter's Hotel, the *Ouachita Herald*, Riley's grocery, Woodward & Heydenfeldt's attorney's office, Dr. McElrath's, the Camden Foundry Company, Jennings's marble quarry, a livery, wagon yard, another grocery, Morgan's Apothecary, even Kroger's Mercantile & Post Office. To my surprise, the buggy kept right on going down the street.

I glanced at Miss Mary, who just stared ahead. So I returned to watching the people, taking in the scent of town, of baking bread, of mud and manure, of cigar and pipe smoke, and of the stink of soldiers marching through the bog.

"Here, Mowbray," Miss Mary said, and I turned back as the slave pulled on the lines, eased the carriage off the street, and set the brake. He was up and in the mud in an instant, helping me from the carriage, swinging me onto the boardwalk, then assisting Miss Mary onto the plank that served as a bridge across the mud that was Washington Street.

"I could use something new to read, Travis," Miss Mary said. "What about you?" Without waiting for my reply, she opened the door, telling Mowbray that we would not be long and if the constable gave him any trouble about hogging the street with the carriage, he should remind him that this was Miss Mary Frederick's carriage, and that was Miss Mary Frederick of the Cincinnati Fredericks whose father was Jonathan Frederick and need anyone say more.

"Come along, Travis." She was holding open the door for me. Miss Mary was. Miss Mary of the Cincinnati Fredericks and before that the Fredericks of Virginia and Pennsylvania. Excitedly I entered J.D. Mendenhall's, the reason I loved coming to Camden with Miss Mary. Even if Uncle Willard thought she was an addle-brained fool lady, crazy as a loon. But she knew me. Probably better than Mama or Papa.

"Why, Miss Mary Frederick," Mr. Mendenhall said in his English accent. "What a delight to have you in our store again." Removing his monocle, he stepped away from the shelf he was sorting through, and, bowing, he lifted Miss Mary's proffered hand to his lips. "And young Travis Ford. What may I do for you this fine afternoon?"

I stuttered.

"Look around, Travis," Miss Mary said. "I shall do the same. Do you have the latest *Home Journal,* Mister Mendenhall?"

As the proprietor began apologizing about the difficulty of getting current magazines these days, but saying he did have a new translation of Homer's *The Iliad,* I wandered among the towering shelves. A short while later, the Englishman and the wealthy woman were conversing in French. Quickly, however, I no longer cared what language they were speaking. I wasn't listening because I was too focused on all the books.

To me, there was nothing better than browsing through a bookstore, especially Mr. J.D. Mendenhall's. He never said anything. Maybe he knew I couldn't afford a book, not those yellow-backed dreadfuls, or even a magazine or newspaper. He let me sit in one of the jury chairs by the window, reading whatever I wanted to read. Sometimes he even brought me a book while he and Miss Mary chatted and sipped tea.

I loved the smell of books, of paper, of leather. I loved the feel of a book in my hands, the gilt shining like gold, the touch of the paper, the smoothness of the leather covers. I loved the feeling I got when I opened a book for the first time, the noise of the spine cracking, the stiff pages. Mostly I loved reading. The adventure. The promise. The joy of learning something new. I would pick up a copy, read the title, and imagine what it must feel like for the author to see his name on the spine. I would imagine seeing my name. I picked up a book and silently mouthed: "*Jane Eyre* by Travis Ford." Then I moved to the shelf I knew all so well.

The Partisan. The Yemassee. Border Beagles. The Tennessean's Story. Eutaw.

I had read everything William Gilmore Simms had ever written, fiction and nonfiction, or at least 'most everything J.D. Mendenhall had ever sold. Then I remembered something. I looked, fingering the spines, studying the titles, then sighed with disappointment. *The Cassique of Kiawah* was gone. I imagined Mr. Mendenhall had sold the one I had been reading on my visits to town with Miss Mary. That was one I would never finish, unless he got another copy to sell. It was William Gilmore Simms, Esquire, who had introduced me to South Carolina's Swamp Fox in *The Life of Francis Marion*. And Nathanael Greene in *The Life of Nathanael Greene, Major-General in the Army of the Revolution*. He wrote of adventure, and romance, of the olden times of the Revolutionary War in the South, and the frontier of the Carolinas, Alabama, and Mississippi. I had even enjoyed Simms's poetry.

Other books were missing. In fact, the shelves, usually overflowing, had plenty of spaces. It resembled Mama's cupboard back home.

The few titles of Simms I had already read, but that was all right. I moved on to Dumas.

I loved Simms, but he wrote about the South, a South not that far removed from my current home and times. Dumas, however, wrote about France and Europe, and that was a long, long way from Washington County, Arkansas.

I had devoured *The Three Musketeers, Twenty Years After, The Vicomte de Bragelonne,* and *The Count of Monte Cristo,* but where I had hoped to find *The Black Tulip,* of which I had read the first twenty or thirty pages, I found only one book, and it wasn't even Dumas. It was something from Charles Dickens. I had heard of Dickens, but had never read anything by him, although Mr. Mendenhall had suggested that I try *David Copperfield* or *A Christmas Carol*. This book, however, was titled *A Tale of Two Cities*.

With no new Simms or Dumas to guide my way, I walked to the window with Charles Dickens, and read.

BOOK THE FIRST. RECALLED TO LIFE.
Chapter 1.
THE PERIOD.

It was the best of times, it was the worst of times, it was the age of wisdom, it was the age of foolishness, it was the epoch of belief, it was the epoch of incredulity . . .

"Epoch" and "incredulity". Two new words for Webster's when I returned home.

. . . it was the season of light, it was the season of darkness, it was the spring of hope. . . .

I looked up, and stared out the window. The cannon and caisson were out of the bog, moving down Washington at a fast clip, the officer still cursing his men and waving his saber.

"It was the spring of hope," I said aloud.

That afternoon, I never read another word. Rare for me in Mr. Mendenhall's store. I had devoured Simms and Dumas and Shakespeare and Milton and Hawthorne and Cooper and Poe and Lord Byron. Or thumbed through *Harper's Monthly Magazine* or *Phunny Fellow* or *National Police Gazette* or the newspapers from Arkansas, Texas, Missouri, and Tennessee. Once, Mr. Mendenhall had even handed me a copy of *Uncle Tom's Cabin* by Harriet Beecher Stowe, with a warning. "Put this away when Miss Mary comes to say it's time to take your leave. Hide it under the cushion and show her *The Big Bear of Arkansas* instead. I dare say it would be a trifle unpleasant to be run out of town on a rail and see my bookstore burned."

I watched soldiers marching or riding through the mud. I studied the faces of the civilians, women in their calico dresses, men in their top hats and suits, children, even the preachers. I tried to imagine what they were thinking. Then I saw Uncle Willard walking down the boardwalk, spitting tobacco juice into the mud, and I looked away, turned from the window, buried my face in *A Tale of Two Cities* but not reading a word, praying that he would not recognize Miss Mary's carriage or Mowbray, who was leaning against the hitching rail in front of Stinson and Dodge's Jewelers, not daring to make eye contact with anyone passing by.

Uncle Willard must have been too preoccupied, because after an eternity of thirty or forty seconds I looked up and carefully turned around. He wasn't standing there, glowering. Nobody passed by, but then I almost leaped off the chair when the door opened and the bell chimed.

The door closed quickly, shutting out the noise of soldiers and horses. Light steps sounded across the hardwood floor before a timid voice called out: "Mister Mendenhall?"

It was a woman. My heart resumed beating. I closed Dickens, and heard Miss Mary greeting the newcomer, who spoke so excitedly her voice rose and cracked.

"Mary, Mister Mendenhall, those soldiers . . . I think they are preparing to leave."

I had started to reopen *A Tale of Two Cities.* Now I listened.

"Does Old Pap confide that much in you, Missus Andersen?" the bookstore owner said lightly.

"I have not spoken to General Price," the woman said. "But the soldiers speak plainly. They speak bluntly. The Yankees are moving toward the capital."

Little Rock? I shook my head. The Yankees already controlled Little Rock. Then it struck me. Washington. The new Confederate capital of Arkansas.

"And if Price leaves us to those horrid, horrid barbarians . . . I . . . I fear for my . . . for our safety."

"Now, now, Joyce." That was Miss Mary. "I think the Yankees will leave you alone. Mayhap they will even leave Camden alone. Don't you think so, Mister Mendenhall?"

His silence betrayed any confidence felt by anyone in the store, probably in the entire city.

"But . . . ," Mrs. Andersen said, "I've heard that the Yankees have darkies fighting for them. Darkies! I am a white woman, a widow living alone. I fear for my very life."

I shook my head, and reopened Dickens. Mrs. Andersen was just another crazy old lady living in troubled times. She likely feared what the Confederate soldiers under Price would do to her when they first returned to Camden.

Still I didn't read. Mr. Mendenhall suggested to Mrs. Andersen that some hot tea might steady her nerves, and then Miss Mary bid them both good day. It was time for us to leave on our other errands. Miss Mary had a package, wrapped in brown paper and secured with twine, and the *Ouachita Herald* in her hand. I offered to take it, but she said she was not old and feeble although she thanked me for my kindness and consideration. We stepped outside, leaving behind the worlds of Dumas and Dickens and Simms. She handed me the newspaper, which felt funny in my hand.

"It's printed on foolscap," she announced. "As it was when Joshua Ruth published his first edition almost twenty years ago." She sighed. " 'What goes around, comes around', as the saying goes. Paper is hard to find, too." She held up a $5 Arkansas banknote. It had been printed on the back of wallpaper.

Back down the street we rode to Mr. Kroger's mercantile.

"Don't be disappointed, Travis," Miss Mary said, "if there's no letter from your father."

"I won't be," I said, but I would be. Miss Mary knew. She put her hand on my shoulder and squeezed, and said hopefully: "If not today, then maybe tomorrow, Travis."

Tomorrow was Sunday. I was beginning to fear there would never be another letter from Papa.

At the store, Miss Mary stocked up on tea, flour, beans, and bacon, never balking at the outrageous prices Mr. Kroger charged, although he was apologetic, noting how everything was hard to get these days. Except bacon.

And wood, I thought, thinking back to Mama's crazy idea about reopening the sawmill.

We never even looked at fabric for drapes in the formal parlor. I imagine Miss Mary didn't care a whit if the drapes were red or brown or blue. That had been just her way of getting me to Mr. Mendenhall's, or maybe she had just wanted someone to talk to on the drive to and from Camden.

"Well, Travis, there's one more stop, then it's back home for you," she said.

I became curious immediately, hoping our last stop would be at one of the restaurants, but instead we went out of town to the Fountain Timber Company.

When we turned off the pike, even though the mill lay two miles down the woods road, I could hear the saws whirling. Circular rotary saws, not old muleys. I could smell smoke, see the white plumes rising above the pines that shaded the road, coming from the giant incinerator where the Fountains burned sawdust and small wood pieces.

"I warrant that Ezekial wouldn't charge Confederate rates for some sawdust, do you, Travis?" Miss Mary said.

"Ma'am?"

"Sawdust," she said. "What do you think a fair rate for sawdust would be?"

"I don't know."

"You're a sawyer, aren't you?"

I shrugged for an answer, then said: "Papa was one. *Is* one."

"Yes. He *is*. But you're not?"

This time I let my shrug suffice.

"I'm building a new carriage house," she said. "And I would like Mowbray to be warm in the winter. Wouldn't you like that, Mowbray?" addressing her driver.

"You don't have to worry about ol' Mowbray, Miss Mary," he answered, keeping the grays focused on getting us down the road.

Back to me, Miss Mary said: "So I need sawdust."

"What for?"

"Insulation."

Insulation? That was another new word for me and Webster's, along with epoch and incredulity. Then I forgot about spelling and vocabulary and the "spring of hope". I thought about Mama, and her far-fetched dream.

"You need sawdust?" I said.

"For insulation."

"Well, Miss Mary, we can get you sawdust. At Papa's mill. There's plenty of it there. And you can use it for your incredulity."

"My what?"

I muttered an apology. I was too excited. "Your insulation," I corrected. "How much do you reckon you'd need?" Before she could answer, I fired out: "It don't matter. Doesn't matter. We have tons. We could haul it to. . . ."

I had hit a snag. Our mules were gone. Those wagons I'd seen at the mill weren't good for anything except firewood.

"Well . . . ," I said, determined. "Well, we can get it to your place."

The wagon kept taking us down the path toward the Fountain Timber Company. Miss Mary stared at me until I looked away, embarrassed. Suddenly the woman everyone thought was crazy did something absolutely insane.

"Mowbray," she said, "turn this wagon around. I shall do business with Master Ford. It's much better to do business with a neighbor, and, honestly, I despise Ezekial Fountain and his loathsome brood."

CHAPTER FIVE

The ride home turned pleasant. I evolved from thirteen-year-old boy to entrepreneur. I stopped imagining an adventure story called "the spring of hope" and began thinking of how Mama, Edith, and I could get barrels of sawdust to Miss Mary's place, five miles down the road from our home, even farther from Papa's sawmill.

Put lids on the barrels? Roll them from the mill up the road to the Camden-Washington Pike, then roll them down to Miss Mary's? But there were a lot of hills. Rolling them uphill would prove backbreaking. Rolling them down? I could picture them smashing into a pine, spraying sawdust like grapeshot. I saw them rolling down the hills and wiping out a group of Yankees marching to Camden. I liked that idea. I hoped I could remember it later. Well, rolling barrels of sawdust might make for a good adventure, a scene worthy of Simms or Dumas, but for transporting insulation, it wasn't practical. Those barrels could hold forty-two gallons, and I recalled Papa's workers moving the barrels, their muscles bulging, straining, their grunting and groaning, until they finally just dragged them over the floor. A hundred pounds? Maybe. And wet sawdust would weigh even more.

We had no mules. We had no wagon. But I was bound and determined to figure out a way to make this deal work. If I possessed one talent, it was imagination, which I would definitely need for Mama to agree to my idea.

"Sawdust?" Mama said.

She sat in her chair on the porch, staring down the road as Miss Mary rode back home in her fancy carriage. Miss Mary hadn't mentioned my scheme again, even when dropping me off. I reckon she figured that would best be left to me.

"Yes, ma'am. We got plenty of it."

Edith and Baby Hugh stood silently in the shade. I was kneeling in front of the steps.

"And she needs this for . . . ?"

"Insulation." I remembered the word. "She's building a new carriage house. The insulation would keep Mowbray warm." That's when it began to hit me. I had thought maybe the sawdust would be used for fuel for the fire. We had used it often ourselves, but now I began to see the purpose, and the definition of insulation. Miss Mary was building a frame house, not a cabin like we lived in, and not brick like her mansion. She had told me that on the fifteen-mile ride home. The outside of the house would be plank boards, nailed to the two-by-four frames. The sawdust would fill the gap between the outside and inside walls. Or maybe in the roof. Or underneath the floor. Insulation. I'd look it up in the Webster's just to make sure.

"Do we have enough sawdust?" Mama asked. She glanced at the brown-paper package Miss Mary had left with her as if she might find the answer there.

"There's a lot." It was as specific as I could be. "If we don't, we can always get some from the other sawyers in the area. They usually just burn theirs. They'd probably just give it away."

"And how much would you charge Mary?"

"We ain't . . . we haven't gotten to dickering yet."

"You won't dicker with Mary Frederick, Travis. She has been

45

too good of a neighbor."

"Yes, ma'am. I'll ask her what she thinks is fair, and that'll be it."

"I think it's a good idea, Mama," said Edith, speaking as the oldest child.

"I ate all the pound cake," Baby Hugh said. "Didn't save none for you." He stuck out his tongue.

"Be quiet, Hugh," Mother said, contemplating, and I knew her next question would likely sink my money-making idea.

"How do we get the sawdust to Mary's? That's seven, eight miles from the mill."

"The wagons!" Edith sang out. She hadn't seen the condition of those wagons. "The wagons Papa always used to haul. . . ." Then she remembered. "Oh. . . ."

Even if those timber wagons could carry one-hundred-pound barrels of sawdust up the woods lane and down the main pike to Miss Mary's plantation, we didn't have the livestock to pull the wagons. Yet Edith, like me, wasn't about to let the idea go.

"We could borrow a team of mules from Miss Mary."

"I suppose so," Mama said.

"We'd have to borrow a wagon, too." I let out a heavy, dream-killing sigh.

Edith and Hugh looked at me in disbelief.

"Those wagons at Papa's mill couldn't carry a pine cone," I said.

"But . . . ," Edith began.

"Travis is right," Mama said. "I suppose we should just offer to give the sawdust to Mary. She's been such a wonderful neighbor."

"I offered that, Mama," I lied. "But you know Miss Mary. She's a prideful woman. Wouldn't hear of it."

"Yes," Mama said, "but if we're using her mules and her wagon, it would only be fitting. . . ."

"How about Uncle Willard?" Baby Hugh interrupted, and my stomach turned. I had thought of him, too, but couldn't see him at Papa's mill, working his slaves.

Mama, thank the good Lord, couldn't see that, either.

"No," she said. "Not Willard. He'd take over the mill, run it with his slave labor." Her Abolitionist was up. "By the time Connor came home, Willard would be running the mill. No, we won't use him. But . . . there is . . . Reverend White." I didn't know what she meant, but the subject had been tabled. "It's time for supper," Mama said as she rose, and held out the package Miss Mary had given her. "This is for you, Travis."

Baby Hugh's previous smug look became one of envy. All he had gotten was pound cake. I had something wrapped, something solid, something that would last a lot longer than a full belly, or so I imagined.

"What is it?" I asked.

Mama smiled. "It's a present. I don't know what it is."

"But it's not his birthday," Edith argued. "I would know."

"Hush," Mother said, still holding out the package.

I moved toward her, and took the package as if I thought it would disappear.

"Open it," Baby Hugh said, and my mother stepped back, folding her arms, smiling.

The bow was easy to undo. I handed Baby Hugh the twine, and then pulled back the brown paper. That I gave to Edith, who muttered something under her breath that she was really lucky Mama had not heard, or at least had pretended not to hear.

"That ain't no present," Baby Hugh said, and the smug look returned. "That's for schooling."

I held a writing tablet and a box of pencils.

"Mary Frederick must know you well," Mama said softly.

I studied Mama closely. Did she know my secret, too?

"She should," Edith complained. "She takes him to Camden once a month."

"I'd rather go to Little Rock," Baby Hugh said. "And I'd rather eat leftover pound cake."

Miss Mary did know me well. I wondered how. Had she read my mind when I had imagined all those adventures—pirates hanging out in the pine trees, the carriage Mowbray drove a balloon full of wild Argonauts. I had always imagined those stories. Now, at last, I could try to write one down.

"You'll write her a note thanking her for her kindness," Mama said. "And you'll keep this in mind when she tells you what she considers a fair price for the sawdust."

After supper, I retired with my writing tablet and newly sharpened pencil. Having referred to my Webster's, on the first page of the tablet, I wrote:

epoch: In chronology, a fixed point of time.

Which was one of the bothersome things about Webster's. I kept reading the definition, writing down the examples—*The exodus of the Israelites from Egypt, and the Babylonish captivity. . . .*—then turned to chronology. And wrote:

chronology: The science of time; the method of measuring or computing time by regular divisions or periods.

I didn't write the rest. I found insulation, and decided that my definition was right. Incredulity took longer, because I didn't have an inkling how to spell it, but eventually I located it.

incredulity: The quality of not believing.

That was a good word, I decided. I'd likely use it a lot more than insulation or chronology, but I liked epoch the best.

So once I was sure no one was watching me, I turned the page and wrote,:

THE SPRING OF HOPE
By Travis Ford

It was the epoch of adventure.

Sunday morning we walked to the meeting house.

Mama made a vinegar pie, and made Edith carry it on the long, wet walk to church. The Reverend White was like most preachers, and I found his sermon boring—like most sermons—until he began preaching of the dark days that lay ahead for all of us. The Yankees were marching toward Washington. General Price was sure to meet the enemy. The South could not, would not, be defeated. Arkansas was just. Arkansas was Eden. Arkansas would prevail.

Although he did not cite chapter and verse, he then said something that I considered divine. "Last Sunday, y'all might recollect, was a day we call Easter." He waited for the chuckling, mostly his own, to subside. "This is a spring of hope, my friends. A spring of hope."

A spring of hope. I didn't hear anything else. My mind went to the story I had begun. An adventure story. Full of sword fights. The Reverend White had put me in a Dumas frame of mind, mostly because he had always reminded me of Porthos. Without a doubt, he was the biggest, jowliest man I'd ever seen. Whenever I pretended to be d'Artagnan or read *The Three Musketeers* in Mr. Mendenhall's bookstore, I always imagined the Reverend White as Porthos. 'Course, he didn't speak in a French accent—he had a molasses-thick drawl—nor, as far as I knew, did he partake of wine, and instead of wielding a sword nicknamed Balizarde, he carried a big, well-used Bible.

A spring of hope. That's about all I got out of the sermon or the service itself. After all, I didn't like to sing. I wasn't that great at praying—my mind wandered. And the meeting house was stuffy, full of stiff-backed old men and women, two or three who pressed hearing horns to their ears, rich folks who fanned themselves, poor folks who sweated in homespun muslin and duck trousers, fidgeting children, and those who fell asleep in the back pews well before the doxology. I let my imagination carry me out of the meeting house and to Paris.

After services, Mama made us stay put in the first row, letting the crowd scatter to their Sunday roasts and Bible studies. That annoyed Baby Hugh to no end, but he knew better than to act up in public, especially in church. Finally we rose, and met with the Reverend White at the door.

Mama presented him with the vinegar pie.

"Why, thank y'all. Thank all y'all. From the bottom of my heart. It's good to see y'all. How you been farin', Missus Ford?"

"We are fine in health and spirits, Reverend."

"And Connor?"

Her smile faded. "No word," she said hollowly.

He set the pie on the bench by the door, and put a massive arm on Mama's shoulder. "I've prayed for him and all the young men fightin'," he said. "The Lord'll look after him. He'll see him home. God is on our side, for our side is just."

"I'm sure you are right." She said it without feeling, though.

"Well. . . ." It was noon. The reverend looked hungry. He likely wanted to get back to his cabin and the vinegar pie.

"Reverend," Mama said, "I hate to impose, but we need to borrow a good mule." He pursed his fat lips, as she continued. "One that can haul two barrels of sawdust from Connor's mill to Mary Frederick's plantation. That is per trip. Twelve miles round trip. I cannot fathom how many trips. Well, that would depend on the sawdust."

"Sawdust?" His belly rumbled.

"Sawdust. For insulation."

His face shook with laughter. "That Mary Frederick. She is always up to somethin'. Sawdust. For insulation."

"Yes. And you remember that our mules were stolen. . . ."

"By runaway slaves!" the reverend thundered, no longer laughing, his face now contorted with rage.

"By whomever," Mama said. "Confederate deserters or just plain white trash."

Which, to me, didn't seem like the right thing to say when one wanted to borrow a mule from a Southern sympathizer, but the Reverend White apparently did not hear. He whipped off his wide-brimmed black hat, ran fingers through his thick, sweaty locks of brown hair, and frowned hard.

"How long do you reckon you'd need my Betsy?" he asked once the hat was atop his head again.

"Two days," she said, sounding uncertain. "We can haul the . . . well, Travis can haul the sawdust, dump the barrels in Mary Frederick's stables, and the carpenters building her carriage house can place the sawdust where best used for insulation."

I wasn't sure our supply of sawdust would take two days to haul.

"Well," he said, glancing at the pie again, beaming. "I reckon for vinegar pie, I could loan y'all my Betsy for two days." He turned to me. "Boy, you recollect where I live?" I nodded. "Good. You come on 'round my place on Tuesday. I need Betsy on Monday to get me on my prayer calls. Lots of prayin' needed durin' these dark days of war and pestilence. Can you ride a mule? Good. You can ride Betsy bareback to your place. Bareback, I say. Don't think you'd fit in my saddle nohow. But you'll need to bring Betsy back Thursday evenin'. On account that I got more prayer rounds to make Friday. That suit y'all?"

"Yes, Reverend," Mother answered. "We thank you for your generosity."

"Shucks, Missus Ford, it's the Christian thing to do. And . . . ," he winked, and added in a conspiratorial tone, "some folks say I'd sell my soul for one of your vinegar pies."

Mama put her arm on his shoulder. "Now, Reverend," she said, thickening her accent so that she sounded more like Miss Mary than our mother, "I don't think that's true at all. Not at all."

They both laughed.

CHAPTER SIX

On the morning of Monday, April 4th, I walked alone to Papa's sawmill to begin my new career as businessman. Mama didn't want Edith in the sawmill—not that Edith wanted to be there—and, besides, someone had to look after Baby Hugh, so I volunteered to begin filling the barrels and inspecting those that already contained sawdust, so they would be ready for Tuesday, when we would have the Reverend White's mule to haul the sawdust to Miss Mary's.

Mama packed a lunch of a raw potato and some carrots, some leftover cornbread, and a half-full jar of apple preserves. I tried to slip my writing tablet and two pencils in the knapsack, but you couldn't get anything past Edith's keen eyes.

"You going to write or doodle?" she asked snidely. "Or do some actual work?"

"Work," I snapped, thinking: *Writing is work.* Though I didn't know that for certain. Criminy, I'd never tried writing except when practicing my letters or scribbling a letter to some friend or relative.

"Leave him alone." Mama had come to my rescue. "But, Travis, you cannot idle away the hours. We will only have the Reverend White's mule for two days."

"I know, Mama." I let her kiss my cheek, smiled at Baby Hugh, and stuck my tongue out at my sister before whistling "Pop Goes the Weasel" as I bounded down the steps and headed up the path to the main road, skipping toward the Ford Family Mill.

I didn't know if King Louis's Musketeers of the Guard wore knapsacks like those Confederate soldiers I had seen in Camden, but mine did. Twenty-three-year-old Travis Ford—it sounded French to me—left his farm in Gascony, armed with a musket (the broom Mama had given me) over his shoulder, and rapier (a sapling I had snapped off in the bar ditch).

I dueled with Comte de Rochefort and Cardinal Richelieu's guards, running several through with sword, piercing others with well-aimed balls from the musket. The mysterious Milady de Winter tried to poison me, but I switched goblets and watched her cough, gag, and fall into the bar ditch to be eaten by crocodiles.

Then I thought: *It was the spring of hope. It was the epoch of adventure.*

I had adventure, but where was the hope? Tossing away the rapier, I studied on my conundrum. *Monsieur* Travis Ford, poor nobleman from Gascony, hoped to become a musketeer. That didn't strike me as reason enough to title a whole story, possibly even a book, *The Spring of Hope.* Soon another problem struck me. Rochefort, Richelieu, Milady were fine villains for Athos, Porthos, Aramis, and d'Artagnan, but those were Alexandre Dumas's creations, not mine.

A bobwhite quail sang out. I whistled back at him.

A farmer on a bay horse called out a greeting as he rode out from Camden, but I didn't even realize he had spoken, didn't even notice the horse, until he was three rods past me. I turned quickly. "Good morning, sir."

"You're in deep thought, boy," he called back, chuckling. "Best be aware of your surroundings. Yanks could be hiding in them trees."

"Yes, sir. Thank you, sir."

Twenty-three-year-old Monsieur *Travis Ford turns his musket toward the towering forests outside of Meung-sur-Loire. Cardinal Richelieu's . . . no, Cardinal Willard's guards could be hiding behind any tree, waiting to pick him off, to steal his letter of introduction to* Monsieur *Mowbray, commander of the king's musketeers.*

More adventures await the hero as he turns down the woods lane.

Even sight of the rundown mill failed to dampen my spirits.

I stormed the castle, killing one guard with a musket ball, beating two others with the butt of the gun, and then was safe inside the walls. Out of breath, I reloaded the musket, peeked through the window, and saw the squirrel staring at me as if I were crazy.

My laugh startled him, and he scurried up an oak, but soon he, and plenty of his friends, had resumed their quest to find the acorns that littered the ground. They could clean up the nuts, but I had a far more daunting task. I slung the knapsack off my back, leaned the broom in the corner, and looked around me.

"It would take five grown-ups a week to do this work," I said aloud. "I've only got today."

I got at it, though, still whistling, knowing *The Spring of Hope* would have to wait until I stopped to eat.

The first full barrel was so rotted, the top broke off in my hand, spilling wet sawdust onto the top of my brogans. Three others looked to be in fair shape, so I went back to the first barrel, and, somehow, using a shovel from the tool shed as a level, managed to tip it over. I overturned an empty barrel, and began rolling it across the floor when my right foot smashed through a rotted board. Luckily I didn't break my leg or anything else.

★　★　★　★　★

The castle is filled with traps. That would keep French swordsman Travis Ford on his adventure.

Carefully I picked my way across the floor, dreaming up other adventures, then forgot all about my story as I began shoveling sawdust into the barrel.

I worked until well after noon, dumping sawdust from baskets into barrels, sweeping, shoveling, sweating. Two barrels. The bottom fell out of the third when I moved it. Only two barrels, but that would work. It would have to.

My trousers were covered with sawdust and my hands rough from the shovel and broom. Finally I decided it was time to eat. Thinking I would write and eat, I ate instead, famished, washing it down with water from the well. A fish jumped up in the nearby pond. Birds sang. Thunder rolled, and I stepped outside and looked at the sky, most of which was blocked out by the pines. I saw no clouds, but thunder did not lie. I should have brought my poncho with me.

Travis Ford, King's Musketeer, made his way through the streets of Paris, a violent thunderstorm raging, following his lovely Constance, wondering what intrigue she was involved with, fighting highwaymen along the route.

When I had swallowed the last of the cornbread and fingered out the remaining preserves, I went back to work, testing the two barrels, and sweeping up mounds of sawdust mixed with the droppings of squirrels, mice, rabbits, and rats. Late that afternoon, I decided that I had worked enough. I moved to the millpond, washed the sweat and sawdust off my hair, face, neck, and hands, and dried myself off with the rag I'd stuck in a trouser pocket.

The pines rustled overhead in the wind, and I knew a storm was coming. Mama would be worried, but, first, I had to write. So I sat down and began my epoch of adventure.

By the time I knew I needed to start for home, I could smell rain in the air, which presented me with another problem. If I got caught in a storm, *The Spring of Hope* might be ruined. Besides, did I really want to bring it home, and have Edith discover it when she was snooping around in the loft? Have her laugh at my literary desires? Worse, have Mama find it?

Stepping inside the tool shed, with its tin roof, I began exploring. There were two toolboxes still full of tools, which might work. A lot of sacks. Saws, shovels, rakes, axes leaning in the corners. I pulled a piece of burlap off a shelf, and found a box. I stepped closer, used the burlap to wipe off the dust, and lifted it. The box was made of wood—not pine, not oak, but something dark. The lid was hinged, and there was a keyhole, although I could see no key. It didn't matter. The lid opened, and I looked inside. Empty, but it smelled of cigars and tobacco. I brought out my tablet, and set it inside. It fit perfectly, and I closed the lid, then stared.

At first, I thought the picture on the lid had been painted, then it struck me that it was a wood engraving, and finally I realized, no, it was something different. The image depicted a man in a funny shirt with a white collar, bending over, picking on some strange-shaped guitar. A lady in a flowery dress sat, hands clasped against her heart, eyes closed, head tilted up toward the minstrel who was serenading her. The moon was crescent. A tree, leaves drooping from the branches, stood behind her. They were on a deck. Ship or palace? I couldn't tell. A lake or river or ocean lay behind them. The lady had blonde hair. The man wore a black cap.

The images had been put together with pieces of wood, like in a puzzle, meticulously fitted to form a piece of art. It was the most wonderful cigar box I had ever seen, and then I saw the signature at the corner: *C.J. Ford, '59.*

Connor Joseph Ford. My father was more than a sawyer, more than a furniture maker, more than a soldier. Staring at the lid, I ran my fingers across the top, feeling the contours, the design, the love. Papa was an artist. After I slipped the box back inside the burlap sack, I placed it back on the shelf.

Once I had broom and knapsack, I sprinted down the woods lane, hoping I would beat the rain home.

I did. It rained most of the night, but the storm had blown past by the time I was up before dawn.

"You know where the Reverend White lives?" Mama inquired.

"Yes, ma'am. Me and Papa delivered him some wood for that shed he was building one time."

"Papa and I," she corrected.

"Papa and I, I mean. I can find it."

We had everything figured out to a T. I would bring the mule home this afternoon, run back to the mill, finish collecting the sawdust—and maybe have time to add a few paragraphs to *The Spring of Hope.* Wednesday, when we began hauling the insulation to Miss Mary's, would require some additional help. I couldn't hoist one-hundred-pound barrels onto the packsaddle. But I had engineered a plan that would work. Leaving Baby Hugh with Edith at home, Mama and I would go to the mill. We could pull the mule up to the open side where the cut timber went spilling out. Then we would harness one barrel on that side, turn the mule around, put the second barrel on the other side, and lead the mule all the way to Miss Mary's. We would do the same thing on Thursday, before I had to take the mule back to the Reverend White's. He lived closer to Miss Mary, anyhow.

Two hours later, the hounds began yipping and howling as I

approached the preacher's cabin. Mama had baked him another vinegar pie, which he greatly appreciated and which I was pleased to be rid of after four miles of traipsing through soaking wet grass and mud. The reverend took me to the barn, where he introduced me to Betsy. He slipped a hackamore and blanket on her, and then boosted me onto her back.

"Good luck, boy." His breath smelled of bacon. "Now, don't you forget to have her back to me Thursday afore dark."

"Yes, sir."

"Got lots of prayin' to be done Friday."

"Yes, sir."

"War's goin' badly for us, boy."

"Yes, sir."

"But it's darkest before the dawn."

"That's what Uncle Willard says." I thanked him again, kicked Betsy into a walk, and ducked on my way out of the barn. A half mile later, out of the woods, and back on the main road, Musketeer Travis Ford was racing his fine black steed through charging lancers, the lady Constance clinging to his back, whispering words of love and encouragement.

In no time I reached home.

"I wanna ride him!" Baby Hugh cried out from the porch.

"It's a her," I said, swinging down, taking off Betsy's blanket, and tossing it over the porch railing to dry.

"How would you know?" my brother asked.

I gave him the look that said: *Are you the dumbest kid in Washington County?*

"Mama!" Baby Hugh wailed. "Can't I ride that horse?"

"It's a mule," Edith and I said at the same time.

Mama broke up the bickering before it turned into a fight. "That mule is here to help us," she told Baby Hugh as she came down the steps, put one hand on the mule's back, and walked around him. In her other hand she had carrots that she offered to Betsy. The mule began munching on the carrots. She seemed to enjoy them. Of course, she hadn't been eating carrots and potatoes all fall, all winter, all spring, like we had.

"It's good to have a mule around again." Mama's face shined brightly. She rubbed her hand in a circular motion on Betsy's neck. When Betsy began peeing, causing Baby Hugh to stagger backward and Edith to scream, Mama merely laughed. "Oh, this is a great spring," she said. "I can feel it."

"It's a spring of hope," I told her, and her smile faded as she began to stare at me. It kind of felt as if she were seeing me as an adult, not a kid, not her son. "That's right, Travis." Her eyes glowed again. "A spring of hope."

"Hope springs eternal," Edith said, just to say something.

"Yes. Yes, it does."

After dinner, I hurried back to the mill, sending squirrels retreating up to the highest limbs as my feet crunched atop the acorns. I secured lids on the barrels, scooped the last shovelful of sawdust into the last fit barrel. Two barrels. I'd have to fill those barrels again. Looking around, I decided there wasn't enough sawdust left to fill more than five barrels, but that was better than nothing.

I didn't know how much insulation Miss Mary's carpenters would need, but this was all we had. Unless Mama decided I could operate the sawmill, which would mean opening the dam to turn the muley, shoving lumber along the carriage, and then listening to the whine of the saw as it cut into the log. It would take a lot of trees to produce enough sawdust to fill even one barrel.

So this was all Miss Mary would be getting from the Ford Family Mill, but it was a start. It might be enough to put something on our plates other than potatoes and carrots. Maybe we could even find and afford a sack of coffee for Mama.

I scribbled only a few paragraphs, hardly even knowing what

I wrote, then returned the tablet to Papa's cigar box, hid it in the shed, and raced home.

The next morning, everyone awakened and dressed before dawn. Dew covered the ground. The weather had turned cooler, I could feel the rain in the air, and I felt in a rush to get to the mill, to begin loading sawdust.

I finished breakfast so quickly, Mama laughed. "If you're in that big of a hurry, Travis," she said, "you go on to the mill and get things ready. I'll bring Betsy along directly, after I am certain"—she put both hands on her hips and stared hard at Edith and Baby Hugh—"that two children in this household begin their baths."

"It ain't Satur-. . . ." The word died in Baby Hugh's throat. He stared at his potatoes and grits. "Yes'm," he muttered meekly.

I snatched hat, broom, and poncho, and raced out of the kitchen, down the steps, and onto the road.

Travis Ford races through Paris, determined to get the diamond necklace to Queen Anne and save her from her husband's wrath and the guillotine.

When I reached the mill, it took a while to catch my breath. Then I checked the barrels, and restrained myself from sneaking into the shed to write some more. Mama might find me. But she didn't come.

I threw stones in the mill pond. I tossed stones at a squirrel. I even cleaned up parts of the mill. Still, Mama didn't show up. That wasn't like her. She wouldn't be late for church, she always had breakfast, dinner, and supper on the table early. After an hour, I became worried. After two, I had stopped playing, stopped working, and perched myself on the steps, staring down the woods lane. Ten minutes later, I was walking back up the lane.

The line of men, their curses, their laughs, stopped me for a moment. Again, I caught my breath. Unsteadily I continued toward the road. The marching men glanced at me. One sent a river of tobacco juice in my direction, and laughed. Horses, wagons, cannon, but mostly men marched on by. All along the Camden-Washington Pike, as far as I could see in both directions, soldiers marched toward Washington.

Once I understood what was happening, I began running alongside the road, on the other side of the bar ditch. Running as fast as I could for home.

Chapter Seven

It wasn't a dashing musketeer or a Confederate spy who ran through the weeds and briars, but a frightened thirteen-year-old boy. Since the start of the war, I had seen soldiers, but never this many. A few cracked jokes as I raced by them. Laughing, some tossed mud clods after me. Others assaulted me with their foolish jokes, light-hearted insults, vile curses.

"What's the hurry, kid?"

"Hey, Sarge, why don't we conscript that cheetah as a runner?"

"McEnroe, I ain't seen a body move that fast since Princeton last December."

"Yeah, Gates, but that was us skedaddlin' then."

A musket popped, and I almost fell, but then came the laughter, and I righted myself, never breaking stride, leaping over a fallen log. The laughter died behind me when an officer yelled: "Who fired that shot? Who fired it?"

By the time anyone admitted to the breach of protocol, I was a hundred yards up the Pike, being greeted by more jokes, dirt clods, and laughter.

I tried to tell myself that there was nothing to worry about. Mama couldn't bring the mule up the road because the Confederate Army hogged the entire lane. She had had to wait, and that's what she was doing. But I couldn't convince myself.

The path ended, and I cut into the woods, zipping through the pines and oaks, feeling the briars tug at my trousers. Out of the woods I shot, and resumed my race through the weeds, next to the cackling soldiers.

Run! I told myself.

Faster!

My lungs burned, and sharp pain pierced my side. Gripping my side, leaning forward, I kept running, though my stride kept lessening. Tears blinded me. Somehow, I refused to quit racing home.

Until a vise gripped my shoulder, and jerked me savagely to the ground.

My head exploded. I wanted to roll over and vomit. My lungs screamed for oxygen, and I sucked in as much air as I could as I rubbed my head, opened my eyes, and waited for the tears to evaporate.

"Where you runnin' to, boy?" a thick voice demanded.

"Answer Mickey, you runt!" A boot slammed into my brogan.

Wincing, I saw what I had run into. Two Confederates had leaped across the bar ditch. I figured it had been the big one who had grabbed my shoulder, flung me to the ground. The runt who had called me a runt didn't look much bigger than me.

He thrust the point of a bayonet under my chin. "I said, runt, you answer Fellman, here. Or you'll taste the steel Steele's gonna taste right soon." He laughed, turned toward the soldiers on the road, and called out: "Hey, did you hear that, Jimmy? 'Taste the steel Steele's gonna taste.' That's funny. That's real funny."

"If you say so, O'Brien."

O'Brien stopped laughing and faced me again, thrusting the bayonet lower. "Where you bound in such a hurry, runt?"

His blouse was denim, patched with plaid in various places, and filthy suspenders held up his green trousers, the hems rolled up revealing bony, hairless legs, no socks, no shoes, and blackened feet. His face was gaunt. In fact, he looked more like a skeleton than a human with his gray eyes sunk well back in his jaundiced face. He wore no hat, and the only thing that identified him as a soldier was the oval brass belt buckle that held his cartridge box, and that, I soon realized, was stamped *US*, not *CS*. He wasn't a Yankee, though.

"You heard him, boy," his partner said. "Where you in such a jo-fired hurry to gets to?"

That man had a dirty brown beard that stretched halfway to his stomach. His long hair was a mess, flowing this way and that, although he did wear a gray porkpie hat. His eyes were dark, his face leather, and he looked like a mountain. Instead of being too loose, his clothes—butternut pants, a shirt that might have once been white, and a shell jacket of patched gray—appeared as if they would split at the seams if the big man sneezed. He had butted his musket against the ground. He thrust a giant finger at me, which seemed more frightening than the bayonet at my throat.

"Answer me!"

"Home," I managed. "I'm going home."

"What you got there, boys?" another soldier called out as he marched past. "A Yankee spy?"

"That's what Fellman and me's tryin' to figure out," said O'Brien, the runt. He grinned without humor at me. "You a Yankee spy, runt?"

"No, sir. I live down the road."

"Where you comin' from?" the giant asked.

"My papa's sawmill."

"Your papa?" O'Brien cursed, and spit phlegm into the ditch. "How come he ain't fightin' with us?"

"He is. He joined Slemons's cavalry."

Runt turned to the giant. "What outfit's that?"

"Second Arkansas, I think."

65

"Cavalry." The runt snorted. "Well, your papa must be a right rich man. Got his own horse. Gets to ride all around. Hey, Fellman, you ever seen a dead hoss soldier?"

"No," the giant said. "Never."

They laughed, and then the runt said: "What's your papa's name?"

"Ford. Connor Ford."

"Fancy name." But the bayonet had been removed. He turned toward the marching soldiers. "Hey, Gene. You know of some sawmill in these here parts run by some uppity hoss soldier named Ford?"

"Criminy, O'Brien, they's more sawmills in this county than they's peoples."

"Well, how come you ain't fightin' with us, boy?" O'Brien asked me.

"I'm . . . I'm only thirteen."

The big one laughed and spit. "Me and O'Brien's buried boys younger'n that."

The runt looked back at me. "I don't know that we can trust him. What you think, Fellman?"

"Looks like a Yank to me."

"Smells like one, too."

"Should I run him through?"

"We ain't kilt nobody today. Might as well."

I had stopped breathing. Then something crashed to the grass behind me, and the giant and the runt snapped to attention.

"Fellman!" a voice roared. "O'Brien! What are you doing? Back in the ranks!"

"We's interrogatin' this runt, Capt'n," the runt said.

"Help him up. Now! Or you'll both be on the wooden horse when we reach Prairie D'Ane."

They both moved—the runt's musket falling into the grass—and lifted me up. The giant's hands roughly brushed the leaves and grass off my back while the runt picked up his musket and ran.

"Sorry," the giant said, and he hurried across the ditch.

I blinked, but caught only a glimpse of my savior as his roan horse leaped across the ditch, parted through the columns of soldiers. His kepi bounced as he rode back down the line, shouting: "Keep moving, lads! Keep moving!"

He was fifty yards back down the road, when I took off running again, passing Fellman, passing O'Brien, who was arguing with a tall gent in a straw hat.

After that, the dirt clods stopped coming my way, and the insults and laughter became only sporadic.

At last, I turned down the lane that led to home.

Soldiers were there. Long before the dogtrot cabin came into view, I understood that much. Horse apples and horse tracks scarred the path. I heard Mama screaming. I ran harder as I saw a group of Confederates circling the well and caught sight of Mama's head in the breaks between their shoulders. Two men were each carrying something in their arms toward the group by the well. On the porch, Edith held Baby Hugh in her arms. Both were sobbing. I saw other men coming out of the root cellar. I couldn't see the barn or coop, but I could hear chickens squawking, so I knew men were there, too.

Soldiers of the Confederate States of America. They were supposed to be protecting us, not robbing us.

I dodged between the picketed horses and mules, ran toward the well, past the two soldiers carrying. . . . My stomach turned as I caught the scent of death. One soldier pushed back the brim of his forage cap. The other laughed and spit tobacco juice. Each carried a dead dog over his right shoulder.

"You . . . are . . . not . . . doing . . . this!" Mama's voice, spaced out, determined, but choking, frightened.

Finally I heard myself yelling—"Leave her alone!"—as I

charged into the men who surrounded my mother and our well.

Tried to anyhow. One of the men, in a gray blouse without buttons, turned, brought up the butt of his musket, which cracked against my jaw. My teeth snapped down, my jaw exploded in pain, and, as I hit the ground hard on my back, I tasted blood in my mouth.

"You idiot, Clyde," another soldier said. "That ain't nothing but a kid."

Then my mother's voice: "Travis!"

My head swam, the earth spun out of control, and I thought again that I would vomit. Mama lifted me into her arms. I turned away from her, spit out blood. My tongue ran around my teeth. By some miracle, it didn't feel like I had lost any. I spit again.

Mama kissed my forehead. I worked my jaw while Mama screamed at the soldiers, calling them brutes, animals.

"Ma-ma," I managed. I had to spit again. "I . . . bit . . . my . . . tongue." I hoped I hadn't bitten it clean in half.

"You rest. Just lie still." Gently she lowered me to the ground and leaped to her feet. "You are not doing this!" she shouted at the soldiers.

As I opened my eyes it seemed as though dozens of my mother's figure spun around hundreds of blurred soldiers. I closed my eyes, spit, moaned.

"Orders, ma'am!"

"Please!"

"Yanks are comin'. Y'all shouldn't be here nohow."

"This is our home!"

"Please, lady. We ain't takin' no pleasure in this, neither, but it's gots to get done."

"You are not poisoning our well!"

I made myself sit up, started to stand, slipped, tried again. A rough hand gripped my arm. I tried to pull away, but the vise tightened, yet the voice was soft. "Easy, kid. Let me help you."

His beard-stubbled face came into view. He chewed on a twig. He was, I soon realized, the same soldier who had cracked my jaw. "Stand easy," he said. "Sorry I knocked you some. You give me a start."

"Don't do this!" Mama yelled, and I stepped away from the man, somehow keeping my feet as I staggered over to Mama, and stood beside her. They'd have to go through both of us to get to our well. Which wouldn't be hard for six or eight . . . or was it sixty or eighty? . . . Confederate soldiers.

"This is war, lady," said a black-bearded man, wearing the chevrons of a sergeant.

"It's not humane," she said.

"If the Yanks got nothin' fit to drink, might could be they'll leave y'all alone."

"And if *we* have nothing fit to drink?"

The sergeant sighed. "Most folks are leavin' Camden already. Y'all might as well follow us down to Washington."

"This is our home," Mama said.

I tried to say something, but my tongue felt ten sizes too big. I spit blood again.

"My husband . . . ," Mama tried, "the father of my children here . . . he's fighting with the Second Arkansas Cavalry. Please don't do this."

"Might be he one of Paine's boys?" the soldier who had walloped me said. "I might know him. I'm from Pine Bluff."

Her head shook. "No, he's with . . . with. . . ." She couldn't think.

"Captain Mason," I said, struggling with the words, and the blood, and the fear.

"That's A Company," another soldier said. "What be your man's name?"

"Ford!" Mama called out hopefully. "Connor Ford."

The man's head shook. I looked at the soldier with the rock-hard musket stock. His head shook, too. I hoped they were saying that they didn't know him, hadn't heard his name, not that he had been killed in battle.

"Well, bully for your husband and Colonel Slemons's horse troopers," the sergeant said, "but we still gots to p'ison the wells. It's policy, is all." His nod sent the two dog-packing soldiers through a gap in the line.

I stumbled, but didn't fall, and stood in front of Mama. "You . . . leave . . . our well . . . alone," I mumbled.

A few soldiers grinned, but not the two with the dead dogs, and not the sergeant.

Hoofs clopped on the lane, and a voice yelled: "Hold on there!"

The line of gray soldiers turned, and the rider in the kepi, the officer on the roan horse, came to the rescue again.

"What's the meaning of this, Sergeant?" the officer asked as he reined up in front of us.

He was young, the blond mustache more peach fuzz than whiskers, the brass buttons brightly polished, the French-braided shell jacket free of mud. His pants were gray, with a blue stripe up the seams, and his boots were shiny all the way up to his knees, although the bottoms were quite muddy.

"Orders, Lieutenant," the sergeant said. "P'isonin' the wells so's the Yanks'll get thirsty."

"Please," Mama said again. "This is our home. We live here. I have three children."

I spit again. Blood dribbled through the corners of my lips. If the lieutenant remembered me from Fellman and O'Brien, his face didn't show it.

"General Price is abandoning Camden, ma'am," the officer said. "We fear Steele is bound for Washington. Most citizens are leaving Camden, too, as you should, ma'am, with your family."

"This is our home." Mama stood straight. I tried to do the same, but now my head was pounding.

The treetops rustled. Baby Hugh and Edith continued to cry softly. The officer looked toward our porch, then back at Mama and me, back to the porch. He stared the longest time, then sighed.

Through the spaces in the line of soldiers, I saw other soldiers coming around the house. One stood in the dogtrot, holding a squawking chicken in each hand, grinning down at Baby Hugh and Edith.

"Sergeant, get your men back to the road. Pack your dead dogs with you."

"But. . . ."

"Do you have mud in your ears, Sergeant?"

"No, sir!" the man barked stiffly, then spun around. "You heard the lieutenant, back to the Pike, boys. Let's go."

They started away from the well, and the officer rode toward the house. "Parole those chickens, Monroe."

"Aw, Lieutenant."

"Now!"

Down went the chickens, making a beeline for the barn, leaving feathers in the dogtrot. The soldier leaped off the porch, grabbing his haversack. "You're gettin' soft, Kane," he said, but good-naturedly.

"I have a daughter her age back in Ashley County, Monroe," the officer said, glancing at Edith. "And so do you."

"Yeah." The would-be chicken thief tipped his hat at my sister, and fell into the line of retreating soldiers.

Mama and I started for the cabin when the last of the Confederates rounded the house. One of them pulled Betsy behind him.

Now, Mama was sprinting again. "Please, you can't take that mule!"

"Sorry," a lean, red-headed soldier said. "She's been conscripted."

"But she's not ours! We borrowed her."

"And we're borrowin' her from y'all."

Mama whirled to the lieutenant. "Must I beg you again, Lieutenant? That's not our mule. She belongs to the Reverend White."

"I've spared your well, ma'am. That's all I can do."

"But. . . ."

"The South needs mules." He choked out a dry laugh. "We need everything."

"It's just one mule. A Jenny used by the preacher. For prayer services at homes. He needs that mule."

Baby Hugh managed to snort: "He's . . . too fat . . . to walk . . . much."

"I'm sorry." The officer motioned the men forward, and they led Betsy away.

"Please!" Tears streamed down my mother's face. She sank onto the steps.

"Tell Reverend White to pray for us, ma'am. Pray for the South. Pray for Arkansas."

He was trotting away, head down, slumped in the saddle. A moment later, and the only sounds were our sobs, and the continuing clucking of the frightened chickens.

"Don't . . . cry . . . Mama," Edith managed to say, but she couldn't stop crying.

I sat down on the steps beside Mama, pulling her close. She buried her head on my shoulder, and her tears soaked my shirt. I tried to wrap my arms around her. Soon, Baby Hugh and Edith were on the steps beside us, Baby Hugh crying, Edith holding him and Mama.

We sat there for the longest while, and it struck me how

wrong this was, how awful this war had become. A mother should never have to cry on her thirteen-year-old son's shoulder.

CHAPTER EIGHT

The world, at least the world that I knew, which was pretty much southern Arkansas, turned upside down. The skies blackened. It rained again.

The day after Price's army left Camden, Mama put on her rubber boots, poncho, and hat, and walked to Reverend White's. She didn't want company, although I told her I would go, that this insulation idea was my own, and that I should tell the preacher why he no longer had his Betsy.

"Stay home, Travis." After making us a breakfast, Mama opened the door, stepped out, and turned back toward the kitchen. "But I do thank you for your offer."

She had scrambled potatoes and eggs together in bacon grease, so Edith, Baby Hugh, and I ate in silence, then retired across the dogtrot to our *Reader*s, but we had no interest. Not in learning. Not in eating. Rain pelted the roof, which began leaking in the northwestern corner by the fireplace, rare for the home Papa had built, but that didn't bother me. It gave me something to do. I went into the kitchen, fetched a pot, and brought it back. Soon the plopping of water drowned out the rain, the wind, Baby Hugh's reading aloud. Drowned out everything, but the gloom.

Suddenly Edith blurted out: "What day is it?"

"Thursday," I said.

"No. I mean the date."

I had to think. "The seventh."

"Mama's birthday is a week from tomorrow," Edith said.

"When's mine?" Baby Hugh asked.

"Not till November. And you know that." I was testy.

"We should get her a present," Edith said.

"Maybe Miss Mary will bake her a chocolate cake," Baby Hugh said.

"Shut up," Edith and I said at the same time.

Pouting, our kid brother slammed his *Reader* shut. "Well, what are you gonna get her? What you gonna do, walk fifteen miles to Camden and buy her something nice? With what? You ain't got no money."

Ignoring Baby Hugh, although everything he said had merit, I asked: "What would Mama want?"

"She'd want Papa to be home!" Again, Baby Hugh was absolutely right.

"Shut up!" Edith and I echoed sharply, and Baby Hugh opened his *Reader* and pretended to read.

"She'd want. . . ." Edith grinned. "She'd want coffee."

"I wonder if we could find some," I said.

The *Reader*'s cover slammed shut again, and Baby Hugh said in disgust: "Coffee ain't much of a birthday present."

"It's what she would want," Edith said. "More than anything . . . except for Papa coming home."

"Well," Hugh went on, "I'd think she'd rather have some of Miss Mary's cake. Or cookies. Or a pie. But if you could find coffee, how you gonna pay for it? With what? A barrel of sawdust? You gonna haul that all the way to Camden? Or maybe you plan on borrowing somebody else's mule and let that one get stole, too. Why don't you . . . ?"

I was up, hurling my *Reader* across the room. Baby Hugh ducked, and the book slammed against the fireplace, knocking a tintype onto the hearth and dropping into the pot of rain water. Hugh threw his book, which hit me in the chest, bouncing off, as I charged.

Edith yelled: "Thrash him, Brother!"

Breaking into tears, Baby Hugh shrieked, and bolted for the door.

"I'll whip you good!" I let him know.

"I'll tell Mama." He pulled a chair over to block my path, and made for the door.

"You won't be able to speak for a month when I'm done with you!"

I leaped over the chair and toward the open door. As Baby Hugh was turning toward the lane, I heard him scream. Bolting through the door, I tried to stop, but I lost my footing on the wet boards, and went sliding toward the kitchen cabin. I pushed myself up, sitting back against the log wall. My face reddened, not with anger, but embarrassment.

Baby Hugh had run straight into the hands of Uncle Willard, who had picked him up and brought him back to the porch in his carriage. After alighting and taking off his soaked, wide-brimmed hat, Uncle Willard grinned, before turning to spray the nearest puddle with tobacco juice.

"Reckon I broke up an interestin' go at fisticuffs." He wiped his mouth with a coat sleeve.

"He was after me, Uncle Willard," Baby Hugh said. "You ought to whup him with your razor strop."

Timidly Edith poked her head out the door.

"Who you fightin', Edith?" Uncle Willard asked.

"Nobody."

"That's good. Ain't lady-like to tussle. What you two fightin' 'bout?"

Baby Hugh's mouth opened, then closed. Mine never opened. We just looked at Uncle Willard, who slapped his thigh and laughed.

"Well, that's good. That's mighty fine indeed. Don't fret none, you two. Me and your pa fought all the time. It's a wonder we growed up at all, spendin' most of our childhood tryin' to tear one another's head off. Part of our adulthood, too." He laughed again at some old memory, sniffed, wiped his nose, and added: "I take it your ma ain't here."

I managed to pull myself up, brushing off my pants. "She went to the Reverend White's." I saw no reason to tell him why she had gone.

"In this weather?" I shrugged. Uncle Willard turned to say something to the slave driving his carriage, and I glared at Baby Hugh, warning him with my eyes that he had better not say anything about my sawdust plan, or why Mama had gone to see the preacher.

When Uncle Willard turned back around, Edith asked: "Are you on patrol, Uncle? You know? For runaway slaves?" She had stepped outside, drying my *Reader* with the sleeve of her dress.

"Only a fish would be out in this weather," he said. "Reckon your ma's half bream." He smiled at his joke. "Just payin' y'all a visit. When will she be back?"

"She just left a couple hours ago," I said.

Uncle Willard turned again to his slave. "Max, you recollect where that tub of lard they call a preacher lives? Right before you get to the Frederick plantation? That little woods lane that turns off to the south?"

"Yes, suh."

"Well, you go fetch my sister-in-law. No sense in her drown-ing for the Lord. I don't reckon that you'll run into no patrols . . . militia or Confederate . . . so I ain't writin' you no pass. If you catch up to Missus Ford before she reaches the fat preacher, go ahead and let her do her visitin', then bring her back here. If she gives you any sass, just toss her inside. But make sure you bring her back here. And don't spend all day with that preacher. You got that, boy?"

"Yes, suh."

"Then get."

Max clucked at the horses, and the carriage turned in the mud and headed down the lane toward the main road.

"Ain't you a-feared that boy'll run off?" Baby Hugh asked, and I saw my sister cringe.

Uncle Willard spit again. "He ain't got the guts."

Baby Hugh laughed. "I'd love to see that boy throw Mama into the wagon. That'd be something funny to see. That would rile her up, I mean to tell you."

As he stepped deeper into the dogtrot, Uncle Willard began shedding his coat. "Iffen Max was to lay a hand on a white woman, even a Yankee-minded petticoat like your mother, I'd flay the skin offen his back, then feed him to my hounds."

Baby Hugh's face paled.

Uncle Willard pointed toward the kitchen. "Don't reckon y'all got no coffee on the stove?"

We kids looked at each other.

"By Jacks," Uncle Willard said. "Nobody's got coffee. Folks've been burnin' acorn or grain, makin' coffee that way. And I knows Anna Louella ain't got no ardent spirits 'round here."

"There's milk," Edith said. "And some leftover potatoes and eggs."

"That'll have to do, I reckon. Let's see if I can't dry out these wet bones of mine, and warm myself up, before Max fetches your ma home."

Waiting in the kitchen with Uncle Willard proved almost intolerable. After twenty minutes, the rain had stopped. He pulled out his chaw of tobacco, and laid the quid atop the crown of his hat, which he had set on the table. He heated up the potatoes and eggs in the skillet in the fireplace, then ate them with his fingers, right out of the cast iron skillet. Standing up, he washed the food down with milk. Then he wiped his fingers on his trousers, moved to the table, and put the tobacco back in his mouth.

Mama would have had one of her hissy fits had she seen any of that.

Next Uncle Willard pulled up a chair, scraping the floor with the legs, which made our skin crawl. He turned the chair around and straddled it, leaning his arms against the back, staring at Baby Hugh, then at me and Edith.

"Y'all know what happened yesterday," he said.

It wasn't a question, but I answered. "Yes, sir. Some soldiers came here while they were marching to Washington."

"Steal anything?"

I ran my tongue over my lips, thinking of how to answer that and not lie.

Edith came to my rescue. "What's there to steal here?"

With a snort, Uncle Willard spit into a tin cup he had liberated from the wash basin.

He seemed to have changed since his last visit, and that hadn't been that long ago. His face was paler, and there was more stubble on his cheeks. The clothes he wore had a disheveled appearance, and red lines rimmed his eyes. It wasn't that Uncle Willard dressed like some Yankee businessman and looked well-groomed when he came visiting, but, I don't know, he just seemed different, and I couldn't blame it all on the rain. Haggard. Nervous. Worried. Bitter. Maybe a combination of all of those emotions.

"Heard the soldiers was poisonin' wells," he said. "That why they come here?"

"I suppose," I said, "but they didn't."

His eyebrows raised. "No?"

"They were gonna drop dead dogs in our well," Baby Hugh said.

"Mama talked them out of it," Edith added.

"Another Confederate defeat by the Yankees," he said, and let out a bitter laugh. "Didn't make off with your cow?"

Our heads shook.

"No chickens?"

"Mama talked them out of that, too," Edith said.

With a grin, Uncle Willard shook his head. "By jacks, that woman should be an officer in the Confederate Army. We might be winnin' this war iffen our boys had her sand."

Though I didn't want to, I grinned.

Uncle Willard shifted the tobacco to his other cheek. "Well," he said, "you know what's happenin'? No army to defend Camden. Yanks is pressin' from Little Rock. Right now, the road out in front of your place looks like Moses leadin' his tribe from the pharaoh. Ain't many folks left in Camden. Soon as Price's boys started pullin' out, they started packin'." He paused to spit. "Y'all should come, too."

We looked at each other, then back at our uncle.

"Are you going?" Edith asked.

"I ain't got no choice. Maybe the Yanks won't come to Camden, but there ain't nothin' to stop 'em. Not yet, nohow. And I ain't about to let some Bluebelly curs take my slaves from me. So I'm packin' up what I can, and lightin' a shuck for Magnolia."

That was a city, maybe thirty or forty miles southeast of us.

"Thought about followin' the army to Washington, but the Yanks'll be marchin' that way, too, I warrant, and I ain't got confidence in none of our soldiers no more."

His tune sure had changed since his last visit, when he'd said General Price could whip any Bluecoat.

"So Magnolia it is. For now." His head shook. "But might be I'll have to keep travelin'. Maybe into Texas. Jefferson, I reckon. Might could wind up in Dallas. I hate to do it, but I ain't got much choice. Not until somebody drives the Yanks up north again. So I figure I wouldn't be much of a brother to Connor if I didn't take y'all with me."

I swallowed.

"Mama won't leave," Edith said.

"She'll have to."

"She won't," I said.

"Stubborn as your ma is, I warrant that you two's probably right. But . . . she might send you kids with me."

She'd never do that. That was my first thought. It became also my first prayer.

The next ninety minutes passed slowly. Uncle Willard bragged again about his dealings with Nathan Bedford Forrest in Memphis, complained about the Arkansas economy, reflected some on growing up with Connor, talked about Mama, mentioned all the reasons he had never married, and criticized generals Sterling Price, J.O. Shelby, and John S. Marmaduke.

"How come you ain't in the Army?" Baby Hugh asked. "Papa is. How come you didn't join up?"

Tobacco spilled out of our uncle's pouch. He had moved from chewing tobacco to pipe tobacco, and had been tamping the clay bowl, but now he cursed, brushing flakes off his thigh and onto the wooden floor.

Baby Hugh wasn't done. "I know Billy Ray Bandy. We play sometimes after church on Sundays. He's about my age. He's got a pa who ain't in the Army, neither. Billy Ray don't say why, but I've heard some grown-ups talking about him. Not to Mama. Just overhear them sometimes after church lets out when they're standing around talking amongst themselves. Billy Ray's pa ain't got no front teeth, but he used to have 'em. The folks at church says he pulled them out himself so he couldn't fight in the Army. No front teeth means he can't bite off the tops of the powder charges, or something like that. So that's why he ain't in the Army. But you gots all your front teeth. One of them's even gold."

Uncle Willard's face reddened, and he shoved the pipe stem between his teeth—indeed, one of the incisors was gold—and fumbled about looking for a match.

"I deal in slaves, boy," he said, still searching for a match. "I'm too important to the economy."

"But you just said the economy's awful."

"Not because of the slave trade." He found a match, but it broke in half when he tried to strike it against his boot.

"And that General Forrest," Baby Hugh went on. "He was a slave trader, too. You said so yourself. But now he's fighting. I think he's even a general. And a bona-fide hero. You said that yourself."

The next match also snapped, but the third fired, and Uncle Willard brought it to the pipe in trembling hands. While he busied himself lighting his pipe, I glanced at Edith. We grinned at each other.

Sometimes, Baby Hugh seemed all right for an ignorant kid brother. I almost even regretted trying to thrash him earlier that morning.

CHAPTER NINE

The carriage's arrival saved Uncle Willard. His pipe going, he shook out the match, dropped it in the skillet, and headed for the door, never answering Baby Hugh's question. Uncle Willard's Negro driver had returned with Mama, who shunned her rain gear. She hung coat and hat on the antler on the outside wall to dry and replaced her rubber boots with her regular shoes, all the while exchanging informal pleasantries with her brother-in-law.

"Hear you drove off Price's army." Uncle Willard's pipe puffed like a chimney.

"There was a nice, young officer," Mama said, combing her hair with her fingers. "He stopped them from poisoning the well . . . if that's what you mean." She shook her head. "That road is a mess! And I've never seen so much traffic on the Pike."

"You will. And it'll get messier," Uncle Willard said. "Yanks'll be marchin' down it, soon enough and sure enough."

Mama sighed.

"Figured you'd like that, Annie Lou," he said just to spite her. "Bein' Yankee born and all."

"I'll be glad when I never see another soldier, Willard," Mama said, "except for Connor coming home."

"Amen to that." Which sounded strange for Uncle Willard.

"Can I fix you something to eat?"

"Already done it myself," he said. "Anna"—his tone changed—"I'm pullin' out. Magnolia."

83

"Magnolia?" Mama wiped her forehead with a handkerchief. "That town south of here?"

He nodded. "Might have to go even farther. But that depends on Old Pap and our boys. But the Yanks'll be here. Nothin' to stop 'em, and I got my property to think of, to protect."

"Well. . . ." Mama put her hand on his shoulder. "We will miss you, Willard." She even sounded like she meant it.

"You ought to come with me, Anna."

She removed her hand, smiled slightly, and said: "We've been over this time and again, Willard. For two years now. I'm not leaving our home."

"Then send the kids with me."

Mama stepped back as if he had slapped her.

"You need to listen to reason, Anna. This is what Connor would want. If the Yanks take Camden, there will be a fight. Not now, but soon. Real soon. I know you've heard all about how them fights have been goin' lately. Shiloh. Sharpsburg. Gettysburg. You don't want to be here, and you'll regret stayin'. But you need to think of these kids, Anna. You don't want 'em to see what's liable to happen."

Edith, Baby Hugh, and I stood together, our differences long forgotten. Uncle Willard spoke with compassion, which was unlike him, too. Then he said something even harder to believe.

"Please, Anna."

She opened the door to the kitchen. "Step inside, Willard." Her eyes went past him and to us. "You three. To the barn. Milk Lucy. Gather the eggs. Clean things up. Now." Her tone meant she'd hear no protest, and we knew the conversation that was about to take place was just for adults. No snooping or eavesdropping, unless we wanted to feel Uncle Willard's razor strop.

★　★　★　★　★

They talked a good long time. So long that we had milked the cow, cleaned the stalls—which didn't take long as we had only the cow since the mules were long gone—even walked around the garden. The rows flowed like ditches, and the sprouts of corn were still green, still growing. We had looked for eggs, but found none after having collected a handful earlier. Leaving the pail of milk in the barn, we stayed away from the cabin.

Finally Mama's voice called us to the front of our home, where Uncle Willard was talking to Max. Dread filled my heart and almost turned my stomach, but my uncle's face was a scowl while Mama grinned.

Another Yankee victory, I thought.

"Willard's bound for Magnolia," Mama said. "So give him a hug and a kiss good bye. We will see you again," she said. "Won't we?"

"In better times, I pray," he said, and he kneeled to accept the hug and kiss on his cheek from Edith. My twin backed away, and I shoved Baby Hugh forward.

Uncle Willard hugged him, felt another quick peck on the cheek, and, as my kid brother backed away, my uncle pulled him closer in an embrace. "I own too many slaves," he said. "That's how come I don't wear the gray, boy. Maybe I should've joined up anyhow, but that's spilt milk. But I ain't no coward like Billy Ray's daddy."

"Of course, you aren't," Mama and Edith said at the same time.

"Willard," Mama added, "you've been very good to us. Connor couldn't have asked for a better brother."

He rose, tousling Baby Hugh's hair, and stepped toward me, saying over his shoulder to Mama: "Connor might have some argument to that statement, Anna." He stopped in front of me, and held out his hand. "You're too big now, Travis, for a hug and a kiss. Reckon a handshake's more in line." And he offered his hand.

His grip hurt, though I know it was unintentional. Then something came over me. Tears welled in my eyes. I pulled myself to my father's brother's chest, and wrapped my arms around him, and smelled the tobacco, the rain. He hugged me back, then stepped away, cursing the rain and wind for putting something in his eye.

Whatever had irritated his eye, he brushed away, and reached into his waistcoat, pulling out more Arkansas script. This time, he didn't sneak it, but held it out for Mama. "Another offerin'," he said, smiling thinly, "for that tub of lard y'all call a preacher."

"Thank you, Willard," Mama said, and took the banknotes.

"It don't have to go to the collection plate, Anna," he said. "It could go to some groceries . . . some clothes."

"It might just do that." Mama smiled. But we all knew she wouldn't spend it on our family. Not even for coffee.

"You got the head of a mule. Like always. I warned Connor about you." Uncle Willard reached over, and pulled Mama close, kissed the top of her head, then cleared his throat, hurried into the back of the carriage, cursing the slave for not leaving fast enough.

Waving, we watched the carriage all the way down the lane, then headed up the steps and into our home. Two hours passed before we remembered the milk we had left in the barn.

"What did the Reverend White say?" I asked after supper.

Mama smiled. "He understood. Soldiers stopped by his cabin, too. He said if they hadn't stolen Betsy from us, they would have made off with her from his place." She patted the pocket in her apron where she had stashed Uncle Willard's latest contribution to the meeting house. "Besides, we have tithed more than most of his parishioners. This might be enough to help him buy another."

"Why don't you buy something, Mama?" I asked.

Her head shook.

"For your birthday."

"No," her lips mouthed.

"Not even coffee?" Edith asked.

"I don't think you could find coffee between Little Rock and Shreveport," she said.

"But we ain't got hardly nothing to eat," Baby Hugh said.

"I think you need to spend another hour with your *Reader*," Mama told him. "Your grammar is atrocious."

"But. . . ."

"No buts, young man. All of you should study some more before bedtime. But don't fret. It is, as Willard always said, darkest before the dawn."

It grew darker.

Over the next few days, after studies and chores, Edith, Baby Hugh, and I would walk up the lane to the road. The ditch was flooding, and we had to make sure our kid brother didn't do something foolish like jump in and drown. We'd stand there, or sit on a log, letting Baby Hugh splash his bare feet in a puddle, and watch the convoy. The exodus. The retreat.

Oxen or mules pulled wagons through the quagmire, deepening and widening the ruts, leaving Camden, heading southwest toward Washington. Maybe Magnolia. Perhaps even Texas. Some noticed us, yet they never waved, barely even acknowledged us. Women in bonnets or straw hats dabbed their eyes. Men focused on the teams pulling the wagons. The children, even those we knew, merely looked at us. Perhaps they'd nod in our direction, but more often they just looked away.

"Do they hate us?" Baby Hugh asked after Hank Kroger, the mercantile owner's ten-year-old grandson, sat on the tailgate of a heavily loaded farm wagon and just shook his head as his family rode by.

"No," Edith said.

"Do they hate Mama? 'Cause she's a Yankee?"

"She's not a Yankee," I said. "And they don't hate her, either."

"Why don't they say nothing then? Hank and me's friends."

I drew a deep breath, trying to think of an answer, a reason.

"They're sad." Edith had found the words. "That's all. They're just sad. Leaving their homes. Not knowing if they'll ever come back."

"Even Uncle Willard said good bye," Baby Hugh said.

"That's different," Edith said. "He's family."

"But they's friends. Don't that mean nothing?"

We couldn't answer. We watched the Kroger wagon round the bend and disappear, then turned to stare at the next passers-by, this one a couple—a white-haired man and a middle-aged woman—trudging through the mud, pulling a pack mule behind them. I didn't recognize them.

"I hate the Yankees," Baby Hugh said. He sniffed, and I put my arm around his shoulder, and pulled him close.

Even darker.

It had started out as a steady progression. Wagons, carts, people on horseback, many on foot. Since Camden was a port city on the Ouachita River, I figured most of the wealthiest ones had fled the city via steamboat, although where they could go, where they could find a port city not controlled by the Union Army, I didn't know. Now, the flood had stopped. Even the water levels in the ditch had lowered.

We had been sitting by the road for two hours, and had not seen anything other than a water snake gliding with the current in the ditch.

"Maybe everybody's gone?" Baby Hugh said.

"I don't think everybody's left Camden," Edith said. She sounded like she was trying to convince herself.

Suddenly we heard the noise. It didn't come from Camden, but from the west. I rose, shielded the sun with my hand against my forehead, and stared. A carriage rounded the bend, pulled by two gray mares. The whip cracked. The horses ran faster, the big wheels at the rear of the wagon spraying mud behind them.

"It's Miss Mary!" Edith said.

"Driving like a crazy woman," I said.

"Maybe Yankees are after her," Baby Hugh said.

Yet no one was behind her. Baby Hugh began waving, but Miss Mary didn't even see us. She pulled hard on the lines, slowing the two mares, their eyes wide with fright, gray coats already lathered. "Turn!" she yelled at the horses. "Turn!" She punctuated the command with a curse, leaning hard to her right, pulling the lines tighter, and the horses moved, the buggy tilted, and Edith screamed, fearing the buggy would flip, catapulting Miss Mary into the pines. Somehow, it righted itself. Miss Mary swore again, the whip slashed, and grays, carriage, and Miss Mary Frederick moved like lightning down the lane to our home.

We were running after her, but I stopped long enough to make sure no blue-coated soldiers were indeed chasing her.

I caught up with Edith and Baby Hugh, passed them, and reached the yard just as Miss Mary began screaming at Mama, who tentatively came down the steps. Miss Mary raised the whip in her hand. She had not come to converse in French with Mama.

"I hided him good!" Miss Mary yelled. "Good, I tell you! I hided him like he's never been whupped before." Her hair was a mess. Mud stained her white dress. Her eyes seemed wilder than those of her horses'.

"Who?" Mama asked. "What are you talking about, Mary? What's wrong?"

Edith and Baby Hugh slowed their running as they neared me. They kept their distance from our neighbor with the whip, who seemed crazy. Mama stayed clear of Miss Mary. So did I.

"Mowbray!" Miss Mary turned around, as if she expected to find her servant. She flipped the whip against her leg. "The miserable darky. I whipped the skin off his back. And he run away. Run away. The black bas-. . . ."

"You whipped Mowbray?" Mama stared at Miss Mary as if she had never seen her before. Well, she hadn't. None of us had ever seen her this way. "Because he ran away?"

"No!" Miss Mary cried, as she flung the whip toward the carriage, missing, but hitting the nearest gray, which took a few nervous steps before Mama walked over and grabbed the harness. She rubbed the horse, trying to steady it, but kept her eyes on our neighbor. Then she moved to the other mare, trying to keep her calm.

"No," Miss Mary said. "He run off after I whipped him."

"Why?" Mama signaled me with her eyes to come over to the team, and once I had the harness tight in my hand and was rubbing the nearest gray's neck, whispering soft words, she inched her way toward Miss Mary, who was walking back and forth in the mud. That's when I noticed another peculiar thing about her.

Like Baby Hugh, Miss Mary was barefoot.

Maybe Uncle Willard had been right all along. That sweet old lady was crazy.

"Why did you beat him?"

"I whipped him till I was worn out," she said.

"But why?"

"Because the South is losing, Anna Louella! Because the Yankees will soon be in Washington County. By thunder, they probably already are. And soon they'll be in Camden. They'll destroy my beautiful home. Leave it in ashes. They'll . . . they'll . . . oh, it's just so horrible."

"But Mowbray. . . ."

"The Yankees killed my brother. Poor Charles. Yankees murdered him. I whipped Mowbray for Charles. Whipped him till I was worn out. Hided him good. Good, I tell you!"

Mama had reached her. "Mary, Charles fell at Murfreesboro. That was more than a year ago."

Almost immediately, Mary collapsed into Mama's arms, and they fell to their knees in the mud. Edith and Baby Hugh ran up to them. I led the mares and carriage away, hitching the team to the post near the well.

"Go on," Mama told my siblings. "Go on. Just leave us alone for a spell."

"But, Mama," Edith said. "Where shall we go?"

"I don't care!" There was such fury in Mama's voice that Edith staggered back. She ran, crying, to the barn, Baby Hugh right behind her.

I just watched. Watched Mama rise, not even knocking the mud off her dress, her shoes. She helped Miss Mary to her feet, led her up the steps, moved toward the kitchen. Maybe I should have gone with my sister and brother, but, instead, I just walked up the lane. I turned toward Camden, and followed the Pike until I turned off onto the path that led to Papa's sawmill.

It was my escape. Or had been. Now I saw the barrels still filled with sawdust, barrels that would never be delivered to Miss Mary's. I looked at the acorns. I looked at the squirrels, and the blue jays. Into the shed, I stepped, and found the burlap sack, which I pulled off the shelf. I carried it and the cigar box into the mill, found an old log to sit on, and withdrew the box from the sack.

Slowly I opened the box, and pulled out the writing tablet. I turned the cover, saw what I had written, which wasn't much. Hadn't even thought of any stories, had hardly played musketeers or Confederate spies. I hadn't even played mumblety-peg or checkers with Baby Hugh or Edith.

I found the pencil in my hand, read the title I had written. Aloud, I said—"The Spring of Hope."—then laughed bitterly, and stared up at the hole in the ceiling, at the pines, the oak that had crashed through part of the roof, at the darkened sky.

The pencil went to work. I drew a line through the title and wrote something that seemed more fitting. After a moment, I lowered tablet, box, sack, dropped the pencil, pulled up my knees, and buried my head in my arms, rocking and crying, crying and rocking.

Finally I dammed those tears, swearing I would never cry again, that I would never write again. I thought about tearing up my story or book or whatever it was I had written.

I looked down, blinked away the tears, and read: *The Spring of Hope.*

Beneath that, the new title: *Poison Spring.*

CHAPTER TEN

Full dark had descended. It was another gloomy evening, and Miss Mary was gone by the time I walked back home in a misting rain. After drying off with the towel over the wash basin, I stepped into the warmth of the kitchen. Well, physically it felt warm, but I remained chilled by everything that had happened earlier that day. There were no greetings, little eye contact. Mama stood over the table, dishing out boiled carrots and cornbread onto our supper plates.

Back before Papa had marched off to war, Mama had always put the food in dishes, and brought those to the table to be passed around. Now she merely emptied what food she had cooked onto plates. There would be no second helpings. We didn't have enough food. Even the cornbread appeared spartan. When I tasted it, I knew we must be out of salt now, too.

She had a plate set for me. I reckon she knew that I'd come home. Edith and Baby Hugh glanced at me, their faces blank, and I slid into my chair without saying a word. In fact, nobody said anything for the longest spell. Mama placed the pot from the carrots in the sink, wiped her forehead with the back of her hand, and returned to the table. Usually she said a blessing before every meal. Even when Papa had been home, Mama always led the prayers. This time, she bowed her head, gripping the back of her chair, and my siblings and I bent our heads, closed our eyes, and waited.

Outside, the wind moaned, and thunder rolled in the

distance. Or was that cannon? Whatever, it seemed far, far away. Inside, silence remained, pressing us with its enormity.

After a while, I heard a sigh, then the scraping of the chair legs over the wood. My eyes opened to find Mama sitting in a chair, shoulders slumped. She placed her elbows on the table—something she always scolded us not to do—and buried her face in her hands. For a moment, I thought she was crying, but she never made a sound.

"Mama?" Edith timidly inquired.

The hands dropped to the table, and her head shook. There was no plate before her. It was set by the sink, no food on it.

"I'm sorry," Mama said. She turned toward Edith. "I'm sorry I yelled."

"It's all right, Mama," Edith said, and Baby Hugh echoed the statement.

"No, it isn't." Her head shook again, harder this time, and she looked at the ceiling as if speaking to the Almighty. "The whole world has gone mad." A heavy sigh escaped her, and she turned toward Edith, then me. "I should have sent you to Magnolia with Willard."

"No, Mama," Edith and I blurted out in unison.

The silence returned, and I could not bear that. Not after today.

"How is . . . ?" I swallowed. "How is Miss Mary?"

Mama shrugged. "As well as could be expected," she said after a moment's thought. "Mary's nerves have always been tightly wound. They just got unwound, I expect. As the world unravels around us."

"Why did she come here?" Edith asked.

This time, Mama's smile seemed genuine. "I am . . . *we* are her friends."

Edith's head dropped. She stirred her carrots with her spoon, but did not eat.

"Did she really whip Mowbray?" Baby Hugh asked.

"I imagine she did."

"Did he really run away?"

Mama's head bobbed.

"I liked Mowbray," Baby Hugh said. "He didn't have no hair."

"*Any* hair," Mama corrected, still smiling.

"One time, he even let me rub the top of his noggin." Baby Hugh grinned at the memory. "It squeaked."

This brought a slight laugh from everyone at the table, but mine lasted shorter than any of the others'. I remembered that day, old Mowbray laughing so hard he toppled off the doorstep, and Baby Hugh staring at his hand that had elicited the squeak as if it were some kind of magician's wand. And I remembered Papa, leaning back in his chair, laughing the hardest of everyone there.

Papa. I could picture his face. I could hear his laugh. But I couldn't remember his voice, what he sounded like.

Mama ended that memory, for which I was glad. "Mowbray was a good man," she told Baby Hugh. "Still is a good man. Maybe he's free now."

"I hope so," Edith said.

Maybe, I thought. *He'd have to make it to Little Rock. Or perhaps not, if the Union Army kept marching south.* Then I felt revulsion. I was a Southerner. My father was fighting with the Confederate cavalry, and here I was, wishing a runaway slave could find his freedom. I glared at my mother, silently cursing her Yankee blood for getting into my veins, my thoughts, but even I couldn't hold such anger for long.

No, I wanted Mowbray away from crazy old Miss Mary and her vicious whip.

"Should we pray for old Mowbray, Mama?" Baby Hugh asked.

"Yes." Firmness returned to Mama's voice. Her face no longer looked so pale. "Yes. Yes, indeed." Bowing her head, she began to pray. For Mowbray and Miss Mary. For Uncle Willard. For Papa. For Hugh, Edith, and Travis. For Washington County. For the United States of America and the Confederate States of America. For Reverend White. For all those poor families fleeing Camden. For President Lincoln and President Davis. At last, she got around to blessing the food and she closed with: "Bless this food to our use, and us to thy service, and make us ever mindful of the needs of others. Amen."

Edith quickly added: "And God bless Mama, too."

"Amen," Baby Hugh and I chimed in.

When our heads raised, Mama's smile brightened our moods. "Thank you," she said.

Life in southern Arkansas, of course, did not return to normal over the next day or two. I don't think I even remembered what normal felt like, but things did get better. We went through our *Reader*s, through the Bible, did our chores. The corn seemed to grow higher. Sometimes, I would even catch Mama humming— "Woodman, Spare That Tree" or "Amazing Grace". For us kids, there were no more trips to the Camden-Washington Pike, merely because few people traveled it any more. Miss Mary didn't return, so on Thursday, April 14th, Mama decided to walk the five muddy miles to the plantation and see how our neighbor was doing. I guess she worried about Miss Mary. I guess, honestly, we all worried about her.

Yes, she had whipped her slave, a good man, always kind, but that had been in a fit of madness, and, like Mama said, the whole world seemed to be turning crazy. It was Miss Mary, after all, who had kept us in leftovers, and somehow she had understood something about me, about my love of books, the need to read, and she had bought me that writing tablet and those pencils. She knew my secret, too. I couldn't hate her. No matter what she had done to Mowbray.

So, early that morning, right after breakfast, Mama left Edith, Baby Hugh, and me to our chores and studies. As soon as she was gone—I mean, I don't think Mama could have cleared the doorsteps—Edith closed her *Reader* and said: "I have a plan."

That was all the encouragement we needed to close our books.

"Mama loves coffee, right?"

Baby Hugh nodded, but I gave my twin the best skeptical look I could muster. First, nobody had coffee. Second, it was fifteen miles one way to Camden, and even if a store there remained open and actually had coffee for sale, we certainly couldn't afford it. Probably not even if we robbed the Reverend White of his church collection plate.

"So we make some for her! For her birthday!" The words rushed out of Edith's mouth. She practically giggled with excitement.

Birthday. I had already forgotten. Tomorrow was Mama's birthday.

"Make coffee?" Baby Hugh said. "But we ain't got no coffee to make for Mama."

"I don't think we have any coffee plants in our garden," I said sarcastically. Which got me thinking: *Does coffee grow on a plant, like corn, or under the ground, like a potato? Is it in a shell like a nut? Maybe in a tree like pecans?* I wondered if there would be any information on it in Webster's, and I was on my way to the table Papa had made where the giant dictionary always rested, when Edith spoke up.

"We don't need a coffee tree," Edith said.

That irritated me. I kept going. How did she know coffee grew on a tree? I hoped Webster's would prove her wrong.

"Acorns," she said. "Isn't that what Uncle Willard said people

97

were burning to make their own coffee?"

"Yeah." I opened the dictionary. "Squirrels."

"No, Travis," Baby Hugh said. "I recollect now. Uncle Willard said that. Burning acorn or grain. That's how folks is making coffee these days. Them that drinks it." He made a sound like gagging. "Sounds horrible."

"Coffee is horrible," Edith said. "But Mama loves it."

"I'd rather have Miss Mary's cake," Baby Hugh said. "You reckon Mama will bring some home with her after she's visited Miss Mary?"

Edith scolded him for his lack of thoughtfulness, and, as if God were directing my fingers, I turned right to page 221, and found the word almost immediately.

> *cof'fee, n., [Fr. café; It. caffe; Sp. café; Port. id.; G. kaffee; D. koffy; Ar. cahuah, or cahoeh, which the Turks pronounce cahveh. This plant is said to be a native of Ethiopia.]*
>
> *1. The berry of a tree belonging to the genus Coffea, growing in Arabia, Persia, and in other warm climates of Asia and America.*

It does come from a tree! I slammed the book shut, started to my chair, but detoured to the door instead, opened it, and looked outside. Mama was gone. We were safe. I returned to my seat to listen to the rest of Edith's plan.

Miss Know-It-All elaborated. "I don't know where we would get grain. But I do know where we can find acorns."

So did I, and despite my jealousy because Edith knew that coffee grew on trees before I did, I heard myself saying: "There is plenty of acorns down by Papa's sawmill."

"Right." Edith clapped her hands.

"It'll take Mama two hours to get to Miss Mary's," she said. "Then they'll most likely visit a while. I dare say she won't be back till this evening. By that time, we will have gone to the sawmill, gathered up plenty of acorns, roasted them or burned them in the skillet. I'm not sure how it's done, but roasted in the oven or cooked on the skillet, it'll be just like coffee."

"Can I put them in the coffee grinder?" Baby Hugh asked. "When they're done?"

"Of course."

"And crank the handle."

"Sure." Her hands clapped again. "We'll do it all together. It'll be our birthday present to Mama. She deserves it."

"Mama deserves better than burned acorns for coffee," I said.

"Oh, Travis," Edith said, "don't be such a spoilsport."

I tried to think of an argument, but my mouth just hung open.

"I'd like to go to the mill," Baby Hugh said. "I ain't seen it in a 'coon's age."

"It's not the same as you remember it, Hugh." I sighed. Maybe the coffee would taste all right. Maybe we wouldn't burn down the house trying to roast it. "Let's go," I said.

"We'll need a sack to bring the coffee. . . ." Edith burst out laughing. "I mean the acorns. We need a sack."

"There are plenty of sacks at the mill." Already I had grabbed my hat.

Baby Hugh was out the door, ignoring Edith's instructions to wear his brogans for such a long walk.

For once that spring, the skies turned clear, a perfect blue, nary a rain cloud to be seen. The weather had warmed, turned humid, and the air remained still. Of course, the road hadn't dried out, but we ran along the grass between the road and the bar ditch.

Despite my vow to retire my pencil and writing tablet, and quit making up stories, I couldn't help but imagine. . . .

After sailing to Persia, Musketeer Travis Ford races through the desert city of Cahua, accompanied by his trusted comrades, Ed and Hugo, searching for the great coffee tree that could save the life of Queen Anne of Austria. The dastardly cardinal had hired a master of poison to kill the queen, and bring France and England to war. The only cure for the slow-acting poison could be found in Cahua, so the musketeers had sailed to Persia. After many seafaring adventures, fighting pirates, and encountering a whale and a hurricane, they had reached the desert lands. Now, they had to find the beans from the world's tallest coffee tree, get back on the boat, and back to France in time.

Travis Ford knew for certain that even this far from Paris, the cardinal was sure to have Arabian knights guarding the tree. There would be a fight.

He unsheathed his rapier.

He was ready.

"What are you doing with that stick?"

Sliding to a stop, I returned from Persia in 1625 to Arkansas in 1864. I tossed away the sapling I had snatched up during our sprint from home.

"Nothing," I answered my sister. "We better hurry." Past her and Baby Hugh, I sprinted down the lane that led to the Ford Family Mill.

The squirrels began chattering, leaping above us in the high limbs of the trees, as if they understood the reason we had arrived.

Edith stopped, staring aghast at the condition of the mill. On the other hand, Baby Hugh said—"Wow!"—and started for the building before Edith jerked him back with two hands.

"Aw," Hugh cried, "come on, Edith. I ain't no baby no more. Let me go inside and do some exploring."

"There are no acorns inside," she said sternly, and I didn't bother to correct her, tell her about an oak that had fallen through the roof, one massive limb punching a hole through the floor toward the back of the building, with a passel of acorns just waiting to be turned into coffee.

"Y'all start picking up the acorns out here," I said. "There are some burlap sacks in the tool shed. I'll get them."

In a matter of seconds, I had stepped into the shed, closing the door behind me. I withdrew Papa's cigar case from its hiding place, and looked around, hoping to find a better place to keep it. I didn't open the lid. Didn't want to be tempted by the writing tablet and pencils. Looking up at the shelves, I saw three oil cans on the top shelf, used to keep the machinery from rusting. I stepped on a keg of nails, reached up, and pulled the cans down, putting them on the shelf below.

"What's keeping you, Travis?" Edith called out.

"I'm coming. Hold your horses."

I slid Papa's cigar box to the top shelf, and started to put the cans on top of it, but then I thought about the top of it—the minstrel singing to the lady, the beauty of the scene, the painstaking detail, the time it must have taken Papa to make it. So down came the box, and back it went inside the burlap.

"Travis!" Edith screamed.

"In a minute!" I yelled back.

After I had slid the covered box back onto the top shelf, I put the oil cans on top of it, hoping the sack would protect the top, but that didn't seem enough. Again, I removed the cans. Finding some old rags and some pine needles, I covered the sack, figuring that the sack, the pine needles, and the rags would protect Papa's cigar box from any leaking oil. Besides, after shaking one of the cans, I knew there wasn't any oil inside them.

I jumped down, decided that two sacks would hold plenty of acorns to turn into coffee for our mother, and grabbed them from the shelf.

"Here I come!" I called as I opened the door, and stepped out of the shed.

Two long, sharp bayonets greeted me, almost running me through.

The burlap sacks dropped to the ground.

Urine dripped down the inside of my left leg.

CHAPTER ELEVEN

Gasping in shock, I sucked in my stomach to keep from getting ripped by those long bayonets. It took every effort of willpower I had not to scream, and I prayed no one noticed how I had wet my pants—thankfully I hadn't had much to drink for breakfast.

"What you doin' in there, kid?" one of the soldiers asked.

I could only stare.

The one who had asked didn't appear much older than me. In fact, I stood an inch or two taller. He wore trousers the color of the sky, and an unbuttoned coat darker than a thunderhead, with brass buttons. His hat was what we called a bummer cap, navy blue. The brogans and belt were black, and the neckerchief around his collarless red-and-white checked shirt featured pink polka dots. His eyes were brown, nose flat, lips tight, head clean shaven. His skin was ebony, with freckles across his nose and cheeks. The musket with the bayonet seemed huge.

The soldier standing next to him was older and much taller, with dark beard stubble on his chin, and his cap secured with a blue silk scarf tied under his chin. He was just as black.

"I asked you a question," the first one said. I backed away from his bayonet and up against the shed's picket wall.

"Easy, Jeremiah," the older one said. "He ain't no bigger'n a corn nubbin." He grinned at me, then eased the bayonet away from my gut. "But I dare say he be bigger'n you."

"Shut your trap, Hammond. You talk too much for a runaway slave." To me, the small Negro said: "Get them hands of your'n up. Up, I say. I ain't kilt no Johnny Reb in three hours."

"You ain't killed nothin' 'ceptin' skeeters and flies, Jeremiah, durin' the two years we been in this man's army."

"Shut up, I say. And I'm tellin' you, up with 'em hands, boy."

Obliging him, I then looked around. Edith sat on the ground, Baby Hugh in her lap, hugging her in fear. Six or eight black soldiers formed a semicircle around them, but no bayonets were threatening them, although every one of the men carried a musket, and every musket had a bayonet affixed to the long barrel. Other soldiers were inside the mill, talking, laughing, although I could only catch snatches of what they were saying. Some had accents so thick, so foreign, I could never have guessed what they were saying.

How could I not have heard them arrive? I kept thinking to myself. *Why hadn't I detected the fear when Edith had shouted my name?*

"I asked you," the small soldier said again, "what was you doin' in there?" He tilted his head at the larger man, who stepped around me and opened the door to the tool shed.

My mouth refused to work. The little soldier grew angrier. "Boy, iffen you don't answers me, I'll spill your guts on the ground here. And whilst you's bleedin' to death, me and Hammond's gonna fill your belly with stones and sinks you in that millpond. Catfish'll be suppin' on you for a month of Sundays."

The door closed behind me. "Ain't nothing in there, Jeremiah. Just tools and cans and rags and such. Tool shed."

"No whiskey in there?" Jeremiah was talking to me.

My head shook.

"Boy, you ain't pullin' no cork?"

Again I shook my head.

The one named Hammond leaned in front of my face and drew a long breath. "Naw," he said, straightening and facing

Jeremiah. "He don't smell like no John Barleycorn. He smells like. . . ." He faced me again, looked at my dark stained trousers. I shifted my legs. He walked back beside Jeremiah. "Smells like nothin' is all."

Jeremiah pulled away his musket, and let loose with a drawn-out curse. "He's a Reb."

"Ain't in no uniform," Hammond pointed out.

"Most of 'em ain't been of late."

"Yeah." With a snort, Hammond hooked his thumb toward Baby Hugh and Edith. "But none of 'em's been enlistin' snot-nosed young 'uns. And none of 'em's been marchin' with little girls."

"Well," Jeremiah said, studying me, "what you chil'ren doin' here?"

Another colored soldier stuck his head out of the mill. "They ain't cuttin' no lumber, Jeremiah. That's certain sure."

"*I'm* interrogatin' the prisoner," Jeremiah said.

Hammond chuckled. "You ain't gettin' much out of 'im."

"On account that he's likely deaf and dumb. Like most white folks in Arkansas. That it, boy? You deaf and dumb?"

My head could only shake, which got all of the soldiers who had started to gather around the tool shed to chuckle. Again I looked around. I didn't see a white face among them, and I recalled the fear in that woman's voice back in Mr. Mendenhall's bookstore. I could hear Mrs. Andersen's voice echoing in my head: *I've heard that the Yankees have darkies fighting for them. Darkies! I am a white woman, a widow living alone. I fear for my very life.*

"Should we torch this place?" a soldier asked from inside the mill.

The breath caught in my throat.

"We'll ask the capt'n," Jeremiah said, before he looked around. "Though iffen you was to ask me, that would be the

105

waste of a match."

Hoofs could be heard clopping down the lane.

"Well, it ain't the capt'n, but here comes Lieutenant Bullis and Sergeant Greene!" another soldier called out.

"Step away from those white children there, men!" a voice called out, and the soldiers backed away from Edith and Baby Hugh. Even Jeremiah backed up some from me, butting the musket on the ground.

"Hey, Sergeant!" Hammond called out. "We's catched us a quiet one over here."

"A Reb?" another voice boomed.

Hammond loosened the scarf under his chin. "Don't rightly know, Sergeant. Ain't in uniform. And he's armed with . . ."—he looked at the burlap I had dropped—"sacks."

The black soldiers laughed.

The lieutenant was a white man. He had dismounted and was kneeling in front of Edith and Baby Hugh. He reached inside his tunic, brought out a brown paper sack, and offered it to them. Edith just stared, but Baby Hugh reached inside, found something, and stuck it in his mouth. The lieutenant pushed back the brim of his black hat, and spoke, but I couldn't hear what he asked.

Then they disappeared from my view. A mountain blocked my vision. All I saw at first were the brass buttons against the blue jacket, the brass breastplate. Then my head tilted up, and I found the black face. This soldier wasn't younger than me. His well-trimmed beard was salt and pepper, thick, and his forehead scarred, his eyes hard. Like the lieutenant, he wore a black campaign hat with a silver *1* pinned on the crown. A saber rattled in its scabbard. One gauntleted hand rested on the ridge around the saber's quillon.

He studied me for a second, then looked around at the ruins that were the Ford Family Mill, and sighed. "That's a shame," he said to no one in particular, before his gaze locked back on me. "Your name Ford, son?"

My head bobbed.

The sergeant grinned. His tone lightened. "Cat got your tongue, Travis?"

Now I stepped back as if he had struck me with his big hands. My back pressing against the shed door, I stared in disbelief. My mouth formed the word, but it took a few seconds before it escaped: "H-h-how?"

This led to an eruption of laughter among the nearest soldiers. Even Jeremiah chortled.

Hammond said: "Reckon he ain't deaf and dumb after all."

"No," the sergeant said, "Travis can talk. Just never had much to say."

Out of the corner of my eye, I saw the white lieutenant standing, leading Baby Hugh and Edith in our direction. I couldn't look away from the towering sergeant.

"You don't remember me, do you, Travis?" the sergeant asked.

My head shook rapidly.

Still grinning, his teeth white and straight, the sergeant took his left hand off the saber, and began tugging on the white deerskin gauntlets, which he stuck inside the belt near the big brass buckle stamped *US*. He held out his right hand to shake, and I stared at it, reaching, slowly understanding. His middle and pointer fingers and his thumb practically swallowed my tiny hand. The ring finger and pinky were missing. That's when I knew.

I remembered shaking his hand all those years ago at the sawmill. Recalled Papa and him beaming with pride after I branded my first two-by-four with the *FFM*.

"Jared. . . ." My voice barely rose above a whisper. "Jared . . . Greene?"

★ ★ ★ ★ ★

"See, Lieutenant Bullis," Sergeant Jared Greene was saying, "I worked for these kids' pap at this sawmill back when I lived around here. His pap's a good man. Real fine sawyer. Real good furniture maker. Married a gal from Iowa, Indiana, Illinois . . . somewhere like that. Lived at that cabin we passed a couple miles back."

The lieutenant nodded. "The cabin where no one was at?"

"Yes, sir."

"Not the brick mansion?"

"No, sir. No, Connor Ford didn't own any slaves." Greene's face hardened. "Unlike his brother. . . ."

"I see." Lieutenant Bullis was middle-aged, with gray eyes and a bulbous nose, his brow always knotted. The lieutenant popped a piece of hard candy into his mouth, then offered me one. I was about to accept, until I saw the officer's teeth. Those not brown were black with rot, and two were missing. Quickly I pulled my hand away, muttering: "No, thanks."

"Mill's fallen on some hard times since those days, Sergeant Greene," said Lieutenant Bullis as he passed the sack to Baby Hugh, who showed no hesitation at filling his mouth with the molasses candy.

"Yes, sir. Like most of this country, I warrant." Jared Greene looked at me again. "Your ma wasn't home."

"You went by our house?" I asked.

"It's on the way to Camden," Greene said. "We helped ourselves to some water. Good and cold, just like I recalled."

"And not poisoned," Hammond said.

My head nodded. "That's because of Mama," I said.

"Then your ma's alive and well?" Greene sounded relieved.

"Yes, sir."

"And your father?" That came from the lieutenant.

I studied him, and fell silent.

"He joined up, I warrant," Jared Greene said without condemnation. "Either that or got conscripted. What outfit is he in?"

I didn't answer, even when Lieutenant Bullis spoke sharply at me. "Answer Sergeant Greene, you low-down Secessionist cur!"

My lips tightened.

"He's. . . ." Edith hesitated, looked at me, and read my eyes.

"Well?" Bullis demanded.

Edith's head shook.

With a curse, Bullis snatched the sack of candy from Baby Hugh's hands, and strode away, barking orders at the men of color.

Greene stood, but he was smiling, and he leaned over and patted my shoulder. "That's a good boy, Travis. Don't tell the enemy a thing." He turned to Edith. "Your pap'll be proud of you. Of all you." He turned back to me. "Connor . . . he's still alive, isn't he? You pap? He's not dead?"

Now my lips trembled, and I had to will myself not to let any tears show. "I . . . we. . . ."

"We don't know," Edith said for me.

Baby Hugh wailed. "Papa ain't dead! Is he?"

The big sergeant kneeled, and put his hand on Baby Hugh's shoulder. " 'Course not, Hugh. Big, strapping man like Connor Ford, why, Grant and Sherman and all their armies couldn't lay a hand on him. If the Rebs had more men like your pap, we'd all be fleeing for Nova Scotia." He put a huge finger under Baby Hugh's chin, and lifted his head. "You don't remember me, do you, Hugh?"

Hugh's head shook.

" 'Course not. You weren't . . . gosh, no more than three years old when I had to leave, had to quit working for your pap at this mill."

"Where did you go?" Edith asked.

"Kansas. Lawrence, Kansas. But now I'm back. Back wearing the blue, fighting for our freedom, to save the Union, to end slavery forever, fighting with the First Kansas Colored Volunteer Infantry."

The black troops stood straighter when Greene said the regiment's name.

"That's right, boy," Jeremiah said. "We's the first Negroes to fight in Mister Lincoln's Army."

"Whupped the Secesh already," Hammond said.

"Toothman's Mound . . . Sherwood . . . Cabin Creek . . . Honey Springs." A bucktoothed, pockmarked mulatto pointed at the flag a soldier held, who stood beside the lieutenant. It was a blue square, with an eagle in the center, banner in its beak, arrows in one talon, something in the other, a red, white, and blue shield over its breast, and words painted above the eagle. But I couldn't make out the letters.

They were proud men. Like musketeers.

"Sergeant Greene!" the lieutenant called out. "There's nothing here. Let us march into Camden."

"Do we burn this mill, sir?" a soldier standing inside the doorway asked.

"Why bother?"

Greene cupped his mangled hand over his lips, asking: "What about these children, Lieutenant?"

"They're too young to shoot, and I can't very well take them prisoners. Leave them here."

"With your permission, sir, I'll take them back to their home. It's just a couple miles down the road."

"They are Secesh trash, Sergeant."

"They're kids, sir," Green replied.

"We've buried kids younger, Sergeant."

I recalled having heard this from a Confederate soldier in the past.

"And I'd hate to bury another, Lieutenant Bullis."

"Well. . . ." Swearing again, Bullis mounted his horse. "Don't take long, Sergeant." He spurred the black, and loped up the lane toward the Camden-Washington Pike.

Greene turned to me. "Where's your ma? Don't fib. I need to know."

"She's at Miss Mary's," Edith answered before I could.

"Mary?" Greene pursed his lips. "Miss Frederick? That Mary? With the big plantation just down the road from you."

Edith nodded.

Concern cracked through Greene's tough countenance, a word I had picked up at Mr. Mendenhall's and had looked up in Webster's.

"All right," Greene said, and turned to the soldiers, barking out orders like Athos. "Hammond, Wilson, you come with me. Rest of you boys, you heard the lieutenant, Camden's waiting to be liberated!"

Cheering soldiers leaped out of the mill and hurried up the lane. They fell into a column of twos, and began singing as they marched away.

> *We'll rally 'round the flag, boys, we'll rally once*
> *again,*
> *Shouting the battle cry of freedom,*
> *We will rally from the hillside, we'll gather from the*
> *plain,*
> *Shouting the battle cry of freedom!*
> *The Union forever! Hurrah, boys, hurrah!*
> *Down with the traitor, up with the star;*
> *While we rally 'round the flag, boys, rally once again,*
> *Shouting the battle cry of freedom!*
> *We are springing to the call of our brothers gone*
> *before,*
> *Shouting the battle cry of freedom!*

And we'll fill our vacant ranks with a million
  freemen more,
Shouting the battle cry of freedom!

When the voices died, when I could no longer make out the lyrics, Greene, Hammond, and Jeremiah stared at me.

"You kids don't play around here, do you?" Sergeant Jared Greene asked.

"It's a right dangersome place for little kids," Hammond said.

"No," Edith answered bluntly. "We didn't come here to play."

"Then what brought you here?" Jeremiah asked.

The candy cracked between Baby Hugh's teeth. "Acorns," he said. "We come for acorns."

"Acorns!" Jeremiah pulled off his cap and scratched his bald head. "What is y'all doin' that for? Y'all collectin' nuts for winter? Y'all squirrels?"

"It's for coffee," Edith told them.

"Coffee?" the three soldiers said at the same time.

"Yes." Edith glared at them. "Coffee. Tomorrow is Mama's birthday. We were going to gather as many acorns as we could, burn them, make them into coffee. Make Mama coffee. For her birthday."

"Acorns?" Shaking his head, Hammond had to spit the taste out of his mouth.

I stared into three black faces.

After a while, Sergeant Jared Greene's determined countenance faded again, broken this time by a huge smile. "Coffee." His head bobbed. "Acorns for coffee. Travis, Miss Edith, Master Hugh . . . I think we can do better than that for your ma."

CHAPTER TWELVE

Since the 1st Kansas Colored Volunteers were infantry, we walked back home. I guess only Lieutenant Bullis rode a horse. To my surprise, when we reached the main road, I didn't see throngs of soldiers marching toward Camden with wagons, cannon, and caisson. I only caught a glimpse of the soldiers under Lieutenant Bullis's command, spread out as they walked up the road.

This is the Union Army that caused General Price to retreat to Washington? I thought. *Maybe twenty men?*

Sergeant Jared Greene must have read my mind. "We're just a foraging patrol," he said. He tilted his head west. "Rest of the army's coming up slowly. Hard to get along these roads."

"What's foraging?" Baby Hugh asked.

"Stealing," Edith answered bitterly.

"Ain't no such thing," Jeremiah snapped. "We's liberating."

"Stealing," my twin said again.

Chuckling, Greene hooked his thumb toward Lieutenant Bullis and his foragers. "Captain Miller's up ahead with a patrol. He's scouting. We expected to have to fight the Rebs in Camden, but, from the looks of this road, they've done vamoosed."

"You should've seen . . . ," Baby Hugh began, but I cut him off.

"They don't need to learn anything from us!"

Pouting at my sharp rebuke, Baby Hugh looked up at Edith. "But ain't that big darky a friend of Papa's?"

"Don't call him a darky, Baby Hugh," Edith said softly. "It's not polite."

"That's all rights, young 'uns," Hammond said. "We's been called a whole lot worser than that."

"By our own officers sometimes," Jeremiah said.

"But ain't he . . . ?" Baby Hugh began, then tilted his head toward Sergeant Greene, who walked behind Edith and my kid brother. I was beside Greene. Jeremiah lagged a few paces behind, and Hammond walked maybe ten yards ahead of Hugh and Edith. "Ain't he a friend of Papa's?"

"He wears the blue," Edith said. "Papa wears the gray. They're enemies."

"We're just on two different sides," Jared Greene said. "I couldn't call me and your pap enemies. Criminy, I always thought of us as friends."

"He's no friend of Papa's, Baby Hugh," I said, just to say something, feeling angry, bitter. "Or ours. He quit Papa. Just up and quit him four or five years ago. Or maybe Papa had to fire him."

" 'Cause I'm a lyin', shiftless, low-down darky?" Greene had raised his voice two octaves, slurred his voice, mimicking the accent and tone I heard often in Washington County.

My face reddened. "Maybe," I said stiffly. "You left."

We walked in silence for a good hundred yards.

Finally Sergeant Greene said: "I didn't have much choice."

"Was you Papa's slave?" Baby Hugh said.

"Hugh!" Edith said. "You know better. . . ."

The three soldiers laughed.

"The sarge is a freedman," Hammond said. "Always been a freedman. Now Jeremiah Wilson and me? We wasn't so fortunate. I run off from Dardanelle. That's up yonder in Yell County. Place just filled with stumps. Stumps ever'where. Stumps and rocks. And I was always tryin' to get 'em stumps

114

outta the ground. So I run off. By my ownself. No Underground Railroad. No Kansas friends of ol' John Brown. Just me fol- lowin' the drinkin' gourd, outrunnin', outsmartin' all them hounds they fetched after me. Run all the way to Topeka, Kansas. Jeremiah? He got hisself liberated by some boys who taken him off that field some place in Missouri and fetched him back to Kansas. Where was that you was a field hand, Jeremiah?"

"Big Joe Obojkski's farm in Cass County, just outside of Harrisonville."

"That's right. So me and Jeremiah, we's nothin' more'n runaway slaves. But sarge, he's always been free."

We kept walking.

After a while Sergeant Greene said: "Depends, I reckon, on how you define *free.*"

"What do you mean?" Edith asked. I wasn't about to ask anything, though begrudgingly I had to admit I was curious.

The sergeant grinned, but said nothing, just kept walking through the mud for a long while. Finally, with Edith still star- ing at him as he walked, he said: "You ever hear of Dred Scott?"

Even I shook my head.

"Figured," Greene said. "Y'all would have been a mite young back then. And I don't think I ever heard your pap speak of politics. Now your mother. . . ." He smiled.

"I ain't heard of Dred Scott, neither, Sergeant," Hammond said.

"I have," Jeremiah said.

"You ain't."

"Have, too."

"Ain't."

"Have. . . ."

"It doesn't matter," Greene said sharply. "Keep your eyes in those trees, Hammond. You, too, Wilson."

"Ain't no Rebs within ten mile of here, Sarge," Jeremiah

complained.

"Maybe not. But seein' a man of color in Yankee blue's liable to provoke a civilian in these parts into firing a shot at us."

We walked, only now a little more nervous and observant.

"Dred Scott," Greene said after we had covered a few rods, "was a slave. In Missouri."

"That's where you's from, Jeremiah," Hammond said. "You ever met that boy?"

"Told you I knowed him."

"You said you'd heard of him."

"Knowed him, too."

"Did not."

"Did, too."

"Did. . . ."

Greene raised his voice and hand. "Let me see if I can get through this story without interruption."

Silence. Just the sucking of mud against our shoes and Baby Hugh's bare feet.

"Way I recall it, Scott tried to buy his freedom. His owner wouldn't let him. Anyhow, I don't know all the particulars, but the case wound up before the United States Supreme Court. United States, I said, not the Confederate States. This happened before there even was a Confederate States of America. Well, the Supreme Court . . . the highest court in the land . . . says that folks of color, like Hammond and O'Brien and Dred Scott and me, have no claim to citizenship. Said we didn't have the rights of a white citizen. No matter if we were free or slave."

We walked.

"That ain't right," Jeremiah said.

Greene shrugged. His saber rattled. "Well, it's what the Supreme Court ruled. 'Way back in 'Fifty-Seven."

"So . . . ," Edith began. "What did that have to do with you?"

"Had everything to do with me. The Supreme Court said I

wasn't a citizen. Despite the fact that I was born free. My mama and daddy were free. Think my mama was always free, but my daddy had to buy his freedom when he was in Kentucky. Went to school. Learned to read, to write, do my cyphers, even learned a bit of French. I worked a spell in Kentucky before I moved down here. Arkansas was the frontier. There were a number of freedmen in Arkansas when I settled here. I paid taxes. Owned a few acres. Had me a cabin. Worked for your pap. Connor Ford treated me fine. Maybe on account of your mama's leanings . . . her upbringing . . . but I think Connor was a good man. *Is* a good man."

"So why did you leave?" I hated myself for asking the question, which just came out of my mouth before I could stop myself.

"The State of Arkansas made me."

We walked.

"Made every freedman in Arkansas leave."

"Why?" Edith asked.

"Well, after the Supreme Court ruled on Dred Scott, a law was passed in Little Rock. The law said every freedman had to get out of Arkansas. Get out by January of Eighteen Sixty or become a slave."

"You might could've joined up with me in Dardanelle, Sergeant," Hammond said. "We'd 'a' took good care of you. The boss lady didn't whup her slaves too much, lessen she got riled."

I pictured Miss Mary Frederick. I imagined her whipping old Mowbray with her buggy whip.

"Might could have," Greene said. "But I told these young 'uns' pap good bye, headed to Lawrence, Kansas."

"You run into any trouble along the way, Sergeant?" Jeremiah asked.

"Man of color on a mule in this state? Riding north? Yeah, I dare say I had some little trouble. Got questioned a lot. Had to show my papers, which didn't help with the white folks who couldn't read. Some boys . . . might have been in Yell County, Hammond . . . wanted to see me die of hemp fever. Had to persuade them otherwise."

"I can imagine how," Hammond said.

"I can't. Lieutenant Bullis, he always says I ain't got no imagination. So tell us how," Jeremiah said.

"Some other time."

We walked.

"But you made it to Kansas," Hammond said, to prompt Greene.

"I made it to Kansas." Greene nodded. "Settled in Lawrence. Good city. Fine place." He spit. "Or was." His voice was soft, but laced with bitterness. "Till Quantrill showed up with his bushwhackers back in August."

"But now Mister Lincoln's showing them Rebs," Hammond said. "He bringin' all us colored folks the jubilee."

"I hope so," Greene said, and turned to me. "Even before Dred Scott." His eyes showed no animosity. In fact, he was still smiling. "Even before all of that, I was free, but only on the paper I had. I owned my place. Paid taxes to Washington County. But I couldn't vote. Had no rights whatsoever. Guess I wasn't a citizen, even before the United States Supreme Court said so."

"Mister Lincoln's changin' all that!" Hammond shouted.

"Maybe." Greene didn't sound convinced.

"So that's what we's fightin' for!" Jeremiah called out. "Our freedom. Freedom for us. For our families. For all us darkies. What's your daddy fightin' for, chil'ren?"

"That's enough, Wilson," Sergeant Greene said.

"But. . . ."

"You heard me."

The rest of our hike was filled with silence. Until Greene yelled to Hammond: "See that lane off to the left?"

"Yes, Sarge. That's the one we taken when we was. . . ."

"Let's take it again." The big sergeant grinned. "That's where the Fords live." He pointed down the road. "My place, just a little shanty, was a few miles down the Pike. It's gone now. Land cleared, shanty torn down, cotton field in its place. Miss Mary's cotton. I was Miss Mary Frederick's neighbor."

"She's a real good neighbor. Brings us leftovers," Baby Hugh sang out. "Cakes sometimes. And cookies. And pies."

Greene grinned. "That's funny. She never brought me anything."

Lifting the hems of her skirt as she ran toward us, Mama met us halfway down the lane, her eyes filled with panic. She slid to a stop a good many yards before us, gasping, bringing up a hand to cover her mouth, before she yelled out our names and continued her sprint.

"Go on," Greene said. "Run to your ma. She must be worried sick."

Baby Hugh didn't need any more encouragement. He dashed past Hammond, and Edith was just behind him. Being the oldest boy, of course, I didn't want the Yankees to see me run, so I just walked. Kind of fast. Mama was squeezing Edith and Hugh hard, and I couldn't hold back any more. I hurried to her, felt her strong arms wrap around me, and pull me close.

"I was so worried," she said.

"We was just . . . at the . . . mill," Baby Hugh managed.

"What in heaven's name were you doing there?" She didn't let us answer. She swallowed, sniffed, wiped the tears off her cheek, and slowly rose, keeping her hands on Baby Hugh's shoulders, motioning Edith and me to step behind her. Edith did. I just turned around to face the three black Yankees.

Hammond, Greene, and Wilson walked slowly toward us, the two runaway slaves shouldering their muskets, and Sergeant Greene holding his hat in his hands.

"Miz Anna," Greene said.

I looked at Mama. She blinked, her lips parted, and in that instant I saw recognition light up her face.

"Jared?" She released her hold on Baby Hugh. "Jared Greene? Is that you?"

"In the flesh, Miz Anna."

She walked up the lane, leaving us kids behind, Holding out her right hand. "It's been a long time, Jared."

They shook hands.

"Yes, ma'am. Lot of water under the bridge."

"I came home," Mama explained. "Ran home. Some of Miss Mary's . . ."—she hesitated—"some of her . . . workers . . . ran into the house, saying Yankees were on the road. Marching to Camden." She shook her head, wiped her forehead. "When I got to the Pike, I saw many, many soldiers in blue. They were maybe two miles away, so I just ran for home."

"That'd be General Thayer with his main force, ma'am," Sergeant Greene said.

"The Frontier Division," Hammond said with pride. "We's part of that."

We were sitting on the porch in front of the sleeping cabin—Mama in the rocking chair, Edith and I on the bench. Baby Hugh sat with his feet dangling over the porch while Sergeant Greene was perched on an overturned keg in front of Mama, and Hammond and Wilson were on the steps.

"I don't think I slowed down all the way here," Mama said. She still patted her forehead and cheeks with a handkerchief. "I'm not sure my feet even touched the ground. And when I got home"—she looked at Edith and me—"and you weren't here. . . ."

"We're sorry, Mama," Baby Hugh said. "We just went to get some acorns."

"Hugh!" Edith and I shouted.

"Acorns?" Mama lowered the handkerchief. She locked her gaze on Edith, then me, then Hugh, then turned to Sergeant Greene. "Anyway," she said after a long while, "I got here and found the doors open, all of the chickens gone. . . ."

"The chickens!" I glared at Sergeant Greene.

"Reckon the boys liberated 'em," Jeremiah offered, and laughed.

I wanted to punch him in the nose.

"Did y'all forage our cow, too?" Edith asked, her voice as bitter as mine.

"No," Mama said. "Lucy's still in the barn."

"Sorry about those chickens, Miz Anna," Sergeant Greene said.

"Oh, I don't care about the chickens," Mama said. "As long as my children are safe."

"You Yankees are nothing but thieves," I snapped.

"Travis," Mama said.

But if Mama's Abolitionist got up, so did my Rebel. "You don't see the Confederates robbing po-. . . ." I couldn't bring myself to say we were poor. Not in front of those black Yanks. "Not robbing people like us. Citizens."

"Travis!" Mama's tone told me to close my mouth, and I did, though I still seethed.

"I recall Confederate foragers here not long ago," Mama said, "who would have made off with our cow, our chickens, and left our well poisoned with the bloating carcasses of two dead dogs."

"Mama!" Edith made a face.

A smug smirk came upon Jared Greene's face. "It's been this way, Miz Anna," the sergeant said. "We've been on half rations for three weeks now . . . since we marched out of Fort Smith. Some of the men are hungry."

So are we, I almost said aloud, but didn't want to make Mama angrier.

Mama gave an understanding nod.

"And them Reb bushwhackers been tormentin' us all the while," Hammond added.

"Bet we lost a man ever' day," Jeremiah added.

Sergeant Greene cleared his throat to get his men to either change the subject or just stop talking.

"Anyway," Greene said at last, "if General Thayer's coming down the Pike, we should be on our way." As he stood, he motioned for Jeremiah and Hammond to rise. They did, slowly removing their hats, bowing politely at Mama and Edith.

"We thank you for your hospitality, ma'am," Hammond said.

"I didn't. . . ." Mama shot up. "My goodness. I didn't offer you water, or something to. . . ."

"Don't fret, Miz Anna." The sergeant had slipped the haversack off his back. He reached inside and withdrew a sack, handing it to Mama.

"It's not much," he said, "but the young 'uns tell me your birthday's tomorrow. So this is from your children. With the compliments of the First Kansas Colored Volunteers."

CHAPTER THIRTEEN

It had been a long time since that smell had greeted me in the kitchen. I never drank coffee, but I had to admit that the aroma, even Yankee coffee, was pleasing.

Papa had always bragged on Mama's special way of making coffee. Usually she wrapped the ground beans in a handkerchief that she then submerged in the pot of water into which she had already poured honey and some cubes of sugar. On that April morning, however, since she didn't know when she'd ever get coffee again—and what Sergeant Greene had given her hadn't been much—she mixed the coffee with a spoonful of cornmeal she had toasted. There was no sugar. No honey, either. She also couldn't float an egg shell in the pot—which kept the grounds at the bottom—because, thanks to those Yankees, we had no eggs.

Mama breathed in the scent, and said—*"Ahhhhh."*—just like Baby Hugh would when Miss Mary had brought over leftovers.

Mama could drink coffee every day, morning, noon, and night. In fact, back when we had coffee—in that epoch when most people could afford it and every store had some on the shelves—she did drink it throughout the day. Papa never drank it after breakfast.

After pouring her first brew since what must have seemed like forever from the pot into a cup, Mama sipped, smiled, and settled into the chair.

"How does it taste?" Edith asked.

"Delicious," Mama answered. "And it didn't cost sixty dollars a pound." She drank some more before slowly setting the cup on the table. "Now what was all that about acorns?"

While Edith and I stared at each other, Baby Hugh told Mama everything. My face flushed, but Mama smiled at us warmly.

"That was very sweet of you," she said. "I bet acorn coffee would have been fabulous. I've heard from other women in church how they've been making coffee. Burning sugar. Even chopping up sweet potatoes, cane seeds, persimmon seeds. I just didn't see myself trying something like that."

Besides, I knew we didn't exactly have an abundance of sugar or sweet potatoes, sugar cane or persimmons, either.

"But," Mama said, "when Jared's coffee runs out, maybe we shall try acorn coffee. It sounds intriguing."

"If"—Edith grinned—"you're a squirrel."

It had been a long time since we had heard Mama laugh. I mean really laugh. Of course, my conniving twin had stolen the joke I had made when she first suggested that stupid idea of acorn coffee. And those 1st Kansas colored soldiers had made similar jokes. I ground my teeth and clenched my fists.

"When do you reckon the Yankees will get to Camden?" Baby Hugh asked.

"Tomorrow," Mama said after a moment's thought. "Most likely."

"Will there be a fight?" he asked.

That brat sure seemed bent on spoiling Mama's good mood.

"I don't know." Mama brought the cup to her lips. "General Price's army has gone. I don't know."

I decided to change the subject. "How's Miss Mary?" As soon as those words left my mouth, I knew I hadn't changed anything. Maybe I had made things worse.

"She was fine." Mama sighed. She finished her coffee, and

stood, starting for the pot in the fireplace, then stopping, putting the empty cup in the sink, and returning to the table. "I think I'll just save the rest of that coffee for breakfast tomorrow. It'll be stronger then."

Edith said cheerily: "Papa used to say you liked your coffee strong enough to float a stern-wheeler's anchor."

She started laughing again, her face bright, eyes dancing. "Yes. Yes, and I would tell Connor that he liked a tablespoon of coffee with his water."

We grinned, until Baby Hugh reminded Mama: "You were talking about Miss Mary."

Again I cringed. So did Edith.

"Yes." Mama pushed her bangs off her forehead. "She was fine. I don't think she even remembered coming to our house, or beating poor Mowbray with that whip. When her field hands came running inside, saying the Yankees were coming, the Yankees were coming, I left. Just ran home."

Mama's birthday came without cake, even without much food, thanks to those 1st Kansas Yankees. But, at least, Mama had coffee. Still in a good mood, she asked us to sing to her, so we gathered on the porch, and serenaded her with "The Blue-Tail Fly", "Listen to the Mockingbird", and a fairly new song Edith had learned from some of her girlfriends at church, "The Southern Soldier Boy".

The way Edith told it, the hero of the song was supposed to be named Bob Roebuck. But we changed it. Changed the girl's name, too. For Mama. And for ourselves.

Edith would sing a line, then we would repeat it.

> *Connor Ford is my sweetheart's name.*
> *He's off to the wars and gone.*
> *He's fighting for his Anna dear.*
> *His sword is buckled on.*

He's fighting for his own true love.
His foes he does defy.
He is the darling of my heart.
My Southern soldier boy.

But when we got to the next verse, Edith stopped when she hit the part—"Oh, if in battle he was slain." We all abruptly quit singing, and the silence grew heavier than Mama's coffee.

"Well," Mama said, refusing to have anything put a damper on her birthday. "How about if we sing . . . ?"

" 'Old Dan Tucker'!" Baby Hugh shouted.

It was his favorite song. Mama couldn't stand it, but she nodded and said cheerily: "Yes. Yes. That is a lively tune. Sing it, Hugh."

Yet before Baby Hugh could begin, we heard someone calling. Baby Hugh dropped to the ground, and ran toward the lane to see who was coming. Mama called out for him to stop, but, Hugh, being Hugh, ignored her. He was pointing and jumping up and down before he tore a path down the lane. "It's Miss Mary!" he yelled. "It's Miss Mary!"

She didn't drive her carriage like a crazy lady. Not this time. She had walked the five miles to our home, and she looked as if she hadn't slept forever.

Edith and I helped her up the steps, while Baby Hugh stood there pouting, kicking at the dirt, complaining that Miss Mary hadn't brought anything to eat.

Mama ended that in a hurry. "Hugh," she said, and my kid brother's doldrums ended immediately.

"I'm sorry. . . ."

"You get inside, young man. Now! You open your *Reader* and you bury your nose in that book, and you sit there, and you don't say a word. Not one word. Now, mister. Now!"

He vanished. Served him right.

"Edith,"—Mama was easing Miss Mary into the rocker—

"pour a cup of coffee for Miss Mary. Bring it out here. Quickly."

"But Miss Mary doesn't like coffee," Edith said, and, quickly realizing her error, muttered: "I'll get it, Mama. I'll bring it right out." She hurried into the dogtrot and to the kitchen.

I dragged the keg over, and Mama lifted Miss Mary's legs, and rested them atop the oaken top. Mama found her handkerchief, wiped Miss Mary's sweaty face.

Her dress was unbuttoned, dirty. No, not dirty. It looked filthy. Even Hugh's bare feet didn't look so bad. One shoe was unbuttoned, the other caked with mud. She shook her head, her eyes blinking rapidly. Edith ran back through the dogtrot, and held the cup out to Mama.

Leaning, Mama brought the tin cup to Miss Mary's pale lips, encouraging her to drink. She did, and she didn't even complain that she didn't like coffee, especially when it was Mama's strong and thick tar-like brew.

"They're all gone," Miss Mary managed to get out, then she drank more coffee, but the cup slipped and the liquid spilled, dripping through the spaces between the planks. "All gone," she whispered, leaning forward and crying. Mama clutched Miss Mary's dirty hands. Tears streamed down Miss Mary's face, and her head shook. "All gone!" she wailed. "Every last one of them."

Edith and I exchanged looks, but we didn't know what Miss Mary was talking about.

"I treated all of 'em fine. Just fine. Sallie . . . my Sallie had been with me since Daddy was alive."

I mouthed to Edith: "Her slaves."

My sister nodded in understanding.

"The Yankees come. They come up yesterday. Bold as brass, the vermin."

"I was there, Mary," Mama said gently. "Remember?"

Her face was a blank. "No." She pulled her hands from

Mama's grip, shaking her head. "No. I don't remember. I can hardly remember a thing. Not any more."

"Your slaves spotted them," Mama reminded her. "I ran back home. They hadn't arrived when I left. Did they mistreat you, Mary? Did they . . . ?"

"They left," Miss Mary cried. "Even Sallie. They just walked behind the soldiers."

Mama wet her lips, drew in a breath. She was patient, but that had always been one of her strongest traits.

"Your slaves left?" Mama said. "With the soldiers?"

"Yes." Her voice seemed so uncertain.

"How's your home, Mary?" Mama prodded.

"It's . . . empty."

"But they didn't . . . they didn't burn it . . . did they? The soldiers, I mean."

"No." Her head shook. She wiped her eyes. "I don't think so."

Edith and I exchanged another look.

"Sallie and all my hands!" Miss Mary cried out, leaning forward, fists balled. "All of them. They just followed those Bluecoats down the road. I called out to some Yankee officer. I said to him . . . 'What are you doing with my slaves?' And he said, he says . . . 'They aren't slaves, madam. They are contrabands of war.' Have you ever heard of such talk, Anna?"

"You just rest, Mary."

Contrabands. I had another word to look up in Webster's.

"Even Mowbray, old Mowbray, he's gone, too."

"Mowbray?" I hadn't seen such fear in Mama's face since Baby Hugh had had the colic real bad. Mama had sat up all night with him, and Papa had talked about God's will, and that if it was Baby Hugh's time to be an angel we must accept that.

"Mowbray," Miss Mary repeated. "I called for him and called for him . . . after the Yankees were gone. I went into every room in the house, even into the carriage house I was building for him. He was gone. Mowbray left me, too."

She didn't remember. Her mind had gone so far, she had forgotten how she had savagely beaten that old man with a whip, how she had almost killed herself the other day racing that team of grays here.

Uncle Willard was right. Perhaps he had always been right. Miss Mary Frederick was mad as a hatter.

"Maybe he'll come back," Mama was saying to Miss Mary, though all of us knew better. Mowbray would never return to Miss Mary's plantation, unless one of the militia patrols caught him.

"Edith," Mama said softly as she turned toward us. "Go inside. Fetch some blankets. Put them on our bed. Miss Mary will sleep there tonight. Travis, bring the rocking chair inside. I'll sit up with her."

Like she had sat up that time when Baby Hugh had the colic.

"They broke open the smokehouse," Miss Mary said, her voice sounding so far away. "Those Bluebellies did. Busted down the door with the stocks of their muskets. They yelled like savages, and they speared hams and everything else they could with those long knives at the end of their muskets. It was horrible. Just horrible." She ran the back of her right hand across her forehead. "Ran out like crazy men. And all my slaves, as well as I treated them, they just walked behind them. Just walked down the road, leaving my cotton, my carriage house, my stables, my smokehouse, leaving everything. Even leaving me. They got rice and sugar and flour and beans and carrots and potatoes. They got everything." She drew a deep breath, and let it out quickly. Her eyes found Mama. "And the worst thing of all, Anna, the absolute horror of it all. Some of those soldiers . . . a lot of them, to tell you the God's honest truth . . . they weren't white men. They were colored. *Colored Yankees!*"

129

con'tra-band, n. Prohibition of trading in goods, contrary to the laws of a state or of nations.
   2. Illegal traffic.

I closed the dictionary, and climbed up into the loft. Downstairs, Mama sat in the rocking chair, as she had since she had put Miss Mary into bed. Miss Mary slept. She'd been sleeping all day, and Mama was worried sick about her. I guess she forgot to fix us supper.

That was all right, though. After that evening, even Baby Hugh had no appetite.

The next morning, we ate grits for breakfast while Miss Mary slept. She would sleep all that morning, and not stir until well into the afternoon. Before she woke, we had another visitor.

Sweating profusely, the Reverend White made his way down the lane. Like Miss Mary, he was walking, but we knew why. I hoped he didn't come to complain about losing Betsy. He hadn't.

"Yanks pay y'all a visit?" he asked Mama after I had fetched him some water from the well.

"They were here," Mama said. "Stole all the chickens we had."

"Contrabands of war," I said, and the two of them studied me without comment.

"And your cow?" the preacher asked.

Mama shook her head. "They left her."

"God's will."

"His will be done."

"Amen."

They were sitting on the porch. The preacher sipped water, wiped the sweat from his forehead, and shook his head. "Been makin' my way 'round. Seein' if anybody needed prayers. 'Course, ever'body needs prayers. The Yanks entered Camden yesterday evenin'. 'Round six o'clock."

Baby Hugh stuck his head out the front door, saying: "Mama's birthday."

"You don't say. Well, happy birthday, Mizzus Ford."

"Thank you." Mama called softly to Hugh: "Is she still asleep?"

Baby Hugh stuck his head out the door again and nodded.

The preacher looked confused.

"Is Edith sick?" he asked.

"I'm fine." My twin came around the corner.

"Mary Frederick came here yesterday," Mama explained. "In a desperate state. She has been sleeping since yesterday evening. The soldiers freed her slaves. I guess she had nowhere to go, except here."

Reverend White drank more water. "You're a good friend, Anna Louella Ford. A fine, Christian lady. I'll pray for poor Mary Frederick. She's Presbyterian?"

"Episcopalian."

"Ah. Yes. Well, I'll still pray for her." He grinned.

I guess it was a joke. We Baptists never understood much humor.

"They were hungry, those Yanks. Went door to door, I am told, demandin' food. Thievin' scum."

"The Confederates weren't much better, Thaddeus," Mama told him.

He looked uncomfortable. "They'll be even hungrier yet, I warrant. Ten thousand hosses and mules to feed. Maybe twelve. Maybe fifteen thousand. All those soldiers, coloreds and whites. They've come to the wrong place if they wants good eats. Ain't that right?"

Maybe it was another joke, but for a family who had been eating potatoes and carrots since forever, and who had just seen the chickens turned into Union contraband, we didn't think much of the preacher's humor.

He leaned toward Mama. "I fear, Anna Louella, however, that somebody . . . a traitorous Judas Iscariot right in our midst in Washington County! . . . has told those Yankee dogs about the hidden corn."

CHAPTER FOURTEEN

Mama just stared.

The Reverend White sat back in the rocking chair, mopped his brow a final time before shoving the rag into his pocket.

"What corn?" Mama asked.

He gave her an incredulous stare. "Haven't you heard?"

Her head—our heads—shook.

"Some of the farmers have corn stored in their cribs."

Now Mama laughed out loud, and, shaking her head, she said: "Yes, well, farmers usually store corn in cribs, shucked or unshucked, to dry. Connor built a crib as soon as he had cleared enough acreage for a cornfield."

The preacher was serious. "Yes, but 'em Yanks have learnt of this, and as they are desperate to feed their hosses and mules, they's sure to be scourin' the country, stealin' from good, honest folks. You should be on the look-out."

Once again, Mama laughed. "Reverend," she said, "we haven't had corn since Connor enlisted. Just a few rows I try to grow to feed us, not. . . ." She stopped. She was about to say our mules, but they were gone, as was the preacher's, which had been seized by Confederates while in our possession. "Reverend," she said, "would you care for some coffee?"

She was changing the subject, and it certainly got Mr. White's attention.

"Coffee?" His hands clapped like thunder. "When in God's glorious name did you happen upon coffee?"

"Come on," she said. Mama wasn't about to tell him the coffee had been given to her by a Yankee, a black Yankee at that. "It should be strong by now."

Into the shade of the dogtrot they went, and then into the kitchen, where that coffee would be thicker than molasses by now. All of our doors and windows had been opened, to allow a breeze, so Edith, Baby Hugh, and I decided to sit close to the door. Not that we were snooping. We were just . . . well . . . snooping.

The liquid was poured, the coffee cups clinked in a toast, and a moment later Reverend White smacked his lips. "By grab, Anna Louella, that's not burnt grain coffee or water poured over year-old grounds, that's real, honest-to-goodness coffee. How did you manage it?"

"It's not all coffee, Reverend White," Mama said proudly. "I toasted cornmeal to mix with the beans I ground . . . to make it last."

"Well, it's strong. And good. Ain't had real coffee in a year now." His lips smacked again. "Did Miss Mary fetch it for you?"

The pause seemed to last forever. I heard a cup settle onto a saucer. It must have been Mama's. "I fear for Mary," she said. "She isn't well."

"God will see to her, Anna Louella. His will be done, and I will pray for her. Pray good, loud, long, strong. But this coffee. How did you manage upon it?"

By that time, I had closed my eyes and was praying, too. Not loud, not long, but strong. *Please, Mama, just tell him that Miss Mary brought you the coffee. Please, God, tell Mama that it's all right to lie. Just this one time. Miss Mary brought the coffee. It was Miss Mary. Miss Mary. Miss Mary. Don't let her tell the truth. Not to him. Not to him.*

My prayer wasn't good enough for the Lord, though.

"A Union soldier brought it, Reverend," she said.

Slam! That must have been the preacher's cup hitting the table. "A Yank?" he said in his fire-and-brimstone, Old Testament tone. "A Yankee!"

"I did not see them as Yankees, but as men."

"Them? More than one?"

"They found my children at Connor's sawmill, Reverend. They had the decency to bring them home."

"And steal your chickens."

"As the Confederates stole your mule."

" 'Traitors, heady, high-minded, lovers of pleasures more than lovers of God!' "

"I am no traitor."

"Sometimes, madam, I forget your Unionist upbringing."

"If I were a Unionist, I would be living in Springfield with my mother and my children. And so would my husband. You seem to forget, Reverend, that he wears the gray. I don't see you in a Confederate uniform, sir." Her Abolitionist was up.

" 'And Judas, the brother of James!' " the preacher shouted, citing Scripture. " 'And Judas Iscariot, which also was the traitor!' It was you, wasn't it, madam, who informed the Yankees about the corn?"

I leaped up, ready to charge, to challenge the preacher to a duel, but Edith grabbed my arm, and, before I could make my way into the kitchen, Mama was laughing.

"Really, Thaddeus? Do you really think I know anything that's going on with my neighbors? Do you think that Willard told me what General Price was doing, where all this alleged corn was stored?"

"That's exactly what I think."

"Corn is stored in cribs, Reverend. If you seek corn, you look in the cribs of farmers."

The fat old man was no Porthos. No fun-loving hero. He was an evil, evil man, unable to see, blinded by hatred.

" 'And he cast down the pieces of silver in the temple, and departed, and went and hanged himself. And the chief priests took the silver pieces, and said, it is not lawful for to put them into the treasury, because it is the price of blood.' "

Somehow, Mama remained calm. "Does this mean that all of the money I have tithed will be returned?"

That shut him up. But not for long.

" 'And the sun stood still, and the moon stayed, until the people had avenged themselves upon their enemies. . . . Our God shall come, and shall not keep silence; a fire shall devour before him, and it shall be very tempestuous round about him.' Perhaps you should leave for Little Rock, madam, and the Blue-bellies there. Or, better yet, return to Illinois."

Mama fired some of the Good Book right back into his face. " 'But I say unto you which hear, Love your enemies, do good to them which hate you.' "

The preacher was out the door by the time Mama had finished, slamming his straw hat on his head, almost tripping over Baby Hugh, and pounding down the steps.

Mama followed him out the door, speaking to his back as he headed up the lane. " 'Bless them that curse you, and pray for them which despitefully use you. And unto him that smiteth thee on the one cheek offer also the other. . . .' "

When she had finished with her scriptures, she turned to us, smiled, and, as if nothing had even happened, she said: "I must check on Mary. You children, run along now, and play."

Play. Not do our chores. Not study. Play.

We looked at one other. Baby Hugh ran down the lane with Edith right behind him. To see if anyone was on the Camden-Washington Pike. I went around the house and climbed into the corncrib. Which, of course, was empty. You needed crops to have corn to store for drying.

Sunlight streaked through the slatted walls, casting shadows on the ground, and I breathed in deeply, but there was no longer the smell of corn. Just dust. And emptiness. I remembered back when Papa would haul the corn in from the field to the crib, parking the wagon underneath, how he would let Edith and me help him put the unshucked corn up in the crib. I remembered playing up here—Robin Hood and his Merry Men, fighting the evil sheriff of Nottingham, dueling him with sword, and falling out, landing hard, the breath whooshing from my lungs, lying there, fearing I was dying, and how nobody could hear me scream for help because I had no breath. I didn't die, of course. Never told anyone about it.

As I climbed back down, I looked at the crib. Papa had built it, too. I didn't remember when. For as long as I remembered, the crib had always been part of our home, and now I wondered if maybe Jared Greene had helped him build it.

Suddenly the mood to write hit me. No, it wasn't a mood. It was like something I just had to do. More than an urge, a need. It felt like I had to write the same as I had to breathe. Down the lane I ran, skirting through the trees before I reached the road to avoid any nagging questions from Edith or Baby Hugh. I cut through the woods until I knew the road had curved, then bulled through brambles, leaped over rotting wood, jumped the ditch, and raced to the lane that led to Papa's sawmill.

As I ran, the story began developing in my head.

Musketeer Travis Ford rescues his lady fair from the Tower of Torment, dueling the evil Cardinal White himself. Thrust. Parry. En garde. *Steel against steel. Lady Constance clutches her chest, brings a delicate, gloved hand to her rosy lips. She is unable to scream, watching as her hero and the evil, sweaty, fat man lunge. Steel clangs. Ford smiles. One of the cardinal's guards leaps through the trap door. No, two. The cardinal smiles, and watches, but then a vile curse escapes his lips when the first guard is run through, doubles over, groaning as he dies. The second is forced back and falls, screaming to his death forty feet below on the cobblestone streets of Paris.*

"And now," Travis Ford boldly proclaims, "it is time for you to join him."

"That is yet to be seen!"

Thrust. Parry. Steel against steel. Blades whistle as they slice through the air. Lady Constance gasps as the cardinal's sword slices through the musketeer hero's white shirt sleeve, but Travis Ford does not even wince. He is moving forward, eyes intense, and the fat, sweaty cardinal backs up and up and up and. . . .

He screams a curse as he falls out of the open window. A sickening thud sounds as the cardinal lands on the rocks, then splashes into the Paris River, and the crocodiles enjoy their supper.

Yet there is no time to spare. Sheathing his rapier, Ford grabs Constance's hand. They hurry down the rickety ladder, touch the streets of Paris, and are running through dark alleys, up buildings, across a moat.

They enter the forest of gloom, and reach the ruins of the Fortress Connor.

The door to the tool shed banged open, sending a rat scurrying over my feet, but I didn't even flinch. Stepping inside, I found the shed exactly as I had left it. Despite some trouble, I finally managed to get the empty oil cans off Papa's cigar box, which I brought into the mill, pulled out of the sack, and opened. Miss Mary's gift still lay inside, and I pulled the tablet from the box, closed the lid, and stared at the musician serenading the lovely lady.

Travis Ford, King's Musketeer, exchanges his rapier for a guitar, and he begins to sing to Lady Constance. "Old Dan Tucker was a funny old man. He washed his face with a frying pan. He combed his hair with a wagon wheel. Died with a toothache in his heel."

I laughed. Why I was in such high spirits, I couldn't explain. Maybe it was this insanity to write. Maybe I thought I had just seen how a real hero could stand up to a tyrant. Then I opened the tablet and saw what I had written, what I had scratched out, what I had written again:

The Spring of Hope
Poison Spring

Closing the tablet, I sat, legs dangling over the side, staring into the forest. A fish jumped in the millpond. A frog croaked. Above my head, the wind rustled the branches, the pine needles, the leaves of the oaks. I listened, taking in every sound. Birds, the wind, squirrels, a woodpecker somewhere deeper into the woods, another fish jumping, that frog still croaking. I breathed, smelling every scent. Pine and dust and pitch and mud. I looked, studying everything I could see. The acorns Edith and Baby Hugh had gathered. The droppings of the horse Lieutenant Bullis had ridden. One mound had been flattened by a boot or a shoe, and I grinned, thinking about how all of those soldiers must have picked on the unfortunate Yankee who had put his foot in the wrong place.

A sentence flashed through my brain: *The epoch of adventure is now.*

Then the thought: *Tell the truth, Travis.*

I pictured Miss Mary, sitting down beside me at the window of Mr. Mendenhall's store, watching me as I tried to make my way through some passage in *The Count of Monte Cristo.* I heard myself telling her: "There sure are a lot of stories in France. Lot of adventures."

Then her voice came to me clearly, even though that had to

have been almost two years ago, only three months or so after Papa had ridden off to join the Confederate cavalry. I could smell the leather and the paper in the bookstore, could hear Miss Mary laughing, and, if I turned my head, I knew I would see her sitting beside me—not in Papa's mill, but at Mr. Mendenhall's—and I held my breath as she spoke to me.

"There are a lot of stories right here, Travis Ford." She had tapped my head. "Just wanting to be put down on paper."

I had closed Dumas, turned to her, and asked: "How do you know?"

Smiling, she shook her head, and I thought she wasn't going to answer, but she had. "I had a lot of stories that I wanted to put down on paper. About Daddy. About Virginia. Even maybe some about Washington County. I just never had the courage, Travis. And probably not the imagination. To tell the truth."

I remember laughing, and telling her: "You don't need imagination to tell the truth, Miss Mary."

"Yes," she had said. "You do."

It struck me then, and I slipped off the edge of the mill, pulling the sack and Papa's cigar box with me. She didn't want me to write make-believe adventures about musketeers and Robin Hood and pirates. She wanted me to write about what's happening now.

The Spring of Hope. Poison Spring.

I shoved the tablet into the box, and the box went into the burlap, and the sack went into the shed, not on the top shelf. I simply flung it inside, slammed the door, and walked away from the mill.

Those kind of guts I knew I didn't have. Would never have.

Chapter Fifteen

The menfolk from the Reverend White's meeting house came that night, and the Yankees arrived the next morning. As was her nature, Mama was ready for them both.

I had not written anything in that tablet, which I had put back in the box, back in the bag, back in the shed. Write the truth? Write about my family, my neighbors? No, that wasn't an urge, an impulse, a desire. Not for Travis Ford. When I got home, I milked the cow, even went around trying to see if maybe there might be an egg we hadn't found, or the Yankees hadn't found, but that was another one of those forlorn hopes.

We ate grits for supper, studied our *Readers*, then went to bed while Mama sat beside Miss Mary, who had not budged all day.

"Is she gonna get better?" Baby Hugh asked.

Mama's head shook, and she sighed. "I don't know, Hugh. I just don't know." She knew, though. I could see that in her eyes. She knew about Miss Mary, just wasn't telling us.

"Should we fetch a doctor?" Edith asked.

"I don't think a doctor, any doctor, could cure what ails Miss Mary, Edith." Mama sounded so weary. I guess that little scrap with the Reverend White had taken a lot out of her. After all, it wasn't that we Fords were the most popular folks in the county. Mama hadn't had many friends, especially once the war broke out. There was no school for us to go to, so we did our learning—as did every other kid in the county—at home. I guess the only friend Mama ever really had was Miss Mary. And Papa, of

141

course, but Papa was gone.

The room seemed so empty that evening, so dark, and as hot as it had been that day, now I felt chilled.

"Go to bed," Mama told us.

Up into the loft we climbed, and into our beds we tucked ourselves. We didn't sleep. We listened, but heard nothing, just the melodic sound of the rocking chair as Mama sat by Miss Mary.

"Travis?" Edith whispered.

"Yeah?"

"Where did you go? Today. After the preacher left."

"The mill."

"What for?"

"We should go fishing there," I said. All of a sudden, for no rhyme or reason, the idea just struck me. Here we were, no crops, no chickens, and not much left in the root cellar, with fish jumping in the millpond.

"I like catfish," Baby Hugh said.

"I don't like to clean them," I told him.

"Make Mama clean them."

"That's not right," Edith said.

"Well, she cooks them."

From downstairs, Mama called up: "I'll clean them and cook them, and I'll eat them, if you go to sleep."

We fell silent again. I hadn't realized we'd been talking loud enough for Mama to hear.

"Travis?" Edith again.

"Yeah."

"What's going to become of us?"

"We'll. . . ." *We'll what?*

That was the question. There was a picture I had seen a long time ago in one of those illustrated magazines at Mr. Mendenhall's bookstore in Camden. I guess it was supposed to be some sort of statement against some sort of politics somewhere. I really don't remember the details, or what the writing said, but the image came clearly into my mind. A man, barefoot, wearing rolled-up trousers, shirt, suspenders, and a tall silk hat was walking on the top rail of a really tall split-rail fence. On one side, a bunch of men in city duds shouted up at the man. Some of them raised fists at him, but a bunch were kneeling, holding lances pointed up at him. If that fellow lost his balance and fell off the fence onto that side, he was done for. On the other side, a bunch of men in tall boots and wide-brimmed straw hats shouted up at the man on that fence, and they, too, raised fists and massive knives in his general direction. If that guy toppled onto that side, he was a goner, too. And the man was sweating, and you could see that he was having trouble keeping his balance. Sooner or later, he was going to fall.

The title of the piece was "Make A Stand!" Underneath the illustration, in big, bold black letters were the words: *Try to Balance and You're Doomed to Fall.*

Maybe that's what we were doing. Straddling a fence. Or trying to keep our balance. Union on Mama's side. Confederate— or, at least, Arkansas—with Papa. Jared Greene and his Yankees. Preacher White and Uncle Willard and everybody else in Washington County.

"We'll be fine," I told Edith, but that's not what I believed, and it wasn't what I was thinking when, after the longest time, I finally drifted into a troubled sleep.

"Travis!"

Miss Mary punched my shoulder. She held a whip in her other hand, and she kept demanding that I take it, use it on poor Mowbray, who had been lashed to a post between the quarters for the slaves and the privies. I had seen that post forty times, I figured, but had never known what it was for.

143

Until now.

Somebody had ripped off Mowbray's shirt, which hung in tatters from his waist. All the slaves had gathered around, crying, praying, some of them chanting in some odd tongue. Mama was there, too. So was Uncle Willard. Even Papa, Mr. Mendenhall, Edith, Baby Hugh.

"Get on with it, boy!" the Reverend White yelled. He was there, too.

"Please!" Mowbray cried.

Miss Mary, her face stern, ugly, mean, thrust the whip at me again.

"Travis!" she yelled. She punched my shoulder, hard.

"Travis!" My eyes opened, but I saw only darkness.

"Travis! Get up! People are out there!"

My senses returned. It wasn't Miss Mary, but Edith, who kept shoving my shoulder.

"Who . . . what . . . ?"

Now, Baby Hugh had grabbed my left arm, and was tugging me into a seated position. "For God's sake, get up!" Terror filled his voice, and instantly I pushed the dream into the back of my head, and sat up, swinging my legs over the bunk.

"What?" I said. Then I heard the voices. Not that I could tell what they were saying, but I knew there was anger behind the words. Mama said something, and her tone was sharp, savage. I'd never heard her speak like that, even when I had done something really spiteful to Baby Hugh or Edith.

I wiped sleep from my eyes, pulled my pants up over my nightshirt, slipped the suspenders over my shoulders as I headed for the ladder. "Stay here," I told my sister and brother, and climbed down from the loft, not wearing shoes, no socks.

When Papa had ridden off on Nutmeg to join the cavalry, he had taken with him his rifle, a .42-caliber with an over-and-under swivel barrel, made by some German he had known in

Kentucky. A year earlier, Uncle Willard had brought Mama a revolver, telling her to keep it handy in case the slaves revolted, but I didn't know where she kept it hidden. Baby Hugh was always begging her to show it to him, let him hold it, but she never gave in to those demands. I did know, however, where our shotgun was.

I dragged a chair to the fireplace, climbed up on it, and reached above the mantel. I felt its cold twin barrels. Carefully I pulled it down, and jumped to the floor.

Through the windows, I could see the yellow and orange glow of torches, and heard Mama cut loose with a cuss word, which is something I'd never heard from her before. I could also see Miss Mary, lying under the covers, still as death.

"What are you doing?"

"Shut up, Hugh!"

The shotgun felt heavier than an anvil. Papa had always kept one barrel loaded with buckshot, for deer and varmints, he had always said, and the other with bird shot for quail and doves. Of course, I didn't remember which was which, and right then I couldn't even recall which trigger pulled the left barrel, and which the right. But my sweating hand grabbed the forestock, and I began moving toward the door, slipping my fingers through the trigger guard.

"It's time you Yankee-lovin' wench up and left his county, Anna Louella, with your Yankee-loving curs." That was the preacher. My face flushed. "Else we burn you out."

"This is my home, Reverend." She spat out the last word like Baby Hugh would spit out collard greens. "I'm waiting here for my husband to return. My husband, as you all know, who rides in the Second Arkansas Cavalry."

"Connor's welcome," somebody said. I knew the voice, could remember him singing bass in church, but I didn't recall the name. "You ain't, you God-. . . ."

145

The voice stopped when I stepped through the door. The sound of those two hammers clicking as I thumbed them back even seemed to stop the wind.

"Travis!" Mama said urgently.

I wouldn't let myself look at her. Slowly I brought the shotgun up, bracing the stock against my shoulder, keeping the big weapon as steady as I could as I pointed it at the preacher.

I could see him clearly. He gripped a Bible in his right hand and a hickory cane in his left. Behind him, men held torches, strips of cloth soaked in coal oil, which cast a strange light across our farm. Some of the men held shotguns, and one had a big old Colt Dragoon, but the barrel was aimed at his foot, not at us.

"This is my home," I said, my voice sounding more like Edith's than my own. "And you ain't . . . aren't . . . welcome here."

"That boy ain't got the gumption to pull no trig-. . . ."

"Shut up, Sweeney!" the preacher snapped.

Mama stood on my left. I could see the revolver she held in her right hand, but she wasn't gripping it in a threatening way. It wasn't cocked, and her hand covered the brass frame, which had turned from gold to green, her fingers cupped underneath the trigger guard. Uncle Willard had told us it was a Spiller and Burr, .36-caliber six-shooter, made in Georgia for the Confederacy. The grip had been chipped on one side. Uncle Willard had called it a thumb-buster, and I recalled how hard it had been for even him to cock.

"Anna, get that boy back inside. We ain't here to fight no kids. Get. . . ."

I couldn't tell who was talking. The man stood in the dark behind the torches, but I didn't care. I kept that shotgun pointed at the Reverend White. *If I kill a preacher,* I thought, *does that mean I go straight to hell?*

The man stopped at the sound of footsteps on the porch. I heard Mama gasp, but I just stared at the preacher, shotgun wobbling.

"Edith!" Mama cried. "Hugh. You get back inside this instant. It's. . . ."

"No, Mama."

Edith stepped around beside me. She held a butcher knife in her left hand. Baby Hugh scrambled beside Mama, put his arm around her waist, hugging her real close. Out of the corner of my eye, I could see something in his left hand, but I couldn't tell what it was. I thought it might be one of the saplings I used for a rapier, but later I learned it was a poker from the fireplace.

Now the men fell silent. In the silence I could hear the dancing flames of the torches, my own heart pounding.

The Reverend Thaddeus White brought his Bible up and awkwardly wiped his face with the back of the hand that held the Good Book.

"Mary Frederick is inside," Mama said. "You plan on burning her out, too?"

They didn't answer.

"What's the matter?" I snapped. "You think it's fine to threaten a woman, but not kids?"

"Some men you are," Edith said. "My daddy's in the Confederate Army. Why aren't y'all?"

The man with the torch beside Reverend White shifted his feet uncomfortably.

Mama took up our method of attack. "Will Sweeney. I brought your wife and kids soup when she was sick with the measles. Randall Bandy. Does your wife know where you are tonight? You think she'd approve? Do any of you think your wives, your mothers, would approve? We used to be neighbors. We're still neighbors. When Mister Lincoln talked about a house divided, he was talking about our country, but I never thought

147

he was talking about Washington County, Arkansas."

"It's you . . ."—the Reverend Thaddeus White cleared his throat—"it's you who've done the dividin'. You told the Yanks. . . ."

"I told them nothing!" Mama shouted as she readjusted the .36 in her right hand, shifted a finger until it pressed against the trigger, put her thumb on the hammer, and brought it up. "My family told them nothing. I accepted a bit of coffee from Jared Greene. Do any of you remember him? Jared Greene. Lived down the road from us between our place and Mary Frederick's. Worked for Connor at the sawmill. A freedman from Kentucky. A freedman! Until you, our state government, drove him out of this state." She tossed back her head and laughed. "As God is my witness, when that happened, I should have taken my children and my husband and moved back to Illinois. But I didn't."

"And why not?" the preacher's thundered.

"Because this is my home!" The hammer cocked. She pointed the Spiller and Burr right at the Reverend White's head, and, unlike my shotgun, her weapon wasn't weaving. It was straight and steady. "Our home. It may not be much, and we might not have much food, or money, or anything else, but it's my home. My husband built it with his own hands, cleared the fields, built the barn, and I guess that's what he's fighting for. And I'll fight for it, too. Now I'll ask you kindly to get off my property."

One of the torches dropped a bit, and I thought the man who held it was going for whatever weapon he held, but then the torch turned away.

"C'mon, Milton. I don't won't no part of this."

"Me, neither. Let's go home."

Reverend White whirled around, and moved toward the men that were heading down the lane. "Milton! MacDonald. Get back here. She told the Yanks about the corn . . . !"

"I don't figger she told the Yanks nothin', Preacher," said the man beside White. "As hard-scrabble as this place looks, if she knowed where any corn was, she'd be stealin' it for her own family." He nodded at us, tipped his hat at Mama and Edith, mumbled something that might have been an apology, and followed the others down the lane.

Which left Thaddeus White and two others.

"You owe me for a mule you let get stole!" the preacher shouted, pointing his cane at Mama.

"She don't owe you a blasted thing, White," said one of the remaining men, and then he headed off, too.

"Let's go home, White," the last man told the reverend.

"But. . . ."

"I ain't fighting a woman and three kids," he said. "Never should 'a' let you drag me out of bed this time of night nohow. You coming?"

The preacher's shoulders sagged as the man put his arm through the minister's arm, turned him around, nodded back at us, and then joined the procession with White.

We just stood there, watching the light from the torches disappear, then reappear through the trees, until they were out of view, and we were standing in the darkness.

It wasn't until we had all gone into the kitchen, where Mama lit a candle and began heating up her coffee and fixing us breakfast—even though it was two hours before dawn—that we noticed the shotgun and the revolver. Oh, they were loaded, all right. At least, we assumed they were. But no percussion caps had been set on the nipples.

We had fought off the first attack with weapons that could not have fired.

CHAPTER SIXTEEN

Usually we weren't allowed back up in the loft once we got up each morning, unless we were sick, but Mama sent us back upstairs after we ate grits and cornbread. Baby Hugh was asleep in an instant, snoring like a drunkard, and Edith soon joined him. I couldn't sleep. I lay beside Hugh, head cupped in my hands, staring at the ceiling. It grew lighter.

The rocking of the chair downstairs stopped, and Mama's footsteps moved toward the front door. It was opened, and I heard her on the porch, down the steps, heard her walking toward the garden, the corncrib.

Because this is my home, Mama had told our visitors. *Our home.*

Only it no longer felt like a home, but I couldn't describe in words how I felt. Some writer, I was, some storyteller.

Edith mumbled something in her sleep. Baby Hugh rolled over, which stopped his snores for a moment, but not for long.

Downstairs, I heard Miss Mary call out: "Daddy?" I sat up, then Miss Mary let out a little moan, and she was quiet again. I started to lay back down, but Baby Hugh had rolled over again, hogging the bed we shared. So I just sat on the bed, thinking, wondering, hoping, and praying.

Two or three minutes later, I heard Mama's returning footsteps on the porch. The bed squeaked, Mama sighed, and I rose to go downstairs. By then, it had to be 8:00 or 9:00 in the morning, but my brother and sister did not stir. Not that I could blame them. It had been an exhausting evening.

When I reached the ground floor, I turned to see Mama throw back the covers, get out of her bed, and move unsteadily to the rocking chair. She collapsed into it, bowed her head, clasped her hands. At first I thought the weight of everything that had happened last night—early this morning, rather—had just cracked her armor, but, as I moved closer, I knew it was something else.

I stopped.

Miss Mary still lay in the bed, as she had since . . . since when? I remembered the sound I had heard minutes earlier. I could envision what had happened. "Daddy?" she had called out, then sunk back onto the pillows, and groaned. But had it been a groan? Or had it been death's rattle?

Now her eyes were open, staring up at the loft, and her face looked gray, but she was smiling.

Mama began to cry. Just choking sobs, but, when she heard me, her hands went down, her head went up, and she pushed herself out of the rocking chair. "Hugh . . . Edith . . . ?" Her head shook. "I mean Travis." She came to me then, dropping to her knees, pulling me close to her.

I cried, too, sobbing on my mother's shoulder, feeling her hands and arms on my back, wanting her to clutch me forever.

"It's all right," she whispered. "It's all right."

"She's . . . she's . . . she's . . . dead?" I couldn't believe it.

I felt Mama's head nod. She sniffed. "Her heart just gave out. The poor woman. It just gave out. Now, come on." She stood, keeping her hands on my shoulders, looking down, while I tried to make those blasted tears stop.

Miss Mary Frederick, I had come to understand, knew me better than my mother or my siblings. She knew more about me than I knew myself, and she had been the one true friend our family really had since Papa had gone off to war.

Now she was gone.

"It's all right, Travis." Mama put a finger under my chin, and lifted my head. "She's in a better place now. Away from all these troubles. I need you to be strong."

Which just made me cry even more, and again she dropped to my side, holding me, kissing the side of my head.

"I'm . . . I'm . . . sup- . . . supposed . . . to be. . . ." I sniffed. "I'm supposed to . . . be . . . the . . . man . . . of the house. Now that . . . Papa's . . . not here." I wiped my nose, my cheeks. Me, who had vowed never to cry again.

"You are the man of the house," Mama whispered. "You most certainly are."

Outside, mules snorted and a wagon trace jingled. Mama stood, and somehow I stopped crying. "Stay here," Mama ordered, and she went to the mantel, grabbed the Spiller and Burr, and moved toward the door. "And this time, I mean it."

She didn't carry the revolver loosely, already had pulled back the hammer and slipped a finger into the trigger guard. Percussion caps were on the nipples. She went through the front door, and pulled it shut behind her.

The wagon and mules drew closer to the house, and I heard men talking, a few laughs. Then a friendly voice that I recognized.

"Hello, Miz Anna," Jared Greene said.

"Sergeant," Mama said, not calling him by his Christian name. A metallic click told me that Mama had lowered the hammer on the .36.

"Madam, I bid you good day." I knew that voice, too. Lieutenant Bullis. "We do not wish to impose, but we are. . . ."

"Searching for corn," Mama said.

"*Er* . . . well . . . yes. Um. Well, it's this way, madam . . . you are Secessionist, traitors to the American flag, and it is. . . ."

That must have been the speech he had been giving to every

farm he had stopped at, but his tone let me know that his heart wasn't in it.

"If you find corn in the crib or anywhere else on this property, sir, you are welcome to it. Do your search. The crib's over there. Try not to trample the sprouts in our garden. Or do you want those, too, to feed your horses?"

I heard her moving toward the door, then Lieutenant Bullis began barking orders to his men, and there was more movement, more noise. Though I didn't catch exactly what he was saying, Sergeant Greene began talking to Mama.

Baby Hugh, coming down the ladder, and Edith, wiping sleep from her eyes and getting ready to descend, caught my attention. I sucked in a deep breath, wiped my eyes hard, and went to the bed where Miss Mary lay. I reached over and put a finger and thumb just above Miss Mary's eyes. For a moment I hesitated. I'd never done this before, but I didn't want Baby Hugh to see her like this. Her forehead felt cold, and, as I looked into her eyes, a chill raced up my spine. She couldn't see me, but it looked as if she were seeing into my soul. Like, I guess, she always had. My fingers went down, and her eyelids closed forever.

"What the heck is you doing with Miss Mary?" Baby Hugh asked, and I jerked my hand away, turning.

"Nothing. Just seeing. . . ."

Edith gasped. I guess she saw how red my eyes were. I sniffed.

Baby Hugh stepped closer to the bed, and then Edith began crying, and I turned, pointing at the open door. I tried to tell my sister and brother that the Yankees were back, tried to get their attention away from Miss Mary Frederick, but Edith continued to cry, and Baby Hugh ran to the bed, and reached up for Miss Mary. I grabbed him, pulled him away, only now he was wailing. Edith fell to her knees, sobbing hysterically, but not as hard as Baby Hugh.

We fell into the rocking chair, almost tipping it over. I held him as Mama had held me, somehow managing to turn and free an arm so I could motion for Edith to come. We were crying again, three kids together, a dead neighbor in my parents' bed, and a bunch of Yankees outside.

"She can't be dead!" Hugh screamed. "She can't be dead!"

"Her heart gave out," I told him. "She's in a better place now." My words—Mama's words, really—offered as much comfort to my kid brother as they had brought to me when Mama told me.

The door opened, and Mama came through, revolver in her left hand. She pitched it onto the bed beside Miss Mary, and came toward us. Hugh freed himself from me, backed out of the rocker, and ran to Mama, who swept him into her arms.

"Miss Mary ain't dead. She can't be dead. Tell me she ain't dead, Mama," he pleaded.

Mama kissed his forehead. Then tears blinded me, and I just couldn't be a man. I cried, while holding my sister and listening to our brother wail.

"She can't be dead," he cried over and over.

"It's all right, Hugh. It's all right. Everything will be all right."

"No. No! She can't be dead. I never . . . I never . . . got to thank her. For all them cookies. All them cakes and pies. I never ever once thanked her for all the food she give us!"

"Miz Anna." Sergeant Jared Greene stood in the doorway, hat in his hand. He saw us, then glanced toward the bed that held Miss Mary, and I think he understood.

His presence seemed to stop our tears, even Baby Hugh's. Maybe sight of the big man of color in Yankee blue standing in our doorway snapped him out of it. He clung tighter to Mama, who managed to lift him as she rose, the way she had done when he had been just a baby, and not a seven-year-old.

"Jared," Mama said, as she took Hugh over to the bed, and

set him on the edge. She wiped his face, brushed away her own tears, and put a hand on his shoulder.

"Thank her now, Hugh. Just thank her now."

"She can't hear me." Hugh sniffed.

"Yes, she can. Yes, she can."

She moved to Sergeant Greene. "Mary Frederick died, Jared. I don't know . . . maybe ten minutes, fifteen . . . minutes ago." She was almost whispering, but I could hear her clearly. Could hear the sergeant, too.

"I'm right sorry to hear that, ma'am."

"It's all right. She had been sick for a long while. She told me the doctor in Washington said she didn't have long for this world. So she's no longer suffering."

"Yes, ma'am."

"I'd like to impose on you, Jared."

"It is not an imposition, ma'am."

"Her family plot is on her plantation, five miles down the road. That's where she would like to be buried. Beside her father, her family." Mama drew a breath, had to lean against the wall.

"Are you all right, Miz Anna?"

Mama let out a part laugh, part sigh. "It's been a tiring night and morning, Jared."

"Yes, ma'am."

"I have no way to get her body to the plantation."

Sergeant Jared Greene understood. Turning, he stepped outside, pulled his hat down, and sang out the order: "Hammond, Peavy, Jackson, Cremony! Up here. Up here, now. Wilson! Go get Lieutenant Bullis. Move it, soldier!"

We'd been to funerals before. When someone died in the county, Mama always made us go. Said we had to show our respects. Often I didn't know the person who was dead, but other times—

like when Gregory Hall's two children, one a couple years older than me and the other just a baby, died of cholera—I did. Still, I had never cared much for funerals, mainly because of how the Reverend White conducted them. He never once spoke about the person's life, what that person meant to his or her neighbors. Rarely did he ever mention the deceased's name.

Miss Mary's was different, though Mama didn't make us put on our Sunday-go-to-meeting clothes. The soldiers, with Mama's and Lieutenant Bullis's permission, had wrapped her in the quilt and solemnly carried her to the wagon that was supposed to haul corn. The remaining soldiers stood at attention. It was Lieutenant Bullis who led the wagon, driven by the runaway slave, Hammond. Mama, Edith, Hugh, and I followed, the soldiers marching behind us.

We didn't see anyone on the road.

By the time we reached Miss Mary's plantation, thunder rolled in the distance and the wind blew cold. We turned down the lane. It was almost like we were in a dream. Nothing seemed real. The place stood empty. The gate on the white picket fence banged open and shut with the gusts of wind that moaned through the smokehouse. Its door lay on the ground. There stood the frame of the new carriage house, and the old building, one unfinished, the other abandoned. The horses were gone. So were the mules.

"Lieutenant Bullis!" Mama called out.

We were turning down a narrow road that led past the slave quarters and toward muddy cotton fields.

The Yankee called for a halt, reined in, turned his horse around, and rode back toward Mama.

"Yes, Missus Ford?"

"That is not the way to the Frederick family plot."

Saddle leather creaking, Lieutenant Bullis turned and pointed. I could see a fence beyond the fields, near the woods.

"That appears to be a graveyard over there, ma'am."

"Yes." Mama cleared her throat. At first, she didn't say a word, just wet her lips. Finally she drew in a breath and pointed. "The family plot is that way." It was the opposite from where Lieutenant Bullis had been leading us. "Through the woods over there, then up the hill."

He looked in that direction, then back at the other graveyard, and finally nodded. "Of course, Missus Ford. My apologies."

"You need not apologize, sir."

So we turned around, and continued our funeral march.

"But ain't that a graveyard?" Baby Hugh whispered.

"*Shhhh,*" Edith hushed him. A few rods later, she added, in a softer whisper: "That's where Miss Mary's slaves are buried."

Mama was right. Miss Mary had known she was dying. We all understood that when we reached the Frederick cemetery. There, beside her father's ten-foot high marble monument, was a freshly dug grave. She even had a headstone with hands clasped in prayer etched above:

Here Lies Our Beloved Daughter
Mary Josephine Frederick
1811-1864

Yet I couldn't help wonder what Miss Mary would have thought about all this. No fancy coffin, just Mama's quilt for a shroud. Six colored men serving as her pallbearers, a Union officer with rotten teeth reading the Beatitudes. Instead of a crowd of neighbors, there stood around the grave a bunch of enemy soldiers, and four friends and neighbors who really did cherish her.

Sergeant Jared Greene went up after the lieutenant closed his Bible. Hat in hand, Greene pointed his mangled hand down the road. "I lived just down the road over yonder." He smiled. "I'd see Miss Mary Frederick riding toward Camden, or, once in a while, she'd come by Mister Ford's mill wanting lumber. Now she never looked me in the eye, and I knew better than to look her in the eye, but she always said . . . 'good day' . . . and I'd tell her . . . 'good day, ma'am.' So she was a fine neighbor, even to a man of color. So. . . ." He turned to the grave, and to Miss Mary's wrapped body, and he said: "Good day, Miss Mary Frederick. Good life."

Mama spoke next, smiling at some stories she told, but honestly I don't remember anything she said. Nor what Edith said. I was just remembering all those trips we had made from our farm into Camden and back, all those times in Mr. Mendenhall's store. She had introduced me to Simms and Dumas and Poe and Dickens and Shakespeare and Milton. She had opened my eyes, my imagination.

When Mama asked if I wanted to say anything, all I could do was shake my head.

"That's all right, Travis," she said, and Baby Hugh came up.

"She always brought me food," he said. "Sweets. I hope she's eating now in heaven." Then he ran back and held onto Mama.

We sang "Gently, Lord, Oh, Gently Lead Us" and "Oh, Sing to Me of Heaven", before the lieutenant picked up a handful of dirt and said: " 'In the sweat of thy face shalt thou eat bread, till thou return unto the ground; for out of it wast thou taken: for dust thou art, and unto dust shalt thou return.' " He dropped the dirt into the grave.

The lieutenant and Jared Greene shook our hands, then we walked away—before they laid Miss Mary's body in her grave and began to cover it—walked all the way back home.

I didn't feel bad, not even sad. Oddly enough, right then, I felt comforted, blessed to have known Miss Mary. Yet later I would come to think of Mary Frederick as the first victim of the Battle of Poison Spring.

CHAPTER SEVENTEEN

When we got home, Mama said she was so addled, she couldn't think straight. She wandered about the kitchen, looking for something but couldn't remember what. She said she was nonplused, which sent me to the other cabin to check with Webster's.

    non'plus-ed, n. Puzzled; put to a stand.

By the time I got back, she had found a butcher's knife, and was using it to stir grits in boiling water. Edith glanced at me, but I only shrugged. Baby Hugh looked at both of us and said: "Mama's addled."

"Yes," Mama said, "I am."

That's when I saw that she was crying. "Can we do anything, Mama?" I asked.

"No." She lifted her apron to wipe her tears.

Thunder boomed, and instantly the rain fell, pounding the house.

"Roof's gonna leak again," Baby Hugh said.

"Let it." A smile brightened Mama's face, and, using the oven mittens, she pulled the bowl of grits from the fireplace, dropped the butcher knife on the hearth, and walked to us. Her tears had stopped.

Squeezing between Edith and me, she lifted Baby Hugh onto her lap, kissing his cheek. Hugh hugged her, and Mama reached out, gripping my hand with her left and Edith's with her right.

"It rained like this when Papa and I were married," she said. "In Camden. Fifteen years ago. And I remember the preacher. . . ."

"Was it Reverend White?" Baby Hugh asked.

"No."

"Good."

"No," Mama said. "His name was . . . Murchison. Dark red hair and a Scottish voice born to play the pipes. I don't know whatever became of him. Anyway, it rained hard. . . ."

"Was there a big crowd?"

Mama laughed. "Well, there was your father, me, Willard, the preacher, and my mother, who took a steamboat down to see her favorite daughter be married."

"You were her favorite daughter?" Edith asked.

"As you are mine. I was her only daughter. Anyway, it began pouring, and the preacher, he said . . . 'They say when it rains at a funeral, it means that all the angels are crying tears of joy because a new angel has joined them and received his or her wings from the Lord.' Then the preacher said . . . 'That's for a funeral. But I honestly don't know what this means.' "

Mama erupted in laughter, and we joined in, although it took a moment before I understood the joke.

Sliding Hugh off her lap, she kissed his forehead, then turned to kiss Edith, and lastly me. "I think God has given Mary Frederick her wings, and all the angels in heaven are shedding tears of joy."

Back she went to the fireplace to fix our supper. No longer was she nonplused.

It took forever to find the fishing poles, and it was Baby Hugh who discovered them up in the corncrib, of all places. I had to replace the line on one pole, and the hooks on all three, before Hugh and I went to the garden to dig up earthworms. Edith refused to help.

"We shouldn't let her eat no fish that we catch," my brother whispered.

I rubbed my muddy hands in his hair and agreed with him. He laughed.

"She doesn't like fish," I said.

Good spirits abounded that early Monday morning. We hadn't felt this way in a long time, but Miss Mary was an angel in heaven, and our family seemed to be stronger now. Though I couldn't tell you why.

While Mama packed our dinner—carrots and cornbread— Baby Hugh decided to go fishing in the bar ditch at the road. I shook my head, but baited his hook, anyway, and sent him on his way. One worm. That's all he had, which might last forever in that ditch, or he might lose it before he got halfway up the lane. After placing the can of worms on the porch near Edith's and my poles, I went to the wash basin to clean the mud off my hands, and headed for the kitchen.

"Stay on the shallow end," Mama said.

"Yes, ma'am."

"Hugh cannot swim."

"I know."

"Be back before dark."

"We will."

"Fishing in the millpond!" Mama shook her head. "Why didn't we think of this before?"

"Because Papa always said the only fish in the pond were mudfish," Edith said, "and he said they aren't fit to eat."

"They aren't," I agreed. "But I think there are some bream and catfish in there now. And crappie."

"Be careful with the catfish," Mama said. "Watch their fins."

"Yes, ma'am." I looked at Edith. "Are you coming?"

"Yes," she answered defiantly.

"But you don't even like to eat fish."

"I eat the tails."

Which was all she would eat, just crunching on the tails after Mama fried the fish we used to catch with Papa in the river and creeks.

"This will be wonderful," Mama said. "Fried fish. Just like Saturday nights with Papa." She couldn't stop smiling.

"If we catch any," I had to remind her.

"You will," Mama said.

Somehow, I wish we could have frozen time at that moment. Mama beaming. Everyone happy. The war, the feud with our neighbors, the passing of Miss Mary . . . all of that behind us. A child's fantasy, I guess. It couldn't stay that way.

It didn't.

Baby Hugh's screams reached us, and we burst out of the kitchen, onto the porch. He barreled down that road as if the devil himself chased him, holding his hat in his hand. He must have dropped the fishing pole somewhere up the lane, or left it by the ditch.

Snake must have scared him, I thought. *Or maybe just a crawdad.*

"Ma-ma!" He ran harder. *"Ma-ma!"*

Not even bothering with the steps, she jumped off the porch, and rushed to him.

Edith and I heard him shout—"Soldiers!"—as Mama swept him into her arms. He stuttered something we couldn't understand. Edith and I hurried off the porch, and stared down the lane, expecting to see Lieutenant Bullis or some other Yank come riding down in search of hidden corn.

"Goodness gracious," Mama said. "Those poor Union soldiers are bound and determined to. . . ."

Baby Hugh's head jerked off Mama's shoulder. He wiped his eyes, sniffed, and sang out: "But it ain't Yankees, Mama!"

No longer did I concentrate on our lane. Mouth open, I stared hard at my kid brother. Mama stood, stepped back. "Hugh . . . ?"

"They's Confederates," he shouted.

I could hear the jingling of traces a long way off down the road, muffled voices. I could picture all of General Price's army marching back to Camden. Turns out, it wasn't his whole command, but plenty enough.

"Are you sure, Hugh?" Mama asked.

"They was all dressed in gray and brown and such, and I saw that flag. A bunch of flags. There was one with a big star in the middle of blue, with two big old red and white stripes."

"The Texas flag," Mama said.

"And there was the blue flag with the star . . . the one we sing about . . ."

Lyrics to "The Bonnie Blue Flag" briefly ran through my brain.

". . . and the Confederate flag and. . . ."

"How do you know?" Edith demanded.

Right back, Hugh snapped: "I know what that flag looks like, Sister."

"Be quiet," Mama said. "All of you."

She drew in the deepest breath, held it a long while before grabbing Baby Hugh's hand to lead him toward the cabin. "Inside. All of you."

There was no hesitation, no discussion, certainly no argument. We walked up the steps, leaving our can of worms and the fishing poles leaning against the porch, except for Baby Hugh's.

After marching us into the sleeping quarters, Mama went back into the kitchen for a moment. Quickly she returned, holding the sack filled with the dinner she had planned for us. The door shut, the latch string came in, and she lowered the bar.

"Travis," Mama said, "pull in the other latch string, and bar that door, as well."

As I obeyed, Mama moved to the window. I thought she would close the shutter, but, instead, she dragged her rocking chair beside it, and sat down, staring outside.

Baby Hugh tried to stop crying, and Edith and I looked at each other without speaking. We couldn't hear anything now, except our own heavy breathing and Baby Hugh's sniffling.

"Mama?" Edith spoke in a whisper.

Mama rocked and watched.

"Mama?" Louder this time, but it wasn't until the third try that Mama turned. She looked nonplused.

"Yes. I'm sorry, Edith, what is it?"

Wetting her lips, my sister turned to me as if I knew what to say. I didn't, but I made a stab. "What should we do?"

"Oh . . ."—she brushed her hair off her forehead—"yes, well, just read your *Reader*s. Yes, the *Reader*s. Quietly."

Baby Hugh looked up. "Mama's addled," he said.

She smiled, and went back to rocking and watching.

So I fetched our *McGuffey's Reader*s, handed Baby Hugh his. He wiped his nose, and went to a stool. Once I gave Edith hers, we sat on the hearth. There was no fire, yet with the doors shut, the room quickly turned hot and stuffy.

I started the excerpt from *Robinson Crusoe,* read all about the house he had built after the shipwreck, finished it, and then had to read DeFoe's passage again because I couldn't remember anything I'd read on those six pages, couldn't even describe the illustration.

We read. We waited. Mama watched.

An hour passed. More. It must have been around 10:00 a.m., when Edith and I lowered our books. Mama had stopped rocking, and leaned closer to the window. Baby Hugh kept on reading.

"There," I said, though not meaning to. Turning toward Edith, I started to ask, but she beat me to it.

"Did you hear that?" she said.

I could only nod.

Baby Hugh looked up, and, seeing that we had closed our books, he did the same. "Hear what? I didn't hear nothing."

"Quiet!" Mama called from the window. She had stopped rocking.

The little pop sounded again, was answered, then a few more sounded. This time Baby Hugh heard, and he sprang out of his chair.

"What is it, Mama?"

Mama clasped her hands together. I couldn't hear what she said, but I could read her lips. "My God."

For the next few minutes, the sound continued sporadically, kind of like what we had heard when Papa would walk over to Miss Mary's cornfields in September or October with his shotgun and come back in the evening with a mess of doves for Mama to fry for supper.

We listened. Baby Hugh tried to keep track of the number of the shots he heard, but quickly lost count.

"Are they fighting, Mama?" he asked.

She stood now, against the log walls, wetting her lips, wringing her hands. "Yes," she said, barely audible.

"Fighting the Yankees?"

Her head bobbed slightly.

He grinned, but just for a moment, then he cried out: "I hope they ain't fighting Jared Greene! I kinda like him."

"I hope. . . ."

Mama never finished. The whole cabin trembled, the doors and shutters rattling. Mama reached through the window, and slammed the shutter, fastening it, moving toward the bed.

"Come here," she said.

Our house shook again.

She sat on the floor, leaning against the bed, and we gathered around her, Edith and Hugh the closest to her, me sitting beside my baby brother.

"It sounds like thunder," Edith observed after our cabin shuddered again.

"It's coming from down the road," I said. "Toward Camden."

"Not that far," Mama said.

"That's where those Confederate soldiers was marching to," Baby Hugh said. He waved toward the east.

Edith gasped. "Papa's mill."

Again our house shook.

"Maybe," Mama answered hollowly. "But I think farther up the road. Maybe Lee's plantation." That was another big operation, up the road toward Camden but past Papa's mill.

"Or Poison Spring?" I asked.

She nodded.

A series of muffled explosions shook the cabin again, and Edith cried out: "What is that?"

"Cannon," I answered.

"I seen a bunch of them big guns," Baby Hugh bragged. "They was plowing up the mud. There was a guy just yelling at a mule. He had on a cap just like that one them colored Yankees was wearing, only his was red and not blue, and. . . ."

The cabin quivered.

"Yes, near Poison Spring," Mama guessed, and pulled Baby Hugh and Edith closer. Cannon fire became steady, each series of volleys shaking the mud chinks loose from the logs. Dust rose in the house, irritated our eyes and noses.

"Can you make it stop?" Baby Hugh begged. He sniffled again.

"*Shhhhhh.*"

Mama pulled Baby Hugh closer, and, as faint musketry

166

echoed the cannon fire, I slid nearer to my brother, wishing I were in his place and that Mama was holding me tight against her. Instead, I tried to be the man of the house, so I reached over and grabbed Hugh's thigh, squeezing it while trying to reassure him with: "Everything's all right, Hugh. That's a long way from here. Poison Spring's even past Papa's mill. There's no reason to cry. We're safe here."

I didn't feel safe.

For thirty minutes, which felt like days, booming cannons rocked the cabin. Suddenly the sound quieted.

"Is the battle over, Mama?" Edith asked.

Before Mama could answer, we heard that noise again. Not cannon. Not this time. Instead, the same pops from muskets that had started the battle resumed, only this time, it was not sporadic, but steady. Volley after volley. Volley after volley. Volley after volley.

"Should we pray, Mama?" Edith asked.

"Yes," Mama said. "Pray for everyone there."

If anyone in our house prayed, though, it was silently.

For more than fifteen minutes, those muskets fired and fired and fired. More cannon answered after that, but not as long, not as steadily, and moments later muskets spoke once more. When I blinked, my eyes stung, and I realized that I was sweating.

It felt odd, sitting on the floor with my mother and my siblings, listening to a battle being waged a few miles from our house. We could hear the muskets and cannon, although dulled by distance, hills, and trees. No shouts. No screams. Just the soft shots of long arms, and the dull thud of cannon that rocked our home, our world.

Four hours we sat on the floor, until the sounds died like a thunderstorm moving away from us. A few random pops, then a deathly, eerie quiet.

"Stay here." Mama pulled herself up, walked toward the front door, changed her mind, and went to the dogtrot side. Once she removed the bar, she opened the door, and stepped outside, leaving us alone for maybe five minutes, no more. We never budged. When she came back, the door closed, the bar went back into place, and she said: "I think it's over. Pray it's over, anyway."

"Who do you reckon won?" Baby Hugh sprang to his feet.

"I don't know."

"Can we go out . . . ?"

"No!"

Mama had fetched a bucket of water, and placed it on the hearth. "Let's eat," she announced, and bit into a carrot.

The sack meant for our fishing trip sat untouched. No one had any appetite, though we all drank water. Mama returned to her rocker, and we kids to our *Reader*s. The doors and shutters remained closed, and, around dusk, our stomachs felt strong enough to hold some grub, so we ate cornbread with carrots, washed down with water.

Finally it began to darken, but Mama didn't even light a candle or a lantern. She didn't even get a fire going in the fireplace.

"It's bedtime," she finally announced, but before any of us could stand or move toward the loft, a horse whinnied.

CHAPTER EIGHTEEN

Instantly we froze. I'm not sure anyone even breathed. Darkness stretched across the cabin as the horse's hoofs drew nearer, saddle leather squeaked, and footfalls sounded. Softly at first, then harder as the rider came up the steps and onto the porch.

An eternity passed. Our fear turned palpable. Another new word.

pal'pa-ble, a. [Fr., from L. palpor, to feel; It. palpabile.]
1. Perceptible by the touch; that may be felt; as, a palpable substance, palpable darkness.

Just beyond the front door, a man cleared his throat, then knocked.

Harder.

"Missus Ford?"

A voice no one recognized, but it was Southern, a rich drawl yet commanding.

"Is anyone home?"

More knocking.

"Missus Ford, if you are inside, and I pray that is the case, I mean you and your children no harm. My name is Richard Brodie, corporal with the Second Arkansas Cavalry, and we need your assistance, ma'am. If you are home. . . ."

As soon as she heard Second Arkansas Cavalry, Mama moved for the door.

Papa's regiment.

"Just a minute!" She hefted the bar, turned to us, saying: "Light a candle. Quickly!" The bar went into the corner, and she opened the door as Edith held match to wick.

"Come in," Mama said. She stepped away, allowing a tall stranger inside.

Holding a greasy, gray slouch hat in both hands, he eased inside our cabin. Edith used the candle she had lit to fire up the other candles, bathing our visitor in warm light as he wearily made his way toward the center of the room, Mama walking right behind him, her face anxious.

He nodded in our direction, then turned to face Mama. "My apologies for calling on you at this hour of the evening, Missus Ford."

His shell jacket, gray with yellow trim and gold French braid on the sleeves, was dirty, ripped all along the left sleeve, but I detected no blood. His boots were brown, scuffed, practically worn through, with dirty black trousers tucked inside the tall tops of the boots. The spurs made no noise. He wore no saber, and the holster on his right hip was empty.

The eyes were what caught me when he looked in our direction, nodding again. Mama dragged the rocking chair over, telling him to sit, but his head shook.

"No, ma'am." He grinned. "If I sat, I fear my legs would not allow me again to stand." The eyes, though, weren't grinning. They were dark, dead, bloodshot. Hollow. He looked like a man who had seen a ghost. Or an army of ghosts.

I doubted that he was older than twenty-five, sporting the beginnings of a mustache, but it was hard to tell because his face, the cheeks sunken and lips thin, was covered in black powder and dirt.

"You said you are with the Second Arkansas . . . ," Mama began.

"Yes, ma'am."

"My husband. . . ."

His head nodded. "Sergeant Ford. That's how I knew where to find you. He said you would be here. I feared you would be like most Southerners, and fled after our army abandoned Camden. But the sergeant . . . he was adamant. He. . . ." His hand shot out, stopping Mama from her next question. "Missus Ford, I haven't seen Sergeant Ford since the battle began. I know not where he is . . . where most of my men are, for that matter. Brigadier General Cabell sent most of our regiment to guard the rear, ma'am." His smile tried to reassure us but didn't. "I am sure he is fine, ma'am. But . . ."—he swallowed—"others, I fear, are not as fortunate."

Unable to hold himself up any longer, he sank into the rocking chair.

"Edith," Mama said. "To the kitchen. Bring a cup of coffee."

"It'll be cold, Mama."

"I know." Mama had moved to the bucket from the well, dipped the ladle in it, brought it quickly back to the corporal. Greedily he drank, though most of the water went down his chin, streaking through the grime.

I helped Edith with the bar, and she went through the dogtrot to the kitchen.

"We fought the Yanks today," the soldier was saying.

"Yes, we heard."

"I imagine you did."

Baby Hugh sang out: "Did you whip them?"

"Hugh," Mama said as the corporal hung his head.

"I . . . well. . . ." Richard Brodie shook his head, sipped again from the ladle Mama had refilled with water. "We ambushed the Yanks at Poison Spring. Drove them off in a rout. It was. . . ." Closing his eyes, he shuddered. No one spoke.

I thought he might have died, but his eyes finally opened when Edith ran back inside, holding one of Papa's old beer steins filled with cold coffee. Mama took it, held it to the corporal, who drank it with unsteady hands.

"I'm sorry it's not hot," Mama told him.

"I'm in the cavalry, ma'am," he said. "I'm used to cold coffee, but this . . . this is. . . ." He shook his head again. "It tastes fine. Mighty fine."

"We got it from a. . . ."

In no uncertain terms, Mama told Hugh to shut up.

"How's Papa?" Edith sang out.

Mama didn't tell her to shut up.

"He was well this morning, young lady. He has served the Confederacy and the state of Arkansas proudly. I wish we had more men of his mettle in our regiment."

"He hasn't been . . . ?" Mama began.

He sipped coffee, then made himself smile again, but I doubted that he had felt any reason to feel joy in ages. It's like I've said. His lips smiled. His eyes didn't.

"Well, we have all had ailments, especially of late, but no wounds, nothing grievous. Last I saw him. But. . . ." He handed the stein to Edith, and gripped the arms of Mama's rocker. "Ma'am, we have many wounded soldiers. We could use some assistance."

Mama stepped back. "You don't mean to bring your wounded here?" She shuddered. "It's too small. I. . . ."

Brodie's head shook. "We have turned the Lee plantation into a field hospital, ma'am. And the Frederick farm down the road." His brow knotted. "The latter was all but abandoned. No one, not even a field hand, working the place."

"Miss Mary," Mama told him, "mistress of the plantation, died recently." She didn't tell him how.

"I regret deeply to learn of her passing. Sergeant Ford spoke highly of her, as well. But, ma'am, the sergeant also mentioned

. . . in passing only, Missus Ford . . . that you had training as a nurse."

Mama took two steps back as if she had been slapped. She blinked away her surprise. "Corporal,"—her head shook—"Corporal, I have tended a few sick neighbors, but I would not call it training."

"We could use your help, ma'am. The Confederacy could not pay you, but. . . ."

"I have my children."

He gave us a mere glance. "They look old enough to fend for themselves, if only for a night and a day."

Corporal Brodie looked as if he might fall to his knees and beg, if he could have managed to stand back up. His lips trembled, and I thought he might burst into tears, but Mama reached over, patted a hand that tightly gripped the rocker's arm.

She whispered, but I couldn't hear what she said. When her head moved back, I understood. She was going with the horse soldier. What else could she do?

"You're big boys and a big girl now," Mama said. "I'll be back as soon as I can."

Speechless, we only nodded.

"You can sleep downstairs if you want." She was heading to the kitchen to pack whatever she thought she might need to treat wounded soldiers, leaving us alone with Brodie as he closed his eyes, rocked, and sipped cold coffee.

"You know my papa?" Baby Hugh asked him.

"Yes," he said as if he were about to fall asleep.

"Is he your boss?"

Brodie grinned slightly. "He's a sergeant, son. In the Confederate Army, in any army, the sergeants are everybody's boss. Even generals bow to sergeants."

Before Baby Hugh could ask another question, Edith grabbed

his arm and jerked him back. "Leave him be," she warned.

"He's all right," Brodie said. "I don't mind. Got a brother your age. What's your name, son?"

"Hugh."

"My brother's name is Charles. Four sisters between us. And an older brother, killed at Corinth."

"Did you whip the Yankees?" Baby Hugh asked.

Brodie didn't answer. He tried to push himself out of the rocking chair, but lacked the strength. Edith released her grip on Baby Hugh, and ran to help. I did, too, and we pulled the horse soldier up. He leaned against me, whispered a soft thanks. By that time, Mama was back and ready to leave.

"How many wounded, Corporal?" she asked, tying a bonnet under her chin.

"It's not that many, ma'am. We won handily. Fewer than a hundred." He staggered toward the door.

A hundred wounded seemed like a lot to me.

"And how many Union wounded?" Mama asked him.

He stopped, gripping the doorjamb, and turned to face Mama. Those eyes became even duller. "Fewer, ma'am." A tear rolled down his cheek. "Practically none at all."

"Bar the door," Mama told us before she left. "Don't let anyone in until I'm back. And straight to bed."

After that, Edith and I got the bar back into place, and we stared at each other. Alone.

The horse snorted, someone climbed into the saddle, and we heard them leave. My imagination took over. I wondered whether they rode double, if Mama walked, or if the soldier let Mama ride—even though I'm sure soldiers didn't ride side-saddle—and led the horse.

"What if Papa comes?" Baby Hugh asked. "Could we let him in?"

"Of course," Edith told him. "Don't be silly." She looked at

Mama's bed, then headed up to the loft. "I'm going to sleep."

"Me, too." I let her reach the loft first before I went up the ladder.

"But," Baby Hugh said, "Mama told us we could sleep in the big bed."

"It's all yours!" I called down.

Sitting on our beds, Edith and I waited, but not for long.

"Wait!" Baby Hugh came up that ladder like a terror, knocking me over when he jumped onto me. Edith giggled, blew out the candle she had brought up with her, and pulled the covers over her head.

"Good night," I said, and tossed my brother onto his side of the bed.

"Miss Mary . . . ," he whispered. "She died in that bed."

"I know."

"I ain't sleeping in it."

"Mama did."

"You reckon she was scared?"

Edith was eavesdropping. "Mama? Scared? Ha!"

"You don't reckon her ghost is here, do you?"

"There are no such things as ghosts," Edith snapped. "Go to sleep."

"How about all them soldiers?"

"What soldiers?" I asked.

"At the battle today."

The wind moaned through the cabin, where cannon fire had knocked out the chinking.

"Travis?"

"Go to sleep."

"You reckon Papa's all right?"

"Of course. That corporal said they went to the rear."

"Because they was afraid?"

"No. To protect the rear. From getting attacked there."

"Well, that's good."

"Yes. It is."

"Because. . . ."

The wind moaned. I wished Edith hadn't blown out that candle.

"Because why?" I asked after a while.

"Because it wouldn't be right, would it?"

Edith was still listening. "What wouldn't be right?"

"For Papa to have to fight Mister Greene."

"Go to sleep."

And eventually Hugh did. I, on the other hand, stared into the dark for the longest while.

Morning came, but Mama didn't. The sky was overcast, another gloomy, gray day, and the grass was wet with dew.

We went downstairs, and while Edith fixed breakfast—grits again—Baby Hugh and I did the chores.

After breakfast, we left our *Reader*s alone and went to the porch, staring down at the lane down which Mama did not come.

"How long do you reckon she'll be doctoring?" Baby Hugh asked.

"Nurse," Edith corrected. "She's a nurse."

"Same difference."

The idea hit me instantly. "Fishing. We should go fishing."

"But Mama said . . . ," Baby Hugh began.

"We were going fishing before the battle. We'll leave a note saying we've gone to the millpond, just in case she comes home before we do. And if we get back first, we'll have a mess of catfish fried up and waiting for her. She'll love it."

"But the battle. . . ."

I cut Edith off. "The battle, that soldier said, was at Poison Spring. That's past Papa's mill."

176

"It's close enough." She put her hands on her hips, just like Mama. "Really close."

"Do you want to come or not?" I could be just as stubborn.

"I wanna," Baby Hugh said.

Edith didn't like the idea, but she muttered something underneath her breath, picked up a fishing pole, and said: "You write the note."

Which I did. After that, we grabbed the other pole and the can of worms, and marched down the lane, picking up the pole Baby Hugh had dropped near the ditch yesterday morning. I quickly outdistanced my sister and brother, excited to be out of the house, heading to the mill, to fish, and . . . maybe . . . sneak into the tool shed. Baby Hugh and Edith lagged behind, but soon caught up with me.

Something was wrong, but I didn't realize it until later. There were no birds. This time of morning, birds should be singing, but a quietness filled the country. All we heard was the water flowing through the ditch, and the sucking sound our shoes made in the muddy path.

Five hundred yards down the road, my excitement waned, and my pace slowed to a crawl.

The Camden-Washington Pike was a bog, stinking of mud, stagnant water, and waste. We had seen the road like that before, of course, after the Confederates abandoned Camden, but never so much débris—caps and canteens, a bayonet stuck in the ground, haversacks, a busted musket, overcoats, even a brogan half sticking out of the mud, a filthy sock partly inside.

And a body. . . . He lay face down in the mud on the far side of the road, barefoot, duck trousers, a homespun shirt, his bloody back covered with flies.

Edith gasped.

Baby Hugh called out: "That ain't Papa, is it?"

"Papa wasn't bald," I told him.

177

"We should . . . go . . . back . . . Travis," Edith said.

"It's all . . . right." I had to swallow down the bile rising in my throat. I moved ahead, slower though, never getting far ahead from my siblings.

"Shouldn't they have buried him?" Baby Hugh asked.

Not trusting my mouth, or my stomach, I answered with a nod. A caisson lay on its side. Its axle had busted, and the soldiers, I assumed, had pushed it to the side, and turned it over. More clothing, more gear, but no more bodies.

When we neared the turn-off to the Ford Family Mill, a coyote bolted out of the woods, crossed the road, and hurried into the far woods.

"What was that he had in his mouth?" Baby Hugh asked.

"I don't know," I answered honestly. I didn't want to know.

With relief, we turned down the lane that led to Papa's mill. By the time the mill came into view, I could breathe normally again, though I couldn't shake the image of that dead Confederate soldier. Or the coyote.

Still no birds sang, no frogs croaked, but a fish splashed in the pond, as if telling us we were expected. My mood improved.

"Y'all go to that corner." I pointed.

"I'm not baiting my hook," Edith informed me.

"Me, neither," Baby Hugh said.

"All right. I'll bait them all. Just go on."

"Where are you going?"

"To the shed. There's a sack we can use. I'll meet you there."

"We'll wait," Edith said.

"Great." I leaned the pole against the main building, set the can of worms on the floor, went to the shed, opened the door, and screamed, ducking just in time as a bullet ripped over my head and knocked a chunk out of wall of the mill behind me.

CHAPTER NINETEEN

Over the ringing in my ears, and the pounding of my heart, Edith's and Baby Hugh's shouts reached me. So did a voice.

"You blasted idiot! Give me that revolver!"

My back against the door, I sat, shaking, legs stretched out in front of me. Edith and Baby Hugh started toward me, but I managed to get my muscles to work, and waved at them, telling them to: "Run! Hide!"

A man stepped—no, he staggered—outside, tripping, landing on his side with a grunt. In his right hand he held a revolver, but not threateningly, more the way Mama had first gripped the Spiller and Burr when she stepped out to face the preacher and his group. The hand was bloody, but not from the two missing fingers.

Catching my breath, I got a good look at the man as he managed to pull himself up. "Wait a minute!" I called out to my brother and sister, who had taken my advice, and were running deeper into the woods. "It's . . . it's . . . Sergeant Greene!" I yelled.

He wore no blouse, only a ragged shirt, the side of which was drenched with blood. Greene had ripped off both shirt sleeves, using them to stanch the flow of blood, but, considering all the blood I saw, he hadn't had much success. Sweat beaded his face, his jaw set tight against the pain. Another wound had cut across the left side of his head, just below where his hat would have rested, if he had worn a hat. His bare arms were scratched as if he'd been running through brambles and briars for an eternity.

Smoke drifted out of the barrel of the revolver. He tried to grin at me, but couldn't.

"Sergeant. . . ." A timid voice came from inside the shed.

"Shut up, Wilson. It's young Travis Ford."

"I sorry. . . ."

"You almost blew his head off, fool."

The pistol slipped from his hand. Jared Greene winced in pain.

Slowly I managed to get to my knees, crawling over toward the freedman, glancing inside the shed to find Jeremiah Wilson cowering underneath the shelves, along with another man, this one barefoot and wearing ragged and patched gray trousers. A black man, too.

Jeremiah Wilson grinned weakly at me. A bandage covered much of his head, the white cloth over his left ear blackened with blood. "Hey, boy," he said, his voice trembling in fear. "I'm . . . uh . . . sorry?" The last word came out as a question.

Without answering, I turned away, focused on Jared Greene. I kneeled beside him and reached for the cloth he pressed against his side, but his free hand, the one that had held the revolver, shot out and clamped onto my wrist.

"What the Sam Hill are you doing here?" he asked.

"We were going fishing."

He released his hold, and his hand fell beside the butt of the revolver. "Fishing." He started to laugh, but coughed instead.

By then, Edith and Baby Hugh had gathered around. To my surprise, and to their credit and courage, they didn't gasp, didn't cry, just stood there silently, holding hands.

"What happened?" I managed to ask.

"Had a bit of a scrap with the Rebs," Jared Greene said weakly. "Hit us just down the road."

"We heard the battle," Edith said.

Baby Hugh added: "Cannon and all."

"Wish all I'd done was heard it." Greene tried to slide up, but quickly gave up on moving at all.

"For four hours," Baby Hugh said.

Greene nodded. "Four hours, eh? That all? Felt like forty."

"We give 'em what-for!" Jeremiah Wilson called out from the shed. "At first we did."

"Wasn't much of a fight at first," Greene said. "Till noon, I guess. Rebs hit us with cannon, hit us with everything they had. We just stood there, firing at each other. Giving them buck and ball. Thought we had 'em whipped."

"Then they hit us with cannon again!" Wilson called out.

"And after that, they hit us with the Twenty-Ninth Texas horse soldiers," Greene said. "We'd fought them before. At Honey Creek about a year ago. Captured their colors in that one." His head shook. Sweat must have stung his eyes. "Not this time."

Wilson said: "They called out to us . . . 'You First Kansas darkies now will buck to the Twenty-Ninth Texas.' And then . . . then. . . ." The soldier started to cry.

Greene managed to sit up straighter, both hands clenched into tight fists. "Buck up, Wilson." He swore savagely at the bawling soldier. "Don't you cry, boy. Don't you cry at all. Buck up, I say. Buck up!"

"Yes," Jeremiah Wilson sobbed. "Yes, Sergeant. I'm tryin'."

"Third, I don't know, maybe fourth time they charged. . . ." Greene had to catch his breath. "That was it. Must've hit us with four brigades. It was like a thunderstorm. Only instead of raindrops, the air filled with Minié balls, grapeshot."

"Texians just screamin' their heads off," Wilson said. "Make a body lose his breakfast."

"Caught us in an enfilade." Now the sergeant almost doubled

181

over in pain.

"What's that mean?" I was glad Baby Hugh had asked.

"Means murder," Wilson said.

"That's about right." Greene spit to his side. Just saliva. Not blood. "Shot down the whole line of us." He sighed, and now it wasn't just sweat rolling through the beard stubble but tears. "Then. . . ." He let out the most piteous wail.

I reached over, grabbed his shoulder, tried to squeeze, but it didn't help, didn't stop Sergeant Jared Greene from crying.

"Don't cry, Sergeant," Jeremiah Wilson said.

Greene swore again. Swore, spit, clenched his teeth, shaking his head as if trying to make whatever it was that was hurting him so badly disappear like a bad dream. "Murderers!" he called out, cursing again. "Murdering Rebs." Then he fell back, his breath ragged as he wiped away the tears, cursing himself.

"We tried to give up," Wilson said. "We tried. . . ."

"Shut up!" Greene barked, but this time Jeremiah Wilson didn't listen.

"Throwed down our guns, raised our hands, some of us even fell to our knees and begged. Begged . . . begged the Rebs not to murder us."

"Shut up, I tell you!" Green yelled.

"It was butchery."

I motioned at the man with the bare feet and worn pants. "Is that Hammond?" I remembered the big soldier who had been with Wilson when we first found them at the mill. But I knew it wasn't Hammond; he had worn the uniform of a Yankee.

"Hammond's dead," Greene said hoarsely. "Murdered. It was like the whole Secesh army turned crazy. Crazy for blood."

Everyone fell silent.

Suddenly Edith called out my name, and I heard the pounding of hoofs.

"Rebs!" Jared Greene cried out, and tried to grab his revolver.

"It might be your own . . . ," Edith began, but shouts came from up the lane.

"Come on, First Kansas boys! Come on. Quits hidin' from your masters!"

Followed by Rebel yells.

"Get out of here," Sergeant Greene said, fumbling for his revolver. "Get out, Travis. We'll take as many of them curs with us as we can."

I jerked the gun from his grip. It took no effort. "No," I told him. "Hide."

He tried to resist, but Edith and even Baby Hugh rushed to help me.

"I'm a soldier," he said. "I'm a man. I'm. . . ."

The bloody rag fell, and he passed out, which didn't exactly make it easier for three kids to drag him into the shed. We dropped Greene onto the ground, didn't even look at the man with the bare feet, then rushed back outside.

"The bandage!" I pointed.

The horses were rounding the bend.

Edith ran over, didn't falter a bit, picked up the bloody cloth, and threw the messy wad into the shed. I slammed the door behind me, grabbed the pistol, glanced at Edith.

"Hide your hands," I whispered. "Behind you!"

She glanced at her hands, speckled with blood, and put them behind her back, backing closer to the mill. Baby Hugh looked at his own hands, but they were clean of any blood. I didn't know about myself, and didn't have time to do any checking, because four horsemen slid their lathered mounts to a stop near us. Two revolvers, a shotgun, and a massive Bowie knife were pointing at me, at Edith, at Baby Hugh.

I kept Sergeant Greene's revolver aimed at the ground.

"What you young 'uns doin' here?" The one who spoke wore a gray jacket and black hat, one side pinned up with an ostrich plume that look wilted. He held a massive Dragoon revolver in his right hand. A brown patch covered his left eye, with a white scar running down from the corner of the patch and carving a white ditch through his black beard.

Next to him, the man with the shotgun wore a porkpie hat and the pants of a Union soldier. Beside him slouched a man whose cheeks bulged with chewing tobacco. He held the Bowie knife, which he was busy sheathing once he realized we were three children and not a regiment of enemy soldiers. The last one, on a fine black thoroughbred, eased the hammer down on his small revolver, and leaned forward, dropping his reins over the black's neck, and rubbing the horse with his free hand. He didn't holster the revolver, but he didn't appear to want to kill us.

"Put your cannon away, Dick," he said. "They don't look like Yanks to me."

"Skins the wrong color," the one with the shotgun said, and spit.

"But you will answer Dick's question," Thoroughbred said. It wasn't a question, but an order. The man's blond mustache was well-groomed, and his uniform might have been tailor-made. It looked fancier than the others' clothes, even though wrinkled, dirty, and well-worn. Spectacles covered his eyes. As he straightened, he pushed back his wide-brimmed hat and said: "Well?"

"This is our sawmill," I said.

Bowie Knife sniggered and spit again. "Gotta take your word for it."

"It is our mill!" Edith snapped. I cringed, not wanting any of those Rebels to pay much attention to her with those blood-stained hands behind her. "My papa built it and. . . ."

"You misunderstand me, missy. Meanin' I'm takin' your word that this place is a sawmill."

Everyone except Thoroughbred laughed.

"Papa's Sergeant Connor Ford," I told them, relieved when they all faced me again. "He's with the Second Arkansas Cavalry."

"Is that so?" Eye Patch said. "Boy, I'd feel a mite better if you was to drop that Remington."

I glanced at the pistol, back at Eye Patch, then over at Thoroughbred, who nodded. The gun fell onto the carpet of pine needles.

"Second Arkansas, eh?" Thoroughbred nodded his approval. "We're with DeMorse's Texans."

I nodded as if DeMorse meant something to me.

"Do you know our papa?" Baby Hugh asked.

"Can't say I've made his acquaintance," Thoroughbred said without glancing at my brother. He stared at me.

"Where do y'all live?"

"Down the road. Toward Washington. Couple of miles."

"What brung you here?" He grinned. "Curious about the fight yesterday?"

I pointed at the fishing pole and worm can.

"Man." Bowie Knife smacked his lips. "A mess of catfish sure would hit the spot."

Ignoring him, Thoroughbred pointed the barrel of his revolver at the one I had dropped. "We heard a shot," he said. "You fire it?"

The lie came to me quickly. Never had I been one much to start with falsehoods, so I spoke rapidly and almost believed what I was telling him. "Yes, sir." I grinned. "Found this in the woods right where our lane meets the pike. Never shot a pistol before. Almost"—I attempted a sheepish grin—"blew my head off." I pointed at the hole in the rotting wall behind me.

A few chuckles. I let out a short breath. *Criminy, they believe me.*

Shotgun finally spoke. He was the only one who kept his weapon aimed at me. "You ain't seen no colored boys 'round here, have you?"

Another lie. Well, not really a lie. But it seemed natural. "Miss Mary had some slaves." I pointed west. "She owned the plantation down. . . ."

"Darkies in blue uniforms is what Hilly means," Bowie Knife said, and spit again.

"No, sir," I said respectfully.

"Be a right handy place to hide." Eye Patch nodded, and swung off his blood bay mare. He shoved the revolver into his waistband.

"We're hunting for any Yanks from the First Kansas Colored," Thoroughbred explained, "who turned tail and ran when the fighting got too hot for them yesterday."

"We heard the fight," Baby Hugh said.

"You should 'a' seed it," Bowie Knife said. Leaning back in his saddle, he shouted out: "Where be the First Kansas Charcoals now?"

Shotgun answered, laughing as he said: "All cut to pieces and gone to . . ."—he stopped, bowed at Edith, and continued—"to the hot place run by Mister Lucifer hisself."

Eye Patch stopped beside me. He motioned toward the tool shed. "What's that?"

"Just a shed."

He looked at it, then at the Remington. He bent over, picked it up, shoved it next to the giant horse pistol in his pants. Then he climbed into the main building.

"When did your pa join up?" he asked.

"After Shiloh," I answered.

He jumped down, drew the Dragoon, and moved to his horse, shoving the pistol this time in a scabbard hanging from the horn. "This place went down that far in two short years?" Shaking his head, he climbed back into the saddle.

"What do you expect, Dick?" Thoroughbred said. "The Confederacy has gone pretty far down in two years."

"We ain't whupped yet."

"Not by the First Kansas Colored. No, sir. Not by them black-skinned sons-of-. . . ." Again he stopped, bowed toward Edith, saying: "My apologies for my salty language, missy."

"Ain't nobody here, Capt'n," Eye Patch said, " 'ceptin' these kids."

"I can see that, Dick." Captain Thoroughbred nodded at me.

"Can't I keep the pistol?" I asked.

Eye Patch chuckled. "Sure, boy. Just join up with us. Then you can shoot all the Yanks you find."

My lips flattened. Shotgun and Bowie Knife chuckled, and turned their horses. They were up the road before Thoroughbred and Eye Patch began to follow. Edith brought her hands in front of her, clasped as in prayer, but they quickly returned behind her back. Captain Thoroughbred came riding back toward us. He reined in, looked us over, then his eyes locked once more on me.

"You say your pa's with what outfit?"

"Second Arkansas," I managed to answer. "Slemons's cavalry."

"And his name?"

"Ford. Sergeant Connor Ford."

His head bobbed in acceptance. "Any word you want me to give him? In case I run across him."

Edith answered: "Tell him we love him."

"And miss him," Baby Hugh said.

His smile seemed older than he looked, and wearier than I felt.

"I miss my family, too." He turned the black, and disappeared.

CHAPTER TWENTY

Scared, we waited in silence until we could no longer hear the horses of the Texians. Then, we waited some more, until, from inside the shed, Jeremiah Wilson called out in a plaintive voice: "Is they gone?"

I think so, I thought, then realized I hadn't answered him. I cleared my throat, told him, and slowly, unsteadily stepped toward the shed. This time Edith and Baby Hugh stuck right beside me.

Sergeant Jared Greene hadn't moved from where we had dropped—or rather dumped—his unconscious body.

"Is he dead?" Baby Hugh asked.

Edith answered: "No, but he'll die if we don't stop that bleeding."

"I packed it up good and tight with mud and the likes," Wilson said. "Yesterday. When we got here. But it opened up again this morn."

I looked at Greene's side. Blood flowed steadily out of a thin but wicked-looking gash, pooling underneath him.

"Get a fire started." I didn't speak to anyone in particular, didn't even think about what I was saying. I just knew.

"With what?" Edith asked.

With what? I looked at the shelves, saw the oil cans, but knew they were empty. *With what?* We hadn't thought to bring matches, and nothing looked promising on the shelves or in the corner. I looked at Wilson.

"Do you have matches?"

"No, sir."

"Flint? Steel?"

His head shook. "I ain't got nothin'." His hand came up to the bloody bandage on his head. "Ain't even got no left ear no more."

I paid no mind to his troubles, just stared down at Jared Greene. His belt was gone. No haversack, either, and I couldn't bring myself to go through his pockets.

A weak voice called out. "Looks . . . in . . . my . . . poc- . . . ," said the bare-footed Negro lying in the corner.

Down I went, turning, looking at the old man. I started to reach for the pocket of his patched trousers, but my hands stopped. I studied his tired face.

"Mowbray?"

The old man grinned. "Master Trav-is." A gnarled finger tapped his trousers leg, pointing at the pocket. "Hurry . . . sir."

Seeing the protruding leather cord, I reached for it, tugged slightly, then harder, and finally a pouch came out. I could tell once I lifted it that it held flint, steel, even some bits of tinder to start.

"Grab those sacks on the floor," I told Edith and Hugh. "Rip them up. There's some fat lighter on the other side of this building. I'll get that." Outside, I found the pitch pine, broke off a thin yellow sliver that smelled like coal oil. Moments later, between the shed and the mill, we put the burlap strips over some dried pine needles and pine cones, laid the tinder on top, and the pitch on it. I went to work striking steel and flint, watching the sparks. When they began to catch, Edith and Hugh knew exactly what to do. They blew short, even breaths, and the flames erupted. The strip of pitch quickly blazed to life. Wet as everything seemed to be, I worried that getting a fire burning hot enough would take forever, but the wood inside the sawmill was old, dry, a tinderbox.

Little by little, my sister and brother added to the fire while I ran inside the mill, bringing out handfuls of sawdust that I had once planned to sell to Miss Mary for insulation. Then I went back, getting scraps of lumber. In a short while, the fire burned furiously.

"What are you going to do?" Edith asked.

I didn't have time to answer. I went back into the shed, stepping over Sergeant Greene's body, grabbing the old axe that leaned against cross-cut saws, shovels, wedges, rakes. The blade was rusty, but it would have to do. I turned to Wilson, asking: "Do you have a knife?"

He had moved over to Jared Greene, trying to stop the flow of blood from his sergeant's side with the wadded up sleeves from Jared's shirt. Wilson's head shook. Mowbray had drifted off into unconsciousness. I didn't check Sergeant Greene. His saber would have worked fine, but he had no saber, no gun, and I didn't know how much blood he had left in his body.

Back outside, I kneeled between Edith and Baby Hugh, and laid the rusty blade on the edge of the flames.

"What are you gonna do, Travis?" Baby Hugh asked.

I bit my bottom lip. Somehow, the flames didn't feel hot enough. I grabbed a nearby stick, began poking it. Sparks flew.

"What if them soldiers smell the smoke?" Baby Hugh asked. "They might come back to in- . . . um, in-inves-ti-gate."

"We'll tell them we plan to fry some fish we catch." Which reminded me. "You better go to the pond." I nodded first at him, then at Edith. "Both of you. Start fishing."

"But. . . ."

Edith understood. She rose, took Baby Hugh's hand, and led him away from the fire. They picked up the can of worms, their poles, and disappeared around the side of the sawmill.

I added a few more scraps of wood onto the fire, pushed the

axe blade in deeper, being careful not to burn the handle. The flames warmed my face, and I began sweating, only not because of the heat.

"Son . . . !" Jeremiah Wilson called out from the shed. "You best hurry. Sergeant's still bleedin' like a stuck pig."

I balanced on my knees, dried my palms on my pants legs, and took the hickory handle of the axe into my hands. It felt as if I were lifting one of those barrels full of sawdust. Somehow I managed to get to my feet, carefully avoiding the glowing hot blade, and went to the shed.

I stepped through the doorway, eased onto my knees, and put the blade on the ground. The pool of blood sizzled. Jared Greene didn't move. Nor did old Mowbray. But Jeremiah Wilson backed away quickly, dragging the bloody rag across the dirt floor. I almost threw up.

"You needs to hurry," Wilson said. "Whilst the blade's still hot."

The blade inched closer to the gash in Greene's side. My eyes squeezed shut. Then Wilson came beside me, and his hands gripped the handle above my own.

"We'll do it together," he said.

Together, we pushed. The blade went against the sergeant's skin, and the sound, the stench of burning flesh caused me to tremble. Bile rose in my throat, and this time I couldn't keep it down. I turned away, leaving the axe in Wilson's hands, and managed to slip through the doorway, and violently, urgently retched. Empty, I wove a path inside the shed again.

I stared at Sergeant Jared Greene, thinking about what we had just done.

cau'ter-ize, *v. t.* . . . . *To burn or sear with fire or a hot iron, as morbid flesh.*

Morbid. That's how I felt. Until Jeremiah Wilson glanced at

me. He was sweating profusely, too. He was smiling, also.

"You done good. We done good." He spoke softly, pointing at Greene's side. "Bleedin's stopped. Need some more rags, though, I reckons."

After wiping my mouth with my shirt sleeve, I pulled myself up. The axe lay on the ground. I reached up on the shelf, pulled down the cigar box. After pulling the box from the sack, I handed the burlap to Wilson, and slid the box back on the shelf. I didn't bother to open it, just dropped onto my knees, and helped Wilson bathe the ugly wound.

"You know where any moss is?" Wilson asked.

"Moss?"

"Yeah. My grandmammie used to say it's good for infection. Sucks the p'ison out. Figured to put some on that wound. Just to be safe."

Outside, I found moss, brought it back, and we eased that onto the ugly wound on Greene's side. He shuddered at our touch, moaned something.

"He could use some water," I whispered.

Wilson said: "I could use somethin' a mite stronger."

My smile was weak. "Me, too."

With a laugh, he bandaged the sergeant's side, then moved over to Mowbray.

The old slave's left arm was broken, and not even set in a splint yet. His arms were slashed from briars, and there was a deep hole in his stomach from which blood and puss oozed.

Wilson let out a long sigh. "I don't reckons they's much we can do for him."

"But. . . ." I stared down at the tired old man.

"Gut shot." Wilson's head shook. "Miracle he's lasted this long."

"Did he join up?"

Wilson turned and stared at my question.

"In the Army?" I explained. "The First Kansas?"

"Nah. Told the capt'n he was a runaway slave. His back was all puckered up with scars from a whip. He went to the hospital, then come back, said he knowed this country well, would guide us through it. The capt'n, he said that was a right good idea. Poor ol' man. Should 'a' stayed with the rest of the contrabands."

I studied Mowbray's tired face, then turned around, sank to the floor, leaned against the picket wall. "What happened?" I asked. "At Poison Spring?"

Wilson sat beside me. "You heard. We tried to surrender. Rebs wouldn't let us. Stuck a bayonet through old Hammond's belly, but he didn't die like no coward. No, sir. Last I seen of him, he was bitin' and clawin' and cussin' and they was poundin' him with the butts of their guns." He stopped as if remembering. A tear rolled down his cheek, and he didn't bother to wipe it away. "Ol' Hammond," he said softly. "Sure gonna miss him."

"So you ran here?" I prodded.

His head nodded slightly. "Sergeant Greene knowed it was a good place. Knowed how to find it in the woods. They was six of us when we run, after we knowed it wasn't no use to surrender, that they'd just cut us down, and they was too many for us to fights. That slave yonder, ol' Mowbray, he got shot, and Sergeant Greene just picked him up. He'd already been slashed by a saber. The sergeant, I mean. I feared it would spill his insides out, but he just wouldn't die. Sergeant Greene . . . he can't die. . . . Well, he picks up Mowbray, and we's into the woods."

"Six of you?"

"Six in the First Kansas Colored. Plus him." He tilted his head toward Mowbray. "Rebs kilt four. Don't exactly knows how we made it this far."

He had talked himself silent. For the next several moments, we just sat, exhausted, both of us crying, and not caring who saw our tears.

Another face popped into my mind. "What about Lieutenant Bullis?" I asked.

Wilson's head shook. "He's dead, too. Grapeshot cut him in half. I seed it. Ugly thing to seed. But he died in battle, the lieutenant did. Died game. Died fightin'. He wasn't murdered. Like most of us."

Silence again.

A bird began to sing. Maybe things were returning to normal. *No,* I thought to myself, *things will never be normal again.*

A fish splashed in the millpond, and Wilson looked through the open door. "Reckon your sis or brother just catched somethin'?"

I doubted it. I didn't think that either would have baited their hooks.

"Y'all brings anythings to eat?"

My head shook. We hadn't planned that far ahead. "I'm thirsty."

Wilson had no canteen, but I'd seen some cans scattered about inside the sawmill—if only they could hold water.

"I'll be back," I said, and left the shed.

First, I gathered the cans, then followed the path that stretched alongside the pond. At the corner, I found Edith and Baby Hugh. To my surprise, not only had they baited their own hooks, they had managed to pull in a mess of bream. Baby Hugh tugged the sack out of the shallows, and held it, dripping, for me to inspect.

Granted, Papa would have had a cow had he seen the size of some of those fish. "Too small to keep," he would have admonished. "Throw it back and we'll catch him when he's grown up." Others, however, were the size of Papa's hand.

"That's a good-eating fish," he would have said.

Edith grinned. "I caught the biggest."

"Did not," Baby Hugh said.

"Did, too."

"Not."

"Too."

I closed the sack, raised my hand, and they fell quiet. "It's all right," I said. "Y'all did well."

"How's Mister Greene?" Edith asked.

"Better." *Was he?* "I think so. He's not bleeding."

"And Mowbray?" Baby Hugh inquired.

I couldn't lie. Not to my brother and sister. My head shook. "I . . . he's . . . I don't know. It's . . . Wilson says he's . . . dying."

No response.

"We should cook them some supper," Edith said.

Baby Hugh frowned. "All of them?"

I thrust out the sack for him to carry, saying: "I think there's enough for them . . . and us. . . ."

"And Mama?" Hugh's face brightened.

"Mama, too," I said.

With no frying pan, we skewered the fish—sort of cleaned and gutted them with some old saw blades—and roasted them over the coals.

Wilson ate the two biggest fish, and we left four others for Mowbray and Jared Greene, if they ever awakened.

By then, it was late afternoon, and the skies had darkened again.

"We need to go home," I told Wilson.

Fear shot through his face.

"We'll be back," I said.

"Swear to God?"

"I swear to God."

"And you ain't gonna tell nobody that we's here?"

"I swear."

"When will you be back?"

"Tomorrow. I promise."

Those two miles home might have been the longest two miles we'd ever traveled.

Silently we passed the trash left by the army, past the overturned caisson, the hats, the bayonet, the haversacks. The sock remained in the road, but the brogan was gone. So, thankfully, was the corpse of the bald Confederate soldier.

As we neared our lane, Edith asked: "What are we going to do?"

I kept walking.

"Should we tell Mama?" she asked.

"No." That much I knew.

"But she knows about nursing, and all of those poor men need nursing."

"We can't tell Mama," I said.

"Why not?"

"We just can't is all."

"Well, we can't keep them there forever."

Swinging the sack of fish he proudly carried, Baby Hugh attempted to whistle. He stopped, and said: "I'd like to have a slave."

"Hugh Ford!" Edith shouted.

"Well, I would."

"I'll tell Mama on you."

"You won't tell Mama a thing, Edith," I said. "We have to keep quiet about this."

"We could take them to Miss Mary's," Edith said. "Or up the road to Lee's place. They'd take good care of all three."

My head shook. "They'd be prisoners."

"They'd be cared for," Edith said. "By doctors."

"And a nurse like Mama," Baby Hugh added.

"They'd be murdered," I told them.

We finished the walk home without speaking.

CHAPTER TWENTY-ONE

Mama didn't get home till after dark.

She came into the kitchen to the smell of frying fish—actually more like burning—and the sight of Edith holding the skillet over the coals in the oven, grease popping, coals sizzling, smoke billowing out of the skillet and up the chimney, and me trying to flip a blackened bream with a long fork.

"My goodness," she said as she came to our rescue.

The skillet came out, and she let the coals die down some, sliding the burned fish onto a plate.

"How many did you catch?" she asked.

Instead of answering, we hugged her.

"My goodness," she said again. "Was I gone that long?"

"Felt like forever," Edith said.

Mama let out a weary sigh. "Felt like forever for me, too."

After kissing us all, she pulled off her bonnet, and looked around the kitchen. We had cleaned all of the fish, even the small ones. That much we knew how to do. Papa had shown me and even Edith how, and we had watched him enough to know the proper method of removing the scales, cutting off the head, gutting the insides.

Cooking, on the other hand, was something different.

"Where's the batter?" Mama asked.

"Batter?" Edith said.

She smiled, and went to work, giving us a lesson in coating a fish with cornmeal. "Dip it in milk," she said. "Usually, it's good to beat an egg or two with the milk, but. . . ." She shrugged. "Then dip it in the cornmeal, coating both sides. Then into the skillet in which you've melted bacon grease."

That was one thing we had plenty of, even if Papa hadn't been around to butcher a pig these past couple of falls.

Once Mama had finished cooking, we ate. She insisted on eating the black one, and, grinning at Edith, she said it was quite tasty. "We should have fish every day," she announced as we helped her with the dishes.

Which was perfect as far as I was concerned. "I'll go," I announced.

"Why you?" Baby Hugh demanded. "You didn't catch nothin'. You was too busy. . . ." He stopped himself.

"Too busy doing what?" Mama asked.

"Bossing us around," Edith said.

Mama laughed, as I tried to think how I could repay Edith. She could lie to our mother as well as I could lie to Confederate cavalry.

Dishes done, we moved to the porch to sit and listen to the quiet. Fireflies flickered in the trees beyond the well.

"Can I catch some and put 'em in a jar, Mama?" Baby Hugh asked.

"No." Her voice was soft, as if she were lost in thought. I guess she was. She sighed, and added: "No, let them stay free."

"How was . . . ?" Edith swallowed. "Was it . . . ?"

Mama turned toward us, smiling faintly. "I'd rather not talk about it. Do you understand?"

Our heads nodded.

Hers shook. "Those poor boys," she said. "So young. So proud."

The wind blew. An owl hooted. Inside the barn, our cow lowed.

"So," Mama said after a moment, "what did y'all do today?

Other than fish?"

"We. . . ." I tried to think of something. What had we done? Saved two Union soldiers and a runaway slave from being murdered by Texas horse soldiers. Cauterized the wound on a black soldier.

"Did you read?" she asked, saving me from trying to think of another lie.

"No," we said in unison.

With a sigh, she looked back down the lane. "Well, it's too late to read tonight."

"Did you see Papa?" Baby Hugh blurted out.

"No." Another sigh. "I didn't see one person from his regiment. And I can guarantee you that I asked almost everyone. . . . No, I didn't see your father."

"The fish was good," Edith commented. "Thanks to you."

"Your father showed me how to fry fish," she said. "When we first were married, Connor was a good cook. Still is, I bet."

"Maybe he'll come home," Edith said. "He's near here."

"He's gotta come see us!" Baby Hugh said.

Mama whispered: "Maybe."

In the woods, far away, a coyote called out.

We went to bed.

The next day Mama let me go back to the mill by myself. Edith and Baby Hugh complained, but Mama informed them that they needed to study, and do chores, and since they had caught all of the fish yesterday, I deserved a turn today.

I felt lucky. Till I reached the sawmill.

Sergeant Jared Greene was sitting up, which made me feel hopeful. Still, he seemed in pain, holding his side as sweat poured down his cheeks. But he was alive. Alive and sitting up.

Jeremiah Wilson squatted beside him. He smiled weakly at me, and sat down, breathing a sigh of relief.

When I turned to Mowbray, however, I knew he was dead. My knees gave out, and I dropped onto the dirt floor, knocking over a shovel.

"It's all . . . right . . . Travis." Greene sounded as if every word, every syllable, hurt.

"Mowbray," Wilson added, "he's free now. Free. Got the jubilee."

We had to bury him, of course, and that was a problem. Roots ran deep in the forest, and the ground could be rocky. It wasn't like I could haul his body to Miss Mary's place and bury him in the graveyard for her slaves. Sergeant Greene couldn't help, and I didn't know how strong Jeremiah Wilson was.

"You know . . . where the . . . dam . . . is?" Greene said.

I nodded.

"Good." He winced, tried to find a more comfortable position. "Well . . . about . . . fifty yards . . . upstream. Big pile . . . of rocks."

"Yes, sir."

"Your father's . . . idea." He had to pause to catch his breath. "Case the . . . creek . . . flooded. It did . . . sometimes. . . . Connor said . . . needed rocks . . . to replace those . . . washed . . . away." Wilson and I waited. A minute passed before Jared Greene found enough energy to continue. "Beyond that . . . toward the Pike . . . there's a . . . clearing. Be a . . . good place . . . for . . . Mowbray."

"But the ground . . . ," I started.

His nod silenced me. "I know. Dig deep as . . . you can. Won't be deep. But pile them . . . rocks over . . . him. Best we . . . can do." He wiped his brow, and lay down.

"He won't mind. Mowbray'll . . . under- . . . stand."

I remember Edith and Mama saying that yesterday had felt like forever. For me, this day stretched out even longer.

Wilson and I carried the dead slave to the clearing. I scraped at the earth with a shovel while Wilson brought stones from the creek side. After thirty minutes or so, we switched chores. For a while, we kept that up, and I guess we managed to dig a foot before roots and stones and bedrock stopped us. Then we put Mowbray in the shallow grave, and slowly began covering his body with stones.

Tears blinded us while we worked, which was a good thing since it was hard to bear covering the old man's body with rocks without having wrapped him in a blanket.

When the last rock was in place, Wilson stared at me. "You knows what to say?" he asked.

"Amen," was all I answered.

He nodded. "Amen."

We returned to the shed.

I couldn't fish. Just didn't have the heart after burying Mowbray, or the energy after digging and moving those rocks. My palms sported blisters, and I wondered how I would ever explain those to Mama. They would require the biggest lie I had told her yet. So I sat, while Jared Greene slept, and Jeremiah Wilson went to the pond with my pole and my can of worms.

I didn't know what the fishing was like in Missouri, but Jeremiah Wilson knew what he was doing. He came back with eight bream, all hand-size, explaining how he had caught a tiny fish and used it for bait. With spare hooks he had fashioned, he placed bits of meat from the tiny fish onto the hooks, and dropped them with twine to the bottom of the millpond.

"Get us some catfish come tomorrow," he said.

I cleaned four of the fish—having remembered to bring a knife with me this time—for Wilson and Greene, and took the other four home for Mama to fry.

Which is how things went for almost a week.

Every morning, after I'd gone through some pages of

McGuffey's, milked the cow, maybe hoed the garden, or helped with some other chore, I'd be off to the millpond with a can of worms and a fishing pole or two. I told Mama I might need two poles in case something happened to one. Sometimes Baby Hugh or Edith would come with me, but more often I went alone.

Sometimes I brought back bream or crappie. A few times catfish, which Wilson showed me how to clean. And twice, I brought back nothing. The fish weren't biting, not even in the creek.

One day, I entered the tool shed and stopped, embarrassed by what I saw.

Jeremiah Wilson held the cigar box Papa had carved, holding it as if it were precious, smiling at the minstrel singing to the lady. Jared Greene, however, was reading the tablet. Seeing me, both men sat up straighter. Then Wilson leaped up, and slid the box onto the nearest shelf, muttering rapid-fire apologies.

Jared Greene merely closed the tablet, and held it out to me. "You're a good storyteller, son," he said.

My face flushed.

"No, I mean it."

My trembling hands took the tablet. I wanted to take the cigar box and hide it.

"French adventures. Sword fights. Reminds me of Dumas."

I blinked back surprise, and faced Greene again.

"But what do you mean, Travis, when you write *wee-wee*?"

"It's French," I said. "Means yes."

He laughed. Wilson grinned, but I knew he didn't know what struck the sergeant as so funny. Truth is I didn't, either.

"O-u-i," Greene said.

I stared.

"O-u-i spells *oui*. Not w-e-e," Greene explained.

If I'd read *oui* in Dumas, I'd read right over it. My French came from listening to Mama and Miss Mary.

Wilson got it. He slapped his thigh. "Wee-wee. That means something else, don't it?"

We had a good laugh. At my expense, but it felt good to laugh again.

After six days, Sergeant Jared Greene could stand, and he insisted that we go to Mowbray's grave. He couldn't walk on his own, not even with a cane I'd fashioned from a limb, so Wilson and I helped him. The grave was undisturbed.

Greene bowed his head. I guess he prayed silently for Mowbray. Then he drew in a deep breath, let it out slowly, and said:

> *Whether on the scaffold high,*
> *Or in the battle's van,*
> *The fittest place for man to die*
> *Is where he dies for man.*

I didn't know where those words came from, but they sounded fitting. When we were back in the shed, Greene asked: "Travis, what do you see along the road?"

My shrug didn't appease him.

"Soldiers?"

"Some," I said. "Not many."

"Rebs or Union?"

"Rebs. I guess your army is holed up in Camden."

"Find out what you can, Travis. If you can."

I didn't know what I could find out, but I told him I'd try, and walked back home.

That was April 25th. That was the day of the Battle at Marks' Mill. Maybe thirty miles northwest of Camden, the Yankees and Confederates tangled again. Later, we learned that the Federals were sending a supply train to help the forces in Camden. With all the rains, however, the Camden–Pine Bluff Road proved practically impassible, and at Marks' Mill—an old saw and flour operation up in Cleveland County—the Confederates hit the train, and won another battle, another rout. Word of the battle spread quickly across the county. We didn't hear of any colored troops being massacred, but the Rebs who stopped by our home to water their horses later said they had captured not only the entire train, but scores of food and supplies.

The Confederates were eating well. We Fords weren't.

By that time, we were mighty sick of fish. Mama had even suggested that I give the fish a break, which meant I had to sneak away to bring Jared Greene and Jeremiah Wilson whatever I could sneak out of the house: carrots, potatoes, cold corn-bread, and even congealed grits. I always took the fishing poles and worms with me. Just in case Mama caught me.

Greene and Wilson didn't seem to mind the food. The news about Marks' Mill, however, was another story.

"We was s'posed to be goin' all the way to Shreveport," Jeremiah Wilson said sadly. "Reckon we ain't goin' nowheres now."

I didn't know what he meant.

"Plan for the campaign," Jared Greene explained to me. "Take Shreveport, Louisiana. Did that Secesh tell you anything else?"

Glumly I nodded. "Looks like your army is pulling out of Camden."

Greene nodded. Wilson swore.

"Back to Little Rock?" Greene asked.

"On the Military Road," I said. "But that's just from a soldier, and he wasn't an officer. Just an infantry private. With no shoes."

"Yeah, but I believe what he said." Greene shook his head. "That means the Johnny Rebs'll be back in this area thicker than flies. Means Wilson and me need to join up with our boys."

"What's left of 'em," Wilson added.

"You got a horse?" Greene knew the answer already, so he added: "Or know anybody with one?"

My head shook.

"Got no guns. No horses. My side won't let me march all the way back to Little Rock. And if the Secesh catch us. . . ." He grinned without humor.

I remembered the Spiller and Burr. That I could sneak out of the house, but not the shotgun.

"I can fetch you a revolver," I said.

Their moods brightened.

Greene said: "I don't want to bring no trouble down on you, Travis."

"You won't."

"That'd help." He wet his lips. "Some."

"I wish I could do more."

"You done aplenty," Wilson said. "Wasn't for you, we'd be dead and buried by now. Maybe not even buried."

"Tomorrow," I said, and ran home.

The Camden-Washington Pike was crowded again. Soldiers in gray uniforms moved through the bog, but they weren't alone. Men in civilian clothes had joined them. Marching or riding toward Camden, they ignored a bony boy running on the other side of the bar ditch with a can full of earthworms and a couple of fishing poles.

I reached home, set the fishing gear on the porch, and started up the steps.

Mama met me at the door, and she wasn't happy. "Where've you been?" she snapped.

"Uh. . . ." I pointed at the poles and worm can. "Fishing."

"Fishing?" She didn't believe me.

"I didn't catch anything."

"Did you see soldiers? On the road?"

"Yeah." I nodded. Then remembered my manners. "Yes, ma'am. Plenty."

"Confederate?"

I squinted. "Yes, ma'am."

"Come here!"

She moved past me, down the steps, rounded the house, speaking as she made a beeline to wherever she was going. "I told you we should give the fish a break," she said as I followed.

"Yes, ma'am. I just thought. . . ."

We had reached the corncrib, and Mama was heading up the ladder. I'd always thought I was too big now for a switching, but no longer did I feel such immunity. Mama made it to the top, turned to peer down the lane, then told me to hurry.

When I reached the crib, I gasped at the sight of the man inside it, dressed in denim and gray, leaning against the far wall.

Chapter Twenty-Two

For a moment, I couldn't move. I wasn't even sure my heart still beat. I couldn't look away from the man in the crib.

Wavy dark hair, ragged and greasy, fell past his shoulders. A bandage had been tied across his head, blackened by dried blood on his forehead. His gray woolen tunic, which had no buttons, was splattered with mud, as were his denim trousers. A brown hat, the front brim pinned up with a brass 2, rested between his legs. His boots, spurs still on, had been pulled off and stood in front of his sockless, filthy feet.

Baby Hugh sat next to him, steadying in his lap a bowl full of grits, which the man slowly ate with a big spoon. Edith knelt on the opposite side, holding a ladle over a bucket of water. An over-and-under rifle leaned in the corner.

Laying the spoon in the bowl, the man turned toward me. His face was thin—his whole body looked like it would blow away in a stiff breeze—and his beard was dirty, unkempt. I recognized his eyes, a clear, quiet hazel. And his voice, which I had once feared I had forgotten and would never hear again.

"Hello, old man," my father said.

At first, I just stood there, unable to move, mouth hanging open—"Catching flies," as Papa used to say. Even when Mama told me—"Run hug your father, Travis."—I couldn't. Finally Mama took my hand, and led me across the crib. Baby Hugh moved aside, and Edith dropped the ladle into the bucket.

Papa held out his hand. The hands had been washed, but

plenty of dirt remained underneath his fingernails. I shook his hand.

"Grown some," he said.

There was no stopping the tears. I went to him then, and he pulled me close with a thin but firm arm. I guess I hugged him pretty hard, because he grunted, laughed, and pushed me back just a tad, saying in a hoarse whisper: "Easy, Travis. I got aches all over."

Pushing myself up, I wiped the tears, sniffed.

"Been eating acorns, berries, and roots," he said, "till I got here. Anna Louella's been trying to put some weight back on my bones these past three days."

I blinked. "Three days?"

"Travis," Mama said, as if she were about to begin to explain.

"Papa's been living in the corncrib," Baby Hugh said.

Again I blinked. My head shook. I faced my kid brother. "How long have you known?" My head spun to Edith, who cast her eyes down. I'd been so focused on helping Jared Greene and Jeremiah Wilson that I hadn't noticed anything unusual at my own home.

"Just this morning," Edith finally answered.

"You wasn't here," Baby Hugh said.

"But. . . ." My head shook again, unable to comprehend.

Papa grimaced, and reached up toward the bandage across his head.

"You're hurt," I said.

"I'll be fine."

"But there's a hospital. They've turned Miss Mary's place into a hospital. And there's plenty of soldiers on the road and. . . ."

"Travis!" Mama spoke sharply. "There's no hospital at Mary Frederick's. Not any more. Besides. . . ."

"But. . . ."

A horse whinnied, and a voice called out: "Hello the house!"

For a moment, fear paralyzed everyone in the crib.

"Stay here." Mama brought a finger to her lips, and turned to head down from the crib.

"Travis," Papa whispered. "Best hand me that rifle."

Slowly I moved to the corner. My hand touched the rifle, cold, so cold.

Below, in front of the house, a voice said: "Well, hello there, missy."

"What you doin' up in that corncrib?" called out another.

There were two of them. At least.

"What can I do for you two gentlemen?"

Two. Only two. I hefted the rifle, saw that the nipple was capped. It was the same rifle Papa had carried off to war, the one made by that German in Warren County, Kentucky.

"Like some water," the second voice said, "iffen you ain't got no objections."

"Help yourself," Mama said. "And welcome."

"You gots any grub? Earl and me ain't et in two days."

"Cold grits."

"That ain't right appetizin'."

Mama let out a forced laugh. "Tell me about it. It's all my family's had to eat for about a week now."

"What's in the corncrib?"

"It's empty. I was hoping to find corn, but . . . nothing," Mama said.

"This here mule, she's hungry, too. Corn would be nice. She ain't et, neither. And . . . well . . . seein' how we's ridin' double, this mule. . . ."

The first man cut him off. "You got an extry mule or hoss?"

"Some friends of yours made off with our mules months ago."

Papa whispered my name urgently. "Fetch me that rifle, Son. Now."

"Doesn't the army feed you and your mule?" Mama asked.

"Well," the first man said, "it's like this, missy. The army and us don't exactly see eye to eye no more."

"I'll bring you grits," Mama said. "That's all we have."

"Well, missy, I reckon that's fine. And whilst you's doin' that, Earl'll see what brings a lady like you up into an empty corncrib this time of day. And I'll see if you ain't forgotten some mule in your barn."

"Travis," Papa said.

I heard footsteps below. Then I was moving toward the ladder as Papa was trying to get to his feet.

The ladder moved. So did I. The hammer made a deafening click when I thumbed it back, braced the stock against my shoulder, and aimed down. Upon hearing the ominous click, the man looked up, and froze.

He wore unmatched shoes, threadbare trousers, a dirty plaid shirt, and a black and white checked vest. No hat. His hair was even more tangled than Papa's, and twice as long. His Adam's apple bobbed. "Fletcher . . . !" he wailed.

"Stop right there!" I heard Mama say to the man named Fletcher.

"Now . . . missy . . . you . . . ," he said to her.

"You take one more step toward my barn, and I'll bury you, mister," came Mama's voice.

"Earl!" Fletcher called out. "This wench's aimin' a pistol at me. Come help. Come cut her throat!"

I thought to myself: *Mama must have moved like a tornado to run into the house and grab the Spiller and Burr. Or maybe she had the revolver tucked inside her apron all this time.*

"Hurry up!" Fletcher's voice showed fear. "Now, missy, you don't want. . . ."

Earl called out Fletcher's name, never taking his eyes off me, and added: "They's a boy here pointin' a rifle at my head!"

"Mount your mule," Mama said loud enough for all to hear. "Ride out!"

"But. . . ."

"Or die. The both of you. I honestly don't care one way or the other. It's your choice."

"C'mon, Earl!" Fletcher yelled. "We'll find a more hospitable family that honors those of us who wears the gray."

Earl's Adam's apple moved again. "Is it all right, son?" His voice had risen several octaves. "Is it all right if I climb down this ladder? Rides out with Fletcher?"

"Do you have a knife?" I asked him.

"Yes, sonny. I mean, yes, sir. Just a butcher knife. Part of it's broke off."

"Drop it on the ground." The rifle didn't feel so heavy any more.

Gripping the ladder with his right hand, he reached inside his vest and pulled out what once might have been a decent butcher's knife. It fell into the dirt.

"Any gun?"

"No, sir."

"Any other weapon?" I asked, and Earl shook his head.

"Then get down, and get off my land," I told him. "Our land."

"Just be careful with that cannon, sir." He leaped off the ladder, fell to the ground, scrambled up, and bolted out of the crib. I moved to the window, continuing to aim Papa's rifle as Earl joined Fletcher, who seemed even thinner, even uglier, than his partner. Combined, the two likely weighed more than the mule. I'd never seen a more pathetic animal. Or two more pathetic humans.

Mama stood, both hands steadying the Spiller and Burr, which I could tell was cocked.

The mule put up a fight, didn't want to go—and I couldn't blame it for that—but finally Earl and Fletcher managed to get it to co-operate some, and they hurried down the lane.

Mama lowered the revolver, brought the back of her left hand to her forehead. I felt Papa behind me, and he took the rifle from my hands, easing down the hammer, watching, making sure our two visitors would not come back.

"They were deserters," Edith said. "Weren't they?"

Mama spoke sharply. "They were trash."

He moved back in the corncrib, so he could sit down again and drink water from the ladle. Baby Hugh climbed on his lap. Mama climbed the ladder while I stared out the window, down the lane. I had leaned the rifle in the corner within easy reach. Edith kneeled by the water bucket.

I think I knew then exactly what was going on, why Papa had been hiding in the corncrib for three days, but I had to ask. After sighing heavily, I turned to Papa.

"Are you like them, Papa?"

Mama, stepping off the ladder, spoke my name sharply.

"It's all right, Anna Louella." Papa handed the ladle back to Edith. "Am I a deserter?" His head nodded. "Yeah. That's what I am." He motioned weakly with his right hand. "Sit down. It's about time I laid the truth on you."

"Connor . . . ," Mama said.

"It's all right. They need to know."

I was glad he had asked us to sit. My legs felt weak.

"I was at Poison Spring," he said. Tears welled in his eyes. I'd never seen Papa cry before. He looked away, just staring at the ceiling.

"Corporal Brodie," Edith said. "He said you were sent to the rear."

"Brodie's a good man," Papa said. "Yeah. We got sent back by Cabell. A couple miles. In case the Federals in Camden sent reinforcements. But they didn't. And Lieutenant Tyree sent me back with a message for Major Somervell." He paused.

Mama moved toward Baby Hugh. "Let's go, Hugh," she said.

But Papa waved her off. "No, I want all of them to hear."

"He's too young."

"I ain't too young!" Baby Hugh snapped. "I already know all. . . ."

"We won the battle," Papa said, thankfully cutting off my brother before he blabbed about everything. "We were fighting. . . ."

"Colored boys?" Hugh asked.

Mama whirled, but not at my brother. She glared at me. "How does he know? What . . . ?"

"Soldiers," I said. "Soldiers told us."

Which was not a lie.

"Did they tell you what we did?"

"You didn't do anything, Connor," Mama said.

"I didn't stop it."

I felt sick.

"There was a regiment of Choctaw Indians. They killed. They scalped. But the Texans . . . and Arkansans . . . we weren't any better. The thing is . . . those soldiers . . . the colored ones . . . we had them beaten. They were trying to surrender. To give up." Tears disappeared into his thick beard. "We didn't let them. It was. . . ."

"Murder," I whispered.

He nodded. "Yeah. That's what it was, Travis. Murder."

We said nothing, just watched Papa cry. "Do you understand, Edith? Hugh?"

By that time, all of us were crying.

"But you didn't. . . ." Mama tried to come to Papa's defense.

"I didn't do anything, Anna!" he bellowed. "I just stood there. I just watched. There was a Texas captain standing right beside me, and he said . . . 'Don't take any prisoners, boys. Put 'em all to the sword.' And the sergeant standing right next to me, he laughed. And I just stood there. I just stood there. By God, I laughed with them. I stood there. I watched. I laughed." He swore, and that was something else Papa rarely had done, at least in front of us kids. "I must have lost my mind," he said. "Just went stark raving mad."

Then he was bawling, no longer quietly crying. He wailed like a baby. Edith went to him, and he pulled her close. Baby Hugh said: "Everything's all right. It wasn't. . . ." Mama rushed to Papa, fell to her knees right beside him, while I just stood there.

Oh, I cried, too. Not loud, not like Edith, and Papa, and Baby Hugh. Real quiet, while just standing there, tasting the salty tears as they rolled down my cheeks and fell onto the dirty floor that smelled of must and ancient corn.

And I said something then. I didn't know why. I remembered Miss Mary, always a good and kind and gentle lady, but she had whipped Mowbray. Drove him away. For no good reason. Now Mowbray was dead, not even properly buried. I recalled those soldiers, Northern and Southern, who had visited us, demanding food or corn we didn't have. I remembered Jared Greene saying something. *It was like the whole Secesh army turned crazy. Crazy for blood.* I remembered Mama saying that the world had gone mad. I thought of Reverend White, who once had been a friend. Insanity touched everyone, so why not Papa?

"I guess," I said, "everybody goes crazy in war."

Papa brought up his head, wiped his eyes. "Yeah, Travis. I reckon you're right."

"It's all right, Papa," I said. "Everything'll be all right."

Of course, everything would never be all right. Not now. Papa was a deserter from the 2nd Arkansas Cavalry, and the Union

Army was retreating from Camden back to Little Rock, perhaps all the way out of Arkansas. The Confederates would resume operations, would return to Camden. And Papa was here, hiding.

I knew something else. In the Confederate Army, in any army, they shot deserters.

I knew something else, too. Mama told Papa that maybe he could hide out in the woods. At the millpond. She told him we had been catching bream and crappie there, and that it was a great place to hide. For a while anyway. No one went to the mill any more.

We went to bed in the loft, none of us kids sleepy. Papa stayed in the corncrib, and Mama with him. Which made it easy for me to sneak out before dawn, quiet-like, so as not to wake Edith and Baby Hugh. Mama must have taken the Spiller and Burr with her, and Papa's rifle remained with him, so I had to take the shotgun, the flask of powder, a pouch of shot, and a tin of percussion caps, of which there were ten or twelve. I eased through the door in the darkness well before light, tiptoed off the porch, crept up the lane and to the pike. Then I ran.

"You can't stay here any longer!"

In the tool shed, Jared Greene lit a candle, as Jeremiah Wilson rubbed sleep from his eyes. From his appearance, Sergeant Greene had not slept in days.

"Rebels know where we are?" Greene asked. He shook his head before I could answer. "No, we'd be dead if that were true."

"But they's all along the road," Wilson said. He looked at me. "I been sneakin' up in the woods, spyin', seein' how things is."

"Things aren't good." Greene's head shook. "That road is thick with Secesh, Travis. How do you think two men of color could get out of here alive?"

"Join up with your army," I said.

"Our army is leaving Camden. By way of the Military Road." Wilson's head shook. "No way for us to gets back to our regiment, or any Union force."

"But. . . ." I thought about this for a moment, then my head bobbed, trying to convince myself I was right. "But the Confederates . . . they'll be following you Yanks. . . ." I stopped. "You Federals. They'll be following you, waiting for the right spot to attack."

"But that road out yonder," Greene said, "it goes to Washington. Nothing much but Rebs down that way."

"But if we turn off, toward Arkadelphia . . . ," Wilson began.

"I don't think the Secesh in that burg want to see us again," Greene said.

I kept talking. "Move to Rockport." Uncle Willard had told me once that Rockport had been all but abandoned. "Cross the river there. Then it's an easy trek to Little Rock."

"You plan on guidin' us, Travis?" Wilson asked, grinning. "That how come you brung that shotgun?"

"Yes," I said, and they fell silent, faces hardening.

The shed door slammed open, the candle blew out, and a voice that I instantly recognized bellowed: "I'll kill the first one of you that moves!"

Chapter Twenty-Three

A lantern glowed behind Papa, turning him into a shadowy figure. The lantern moved, a horse snorted, and yellow light bathed the inside of the shed. Wilson shivered, Greene held his breath, and my heart stopped.

"Travis." Mama held the lantern. "What on earth . . . ?" In that moment she recognized Jared Greene.

Whispering something I couldn't make out, she sank to her knees, had to support herself on the doorjamb. The lantern rested by a shovel. Papa stepped closer, and lowered his rifle.

Jared Greene looked up. He didn't recognize my father until Papa said out his name.

"Connor?" Greene asked hesitantly.

Papa leaned against the door. "It's been a long time."

They kept the reunion short, and the stories basic. Papa shared the last of his hardtack with Wilson and Greene.

Gray light began to peak through the pines and oaks.

"What are we going to do?" Mama asked.

"Hide here?" Papa said.

Greene's head shook. "Just be a matter of time before we were dead." His head tilted toward me. "Travis knows. Seems like we've had visitors quite frequently here."

"At our farm, too," Papa said.

"Don't know how long this war'll keep going," Greene said, "but we can't hide till the shooting stops."

"Iffen it ever stops," Jeremiah Wilson said.

We fell quiet.

Then Wilson said: "Your boy's got an idea. Good one. Well, better that anything else I's heard."

Their stares made me uncomfortable, but I told them in an uncertain whisper. Camden-Washington Pike to the Arkadelphia turn-off. Up through there, to Rockport, cross the river, on to Little Rock and the Union forces.

Papa's head shook. "And me winding up in a Yankee prison camp? Think I'd rather be shot or hung. Quicker than rotting to death."

"You won't be a prisoner, Connor," Jared Greene said. "I'll see to that."

"If you live," Mama said. Not out of meanness. Just out of fact. A fact I hadn't thought of.

"It's a risk," Papa said after a while.

"For all of us," Mama said.

"You aren't going," Papa told her.

"I most certainly am. We all have to leave."

Papa started to argue, but she cut him off. "How long do you think we could survive here, Connor? Our neighbors hate us already. Hate me, anyway. I used to think of this place as home, but no more, Connor. No more. I know you put your heart and soul into this mill, into our farm. Give it to Willard. He could make something of it. But it's dead to me. This whole place is just . . . just. . . ."

"Poison," I said.

We fell silent again, although Mama's head bobbed.

Outside, the horse snorted.

"Hey," I said, looking into the early light. "That's Nutmeg."

Papa laughed. "Haven't had to eat her yet. Been hiding her in the hollow."

I stepped outside, went to the old brown mare, rubbed my hand across her neck. Papa had ground-reined her. She was

219

thin, like every other horse I'd seen lately, but she seemed to recognize me, nuzzling me gently. I moved down her side, looked over the saddle, stared at the old sawmill.

The Ford Family Mill.

That's when the idea almost staggered me.

The first risk was if someone took Nutmeg. Scarce as horses were, and as busy as the main road had been, that was a big possibility. That early in the morning, however, Mama and I saw nobody as we rode double to our home. When we got back to the dogtrot, I led Nutmeg into the barn, to eat hay—more straw than hay, actually. I milked Lucy for the last time. I think Nutmeg remembered our cow. It was like a homecoming, of sorts, but it was brief. Inside the cabin, Mama was already waking Baby Hugh and Edith.

After a breakfast of milk and leftover cornbread, we went to Miss Mary's plantation, praying the Confederates hadn't plundered everything. The hospital had moved on; those wounded badly had been transported to Washington or Arkadelphia, maybe Camden since the Yanks had fled. The soldiers who had recuperated followed the army to Marks' Mill and wherever they were now. I hoped far, far from here.

The wind picked up, banging some door in Miss Mary's home open and shut. The wind also blew an ugly smell. The home, which I remembered always smelling of freshly baked bread and sweets and roasting turkey, now stank of death. I wondered if those soldiers who had died were buried here? And where? In Miss Mary's family plot? Or had they been buried in the graveyard alongside those dead slaves? How would a Confederate soldier like to spend eternity lying next to a slave?

Two wagons were parked inside the old carriage house, next to the unfinished structure that Miss Mary had started to build for Mowbray. Her fancy buggy, however, was gone, but that was all right. We needed a wagon. Usually, of course, you pull a farm wagon with two horses, but we had only Nutmeg. We figured it wouldn't be too hard on her, though. And plenty of people in Washington County now used singletrees instead of doubletrees. Like I said before, horses and mules had become scarce.

Quickly we harnessed Nutmeg.

"Has she ever pulled a wagon before?" Edith asked.

"Of course," Mama said.

With Nutmeg hitched, we climbed into the wagon, Mama on the seat, the rest of us in the back. She released the brake, snapped the lines, and off we went, down the road, through the gate, turning onto the main Pike, heading toward Papa's sawmill.

Safe. So far. It wasn't long before Mama tugged on the lines, slowing our pace. I turned to face her back and look ahead. Riders were coming down the road from Camden, but their timing worked for us. She simply turned Nutmeg, and we headed down the road to our home.

"What'll we do if they follow us?" Baby Hugh asked.

"We'll see," Mama said. She was trying to check the Spiller and Burr hidden in her apron without letting anyone see, but we saw. Still, she smiled cheerily, and said: "If there's anything you want to take with you from the house, this is your last chance."

After setting the brake, she stepped off the side of the wagon, helping Edith and Hugh down, while I jumped off. Mama kept looking down the path, but no one came.

"We should get our *Reader*s," Edith suggested.

Baby Hugh complained and kicked his feet.

"Yes." Mama tried to smile. "Yes. Go inside and get your books."

That reminded me of something, so into the house we went, collecting our *McGuffey's Reader*s. I hefted the unabridged dictionary. At the door, I turned back, and stared at the house Papa had built. Then I stepped onto the porch and down the steps one last time.

"What'll become of Lucy?" Baby Hugh asked as Mama helped him back into the wagon.

"The cow'll be fine," Mama said. "Somebody will find her and take care of her."

No more words. No farewells. Mama climbed back into the wagon, and we were turning around, heading back toward the main road, hoping whoever had been riding toward us was well beyond the bend in the road by now.

The Camden-Washington Pike appeared deserted. Mama let out a relieved sigh, and moved Nutmeg at a lively clip. Back toward the mill, turning down the woods lane, not slowing until Papa appeared from behind a tree, rifle ready. He smiled. Sergeant Greene stepped around one of the sawdust barrels, holding the shotgun I had brought him.

Once Mama pulled the wagon up to the mill, I jumped out to help Jeremiah Wilson and Papa move one of the barrels I had filled with sawdust into the wagon. Jared Greene tried to help with the second, but Papa eased him back.

"You rip open that side again, Jared, and you'll be in a heap of trouble."

"With me," Mama added, and Greene stepped back, smiling weakly.

Once the two barrels were in the wagon, I pried off the lid of one. We had scooped out most of the sawdust.

"You certain this'll work?" Wilson asked.

I answered honestly by shaking my head. Wilson grinned, and Papa and me helped him into the barrel, quickly turning toward Jared Greene, who stepped onto the wagon. He held the cigar box in his right hand.

"Figured you might want this, Travis. *Oui?*"

I took the box, ignoring Papa's puzzled look, and said with a smile: *"Oui."* The box went in the corner of the wagon on top of Webster's.

When Greene was in the second barrel, Edith handed the two soldiers wet bandannas to cover their faces. Mama, Papa, me, even Baby Hugh, began scooping sawdust into the barrels, covering the two Yankees as much as possible.

"These barrels are far from solid," Papa told them. "It'll be hot and stuffy, but there should be enough space between the boards for you to breathe."

"And if we can't?" The wet bandanna muffled Wilson's voice.

"Just don't shout out," Papa said. "No telling who'll be nearby."

The lids went back into place.

"What about you, Papa?" Edith asked.

"Two good barrels," he said, climbing over onto the driver's seat. "That's all we have. This'll have to work." He helped Mama onto the seat beside him, motioned for us to sit down. "Probably better this way," he said, and flicked the lines. "Just let me do all the talking."

Thus we started the longest drive of our lives.

I thought of everything that could have happened. We could have bogged down in the quagmire that once had been a road. We could have run into Uncle Willard, coming up from Magnolia since the Yanks were on the run. We could have just been robbed by deserters, trash, anyone. Drowned crossing a river. Been waylaid by the Reverend White. Or we could have just given up, fled back home.

Baby Hugh sniffled when we rode past the lane to our house, and Mama turned around, telling us: "It's all right to cry, children."

But we didn't. Even Baby Hugh stopped crying, dried his

eyes, bit his lip, and just stared at the muddy road behind us.

Past Miss Mary's.

My heart began beating normally again. For an hour. Then it felt like it stopped when Papa began pulling on the lines, and said: "Whoa, Nutmeg!"

Turning, I spotted a dozen or more men in gray uniforms riding up. A black-bearded, bespectacled man stepped toward Papa's side of the wagon.

"Where you bound, Sergeant?"

I cringed. *Why hadn't Papa shed his uniform, tried to pass himself off as a civilian?*

"Arkadelphia." Papa gestured toward the barrels in the back.

Again, I cringed. *Another mistake. Don't let those soldiers see anything, suspect anything,* I told myself.

"What the blazes for? The Yanks are north and east of here."

Papa grinned. "Yeah," he said, "but General Cabell found a house in Arkadelphia that he fancies. And I used to run a sawmill up the road from here."

"So."

Again, Papa pointed toward the barrels. "Sawdust," he said. "I've been ordered to insulate Cabell's new home."

The officer stepped back, pulled off his glasses, began wiping the lenses with a polka-dot bandanna. His clear blue eyes locked on me. I tried to smile.

"This your crew?" he asked, pointing with his glasses.

"My family. Cheap labor."

"O'Ryan," the captain said. "Check those barrels."

Baby Hugh almost said something, but Edith pinched his leg, and I jumped up, saying: "Let me help you, sir."

I was hoping, praying that Papa knew what he was doing, praying that Jeremiah and Jared had burrowed their heads underneath the sawdust.

The lid came off, and the jaundiced soldier named O'Ryan

climbed up with my help, and peered into the barrel.

"Sawdust, Capt'n," he reported.

"For insulation?" The eyeglasses resumed their place on the captain's head.

"Yes, sir," Papa answered.

"I'll help you with the other barrel, sir," I told O'Ryan, but he shook his head, muttering something, and stepped down.

"Check it, too," the captain ordered.

Back up came O'Ryan, and we pulled off the lid together.

"More sawdust, sir."

"Very well."

I pounded both lids back in place.

"Got the Yanks on the run," the captain said.

"Yep," Papa said.

"That Poison Spring was something, I hear. Wish I'd been there."

"It was something," Papa said.

"You were there?"

He nodded.

The captain's grin almost made me vomit. "Kill any colored boys?"

Papa grinned back at him. "As many as I could."

They laughed. My stomach heaved. But the wagon had started moving again, and as soon as we had rounded the next curve, Papa leaned over and spit the disgust out of his mouth.

"You did well, Travis," he told me, wiping his mouth.

"You did, too," I said, adding: "Papa."

The following evening, we endured another search in Arkadelphia, but this time Papa said that Cabell's desired home was in Rockport. And this time, the soldiers only searched one barrel, although I got a fright when that Confederate dipped his hand into the barrel, letting sawdust flow through his fingers to show the sergeant in charge of the guard.

Late the next day, we crossed the river at Rockport.

That's when Papa turned off the road, and removed his uniform, burying it in the woods, putting on duck trousers and a cotton shirt, neither of which fit him any more. While Mama hurriedly helped Papa trim his beard and cut his hair, Edith, Baby Hugh, and I helped Jeremiah Wilson and Jared Greene out of the barrels.

Sawdust stuck to their clothes and hair and faces, which it made us laugh.

Two days later, we rode into Little Rock.

"This is for you, Connor." Jared Greene pinched a white envelope between the thumb and two fingers on his right hand.

We were in a room with hundreds of soldiers, all of us, except Jeremiah Wilson, who was somewhere in the vast warehouse the army had transformed into a hospital.

Papa took the envelope, turned it over, looked at the black sergeant curiously.

"It's a letter of introduction to Joseph Donovan. Says I know you as a fine woodworker, furniture maker." He grinned. "There aren't a lot of sawmills in Lawrence, Kansas, Connor. Not many trees, you understand."

"Well. . . ." Papa didn't know what to say.

Of course, Mama did. "I wonder what Willard would think of that, Connor. His brother receiving a letter of introduction from a man of color."

Grinning, Papa reached over, and shook Jared Greene's hand. "Be careful," he said. "War's not over yet."

"It is for you, Mister Ford," Greene said.

He was shaking all our hands, when a nurse came in, shooing us away, saying this was a hospital for soldiers who were freeing the Negroes and preserving the Union, and not for cowards who didn't have the gumption to fight. She glared at Papa, who merely, and meekly, shrugged. My ears flamed. I was ready to punch that old crone in her nose.

It was then that Jared Greene reached under his pillow, and pulled out a package wrapped in brown paper. "And this is for you, Travis. With thanks from Jeremiah Wilson and all of the First Kansas Colored Infantry."

My trembling hands took it.

"Write well," he said. "Write honest. *Oui?*" Like Miss Mary Frederick was speaking through him.

"*Oui.*"

It would be a long way to Kansas. I didn't know what it would bring. Wasn't even sure we would make it. There were plenty of Confederates in northern Arkansas, and southern Missouri. Plenty of trouble. Mama, however, said we had nothing to worry about. And Mama, we had learned, was never wrong.

So we rode. Out of Little Rock, with a pass from a Yankee major saying that Connor Ford and his family were free to travel to Kansas with the thanks of the First Kansas Colored Infantry. Which wouldn't do us any good if we happened upon Confederates.

As the wagon rolled north, I opened the package. I knew what it was. I hadn't planned on opening it until I was alone, but Baby Hugh and Edith insisted. Mama and Papa just stared ahead.

"That for drawing?" Baby Hugh asked when I showed them all the writing tablet.

"For writing," I told him.

"Stories?" My brother made a face. "Another one of them learning things? Like what Miss Mary give you?"

"Yes, it is." I lifted the cigar box off Webster's. Opened it. Withdrew the tablet Miss Mary had bought me in what seemed like a lifetime ago. The tablet opened, and I glanced at one of my stories about France, cringing as I read my weak attempt at writing, but grinning at my misspelling of *oui*.

"Read a story you wrote," Edith said.

"Some other time," I said.

They frowned.

"Well, maybe tonight."

I turned the page. New thoughts flashed through my head, thoughts about all I had seen in . . . what . . . a month? I leaned back, and put both tablets—one from Sergeant Greene and Wilson, one from Mary Frederick—inside the cigar box. I closed the lid. Sliding closer to my brother and sister, I put my arms around them both. Behind me, Mama reached over and gripped Papa's leg.

"Ain't you gonna write something?" Baby Hugh asked. "Or draw something?"

"Later," I said.

"You ain't gonna write nothing," he said. "I bet you can't write a thing."

"Hugh," Mama admonished.

The wagon rolled. A spring breeze blew.

Oh, I would write. I knew exactly what I would write, not the words, mind you, but the story. Stories, I mean. Not just one.

One story was finished, but another held promise I'd never felt until that moment.

Poison Spring lay behind us.

The Spring of Hope waited ahead.

AUTHOR'S NOTE

Historian Gregory J.W. Urwin has called the Poison Spring massacre "the worst war crime ever committed on Arkansas soil."

The battle—six days after a similar, and more infamous, massacre of black Union soldiers by Confederates at Fort Pillow, Tennessee—resulted in more than three hundred killed, wounded, and missing for the Union Army. Of that number, the 1st Kansas Colored Infantry lost one hundred seventeen killed and sixty-five wounded. Confederate losses totaled fewer than one hundred forty-five.

Less than two weeks later, the 2nd Kansas Colored Infantry got a measure of revenge. On the day after the Battle of Poison Spring (sometimes called Poison Springs), Colonel Samuel J. Crawford, the 2nd's commanding officer, told his men that they "would take no prisoners so long as the Rebels continued to murder our men."

At Jenkins' Ferry on April 30, as the Union Army retreated for Little Rock, the 2nd Kansas met an Arkansas regiment. Crawford ordered his men to "aim low, and give them hell." Shouting "Poison Springs," the black soldiers stormed into the Confederates. In a matter of seconds, the 2nd overran the enemy position, bayoneting as many soldiers as they could, including some who tried to surrender.

A quiet state park rests about ten miles west of Camden off Arkansas Highway 76. I've hiked around it a couple of times, but have never felt that it does justice to the tragedy, the injustice, that happened there. Which might be why I tackled this novel.

Marks' Mill (on Highway 8 near Fordyce) and Jenkins' Ferry (on County Road 317/Forest Road 9010 near Leola), by the way, are also nearby state parks.

Poison Spring is a work of fiction, but the battle, part of the Union's failed Red River campaign, is fact. A fact that has too often been overlooked.

My primary source was *"All Cut to Pieces and Gone to Hell": The Civil War, Race Relations, and the Battle of Poison Spring* (August House, 2003), edited by Mark K. Christ. Other sources include *Biographical and Historical Memoirs of Southern Arkansas* (The Goodspeed Publishing Co., 1890); *"A Rough Introduction to This Sunny Land": The Civil War Diary of Private Henry A. Strong, Co. K, Twelfth Kansas Infantry* (Butler Center Books, 2006), edited by Tom Wing; *Things Grew Beautifully Worse: The Wartime Experiences of Captain John O'Brien, 30th Arkansas Infantry, C.S.A.* (Butler Center Books, 2001), edited by Brian K. Robertson; *Civil War Arkansas: Beyond Battles and Leaders* (University of Arkansas Press, 2000), edited by Anne J. Bailey and Daniel E. Sutherland; and *Rugged and Sublime: The Civil War in Arkansas* (University of Arkansas Press, 1994), edited by Mark K. Christ. I should also thank the Ouachita County Historical Society, based in Camden.

Johnny D. Boggs
Santa Fe, New Mexico

ABOUT THE AUTHOR

Johnny D. Boggs has worked cattle, shot rapids in a canoe, hiked across mountains and deserts, traipsed around ghost towns, and spent hours poring over microfilm in library archives—all in the name of finding a good story. He's also one of the few Western writers to have won six Spur Awards from Western Writers of America (for his novels, *Camp Ford,* in 2006, *Doubtful Cañon,* in 2008, and *Hard Winter* in 2010, *Legacy of a Lawman, West Texas Kill,* both in 2012, and his short story, "A Piano at Dead Man's Crossing", in 2002) as well as the Western Heritage Wrangler Award from the National Cowboy and Western Heritage Museum (for his novel, *Spark on the Prairie: The Trial of the Kiowa Chiefs,* in 2004). A native of South Carolina, Boggs spent almost fifteen years in Texas as a journalist at the *Dallas Times Herald* and *Fort Worth Star-Telegram* before moving to New Mexico in 1998 to concentrate full time on his novels. Author of dozens of published short stories, he has also written for more than fifty newspapers and magazines, and is a frequent contributor to *Boys' Life* and *True West.* His Western novels cover a wide range. *The Lonesome Chisholm Trail* (Five Star Westerns, 2000) is an authentic cattle-drive story, while *Lonely Trumpet* (Five Star Westerns, 2002) is an historical novel about the first black graduate of West Point. *The Despoilers* (Five Star Westerns, 2002) and *Ghost Legion* (Five Star Westerns, 2005) are set in the Carolina backcountry during the Revolutionary War. *The Big Fifty* (Five Star Westerns, 2003) chronicles the slaughter of buffalo on the southern plains in the 1870s, while *East of the Border* (Five Star Westerns, 2004) is a comedy about the theatrical offerings of Buffalo Bill Cody, Wild Bill Hickok, and Texas Jack Omohundro, and *Camp Ford* (Five Star Westerns, 2005) tells about a Civil War baseball game between Union prisoners of war and Confederate guards. "Boggs's narrative voice captures the old-fashioned style of the past," *Publishers Weekly* said, and *Booklist* called him "among the best Western writers at work today." Boggs lives with his wife Lisa and son Jack in Santa Fe. His website is www.johnnydboggs.com. His next Five Star Western will be *The Killing Trail: A Killstraight Story.*